# Coopers Island

## Steve Schach & Sharon Stein

Wandering in the Words Press

2131 Burns St, Nashville, Tennessee, 37216
www.wanderinginthewordspress.com

All characters in this book are fictitious, and any resemblance to
real persons, living or dead, is coincidental.

PUBLISHED BY WANDERING IN THE WORDS PRESS

ISBN-10: 0991078705
ISBN-13: 978-0-9910787-0-7

First Edition

To Jackson and Mikaela

# PROLOGUE

*Bathurst District, Australia*
*Tuesday, July 12th, 1939*

Midnight, midwinter. The crescent moon cast a cold white light over the sheep country of the Central Tableland of New South Wales. Frost coated the grass of the rolling hills.

The door of the rural police station was open; lights were burning. Gretchen Konrad walked into the charge office. She called out, but no one answered. The building was deserted.

Then she noticed the radio transceiver on a table at the back. Gretchen darted behind the wooden counter, grabbed the radio and carried it to her car. She drove away into the darkness.

# CHAPTER ONE

*Alexandria, Egypt*
*Tuesday, August 25th, 1942*

The ornate gold letters on the meticulously varnished wooden sign above the shop spelled out *Aram Kezerian Antiquities.* The corporal pressed the bell embedded in the wooden doorframe and waited. Through the glass door, he saw a woman in a long black dress emerge from the rear of the showroom holding a key in her hand. Her ebony hair was artfully cut to resemble the style worn by the queens of the Pharaohs of the Eighteenth Dynasty. Around her neck, she wore an enamel necklace with bright colors, evocative of the jewelry worn thousands of years ago in Egypt. There was a loud click as she turned the key in the lock, and a softer click as she opened the door.

"Can I help you, sir?" she asked in a subdued voice.

"I'd like to see Mr. Kezerian." The soldier spoke with a heavy Afrikaans accent.

"What name shall I say?"

"Tell him that Klaas van Deventer is my brother-in-law."

"Please come inside. I won't be long."

She carefully locked the door behind him, removed the key and walked back to the rear of the shop. The soldier glanced around the showroom. It was designed to display relatively few items from the period of the Pharaohs. However, each was of the very highest quality, especially a bronze statuette of a priest from the period of Tutankhamun, and a wooden sarcophagus belonging to a young woman who had died during the time of the Twentieth Dynasty. On the wall hung a painting of a hunting scene on papyrus; the colors glowed as if they had been painted that morning, and the numerous hieroglyphics written in the top-right-hand corner that explained the panorama were still pitch black.

The soldier wore the insignia of the South African 1st Infantry Division, including the red shoulder tabs indicating that he had volunteered for service outside the Union of South Africa. The expression on his face and his bodily stance were those of a perennially dissatisfied young man who felt that the world owed him a living. The dull look in his brown eyes and his sullen demeanor revealed that he was utterly bored by the exquisite objects on display in the showroom.

The woman returned a minute or so later. "Mr. Kezerian will see you now."

She escorted the corporal to a spacious office behind the showroom and closed the door behind him. On the left wall was a large steel safe, flanked by equally large wooden filing cabinets. Glass-fronted, ornately carved wooden bookcases lined the right wall. In the center of the room, Aram Kezerian sat behind a capacious Louis XV desk. Kezerian was a tall man, with a large oblong head and wavy gray hair. Heavy black eyebrows loomed over his hooded eyes. His lips were red and fleshy. The Armenian antique dealer did not get up as the corporal entered and he did not invite the young man to sit.

"Can I help you?" he asked. The cultured voice was curt and cold.

The corporal sat down heavily on one of the two Directoire chairs in front of the desk, leaned back lazily and crossed his left ankle over his right knee.

"Klaas van Deventer is my brother-in-law," he said. His Afrikaans accent was stronger than ever.

"I don't seem to recall the name," Kezerian responded.

"I believe you do," the corporal said, raising his chin.

Aram Kezerian arched his left eyebrow interrogatively, but said nothing more.

"About three weeks ago, you paid him one hundred pounds for a photograph of a map of the defenses of part of the El Alamein line."

"You must be mistaken. Everything in my shop is thousands of years old. I deal exclusively in antiquities from the time of the Pharaohs."

"Not so," the young man said. "You also deal in information, and particularly in photographs that would be of the greatest interest to the German troops now only 60 miles from here in Alexandria."

Kezerian rose from his seat. "You're out of your mind. You must have been outside too long in the hot Egyptian sun. Kindly leave my shop at once!"

The corporal ignored the order. From inside the blouse of his battledress he drew out a pile of glossy black-and-white photographs. He laid them on the desk in front of him, arranged them neatly in a pile, turned them so that they were oriented the right way for the antiquities dealer to see them, and pointed to the photograph on the top.

"As you can see, this one depicts the QF 6-pounder, the new British anti-tank gun. It's been used here in North Africa for the past three months against Field Marshal Erwin Rommel's Afrika Corps with great success—I'm sorry to say—especially during the last month. The fact that the Allies have managed to hold the El Alamein line against Rommel, at least for now, seems at least partly due to those 6-pounders.

"But it's going to get even worse for our German and Italian comrades. The effective range of the 6-pounder is 1,650 yards. These photographs on your desk are of a weapons test attended by General Montgomery, General Alexander and a whole host of other top brass— maybe you can identify them in the photographs.

The pictures prove beyond all doubt that the Allies now have an anti-tank shell that's effective from a distance of 3,000 yards and has at least twice the destructive power of the armor-piercing shells they've been using up to now. Yes, that's what I said: They're twice as destructive from twice the distance."

The antique dealer sat down suddenly. From the time that his assistant told him that Klaas van Deventer's brother-in-law wished to see him, Kezerian had been concerned that this could be a trap. But now the soldier had revealed military information of the very highest importance. The Allies might use a photograph of a gun emplacement or a list of troop arrivals in Alexandria Harbor to uncover a spy, but not a secret that would unquestionably change the course of the entire war. Despite his attempts to appear indifferent and uninvolved, Aram Kezerian's eyes now blazed with interest.

"Show me the photographs," he demanded.

The corporal grabbed the pile of prints and replaced them in his blouse. "No. First we talk, then we come to a financial arrangement, and then I show you the photographs."

"Before I buy an antiquity," the dealer said, his voice now calm and soothing, "I want to know its provenance."

"Its what?"

"Its provenance: who found it, where they found it, who owned it previously, and so on. That helps me to avoid buying a pig in a poke."

"So you think these photographs are fakes, do you? Faked photographs of the top generals of the Eighth Army watching a weapons trial?"

This time the soldier stood up. He started to leave the room.

"Sit down, young man, and calm yourself. I'm not suggesting anything at all. Now tell me, who took these photographs?"

"My brother-in-law, Klaas van Deventer. As you well know, he's a combat photographer attached to the Eighth Army."

"If he took the pictures, why did he send you here with them? Why didn't he come himself?"

"Because," the corporal replied as he resumed his seat, "I have a degree in chemistry from the University of Pretoria, and he doesn't."

Kezerian was utterly nonplussed.

"You have a degree in chemistry?"

"Yes."

"From the University of Pretoria?"

"That's what I just said."

"And what does that have to do with anything?"

"It has everything to do with everything. Only someone with my knowledge can explain to you the details regarding the composition of the new anti-tank shell."

There was a long silence. Then Kezerian smiled. "Fine. Let's start at the beginning. What's your name?"

"My name doesn't matter."

"But I have to call you something."

"*Maak nie saak nie.*" Then, realizing he had slipped into Afrikaans, he translated. "It doesn't matter. You can call me whatever you like."

"Well, the commander of your 1st Infantry Division is Major General Dan Pienaar. Can I call you Dan?"

"*Ja-nee,*" the soldier replied, using an Afrikaans idiom for reluctant acceptance.

Kezerian quickly worked out that the corporal had said: "Yes-no." Despite the confusing reply, the antiquities dealer correctly assumed that he could now use that name.

He struggled with himself to relax inwardly and outwardly. If the Allies had developed an anti-tank shell of unimaginable destructive power and range, Germany would surely lose the coming tank battle and be driven out of North Africa, an unthinkable prospect. In particular, when the Allies captured Rommel's headquarters, they would surely find irrefutable evidence proving that Kezerian was a German spy, with fatal consequences for him.

In order to take countermeasures, Field Marshal Rommel would have to learn about this new development quickly. But unless the antiquities dealer could conceal his growing interest and gnawing fears, the soldier might set a price for the prize that Kezerian could not afford, notwithstanding the large amount of money locked away in his safe.

"Dan, tell me more about the photographs. What do they show?"

The corporal once again took the pictures out of his khaki blouse and stacked them carefully on the desk, so that only the top photograph could be seen. Then, as before, he turned the pile so that the pictures were the right way round for Kezerian to view them.

"This first one is just a close-up of a QF 6-pounder anti-tank gun. They used two standard 6-pounders for the weapons trial. Now, this second photograph shows the whole setup of the weapons trial. Don't worry that the details are so small in this picture—I'll show you close-ups of everything in the other pictures I've brought.

"On the left and in the center here are the two 6-pounders I told you about. The close-ups will show the distance markers clearly, and you'll see then that the anti-tank gun on the left has been placed 3,000 yards from its target, and the other one is 1,650 yards away, the stated effective range of the QF 6-pounder.

"Now, on the right of the picture you can see two captured German Panzer Mark IV tanks parked next to one another about 100 yards apart. You'll soon see in some of the other photographs that they're both in perfect condition—the Afrika Korps had to abandon them when they ran out of fuel.

"The British loaded the gun on the left in the photograph with the new anti-tank shell I told you about and aimed it at the left-hand tank. Now look at the gun in the center of the photo, the one placed 1,650 yards from the target. That one they loaded with a standard anti-tank shell and aimed it at the right-hand tank. Do you follow me?"

Aram Kezerian had been listening intently and quickly nodded. His eyes were glued to the photographs. Involuntarily he licked his fleshy lips.

"Now I'll show you some close ups. This next picture shows the one anti-tank gun, and here's the other gun. You can see that they were placed exactly where I just told you. Look at the distance markers—you can easily read the numbers. And the anti-tank guns weren't on special gun platforms. It's obvious in both pictures that they were on the sand, just as in battle conditions. Now, here are two pictures that show the Panzer Mark IV tanks. You can clearly see that they're both in perfect condition—I'm sure you'll agree. And here's a picture of the generals who were watching. Do you recognize any of them?"

"Yes, here's General Harold Alexander, and here's Monty, wearing his famous black beret. And, look, here's your namesake, General Dan Pienaar!"

The corporal did not react to that last remark. Instead, he asked, "Do you recognize anyone else in the photo?"

"No, I don't think so."

"Well, take a close look at the insignia. Do you see anyone under the rank of major general?"

The dealer looked suitably impressed. He said nothing.

"Now," the corporal said, "take a look at these two photographs—I'll put them over there next to one another. They show the two tanks after the guns were fired. The pictures prove exactly what I told you. The tank on the right looks similar to the other German tanks that the Allies destroyed last month in the desert. It's what you'd expect to find when a standard QF 6-pounder at the limit of its effective range fires a standard anti-tank shell at a standard Panzer Mark IV tank and hits it. But look at this next one. That's what happened when the new armor-piercing shell was fired at twice the distance. The Mark IV on the left isn't just scrap metal now; it's been reduced to smithereens."

There was silence for a long while. The corporal gathered the photographs strewn over Kezerian's desk, piled them up one on top of the other all facing the correct way, and yet again straightened the heap. He shifted the pile of pictures a few inches to the right until they were directly in front of him on the desk and then clasped his hands together and placed them firmly on the top of the stack as if to prevent them from being moved out of position.

He could sense that Kezerian was thinking hard. Then the antiquities dealer spoke. "What's your price for the photographs?"

"I want 2,000 pounds sterling in used notes for the photographs. And another 2,000 pounds sterling for the name of the substance in the new shell, together with a detailed explanation that I'll provide. And a final 2,000 pounds sterling if you want to know where to obtain that substance. Oh, I forgot to mention, all three prices are non-negotiable."

Again there was a long silence. Then the dealer changed the subject completely.

"Tell me, Dan, why do you Afrikaners hate the British so bitterly? Is it because of what happened during the Boer War?"

"Don't call it the 'Boer War'—it's the Second War of Liberation. In 1899, the British tried for the second time to conquer the Orange Free State and the Transvaal Republic. The British Empire attempted to crush the Boer guerillas—and for a year, the British redcoats lost battle after battle. Then General Kitchener adopted a scorched earth policy. Our fighters were being supplied with food, horses and ammunition from our farms, so they burned our farms: buildings, crops, livestock, everything. Our women and children now had neither food nor shelter, so the British put them into concentration camps. No, the British didn't kill them in the tents—they just let them die there of cold, disease and meager rations. Those women whose husbands were still fighting the British were issued even less food than the others, which meant almost no food at all. Measles, typhoid, dysentery and starvation killed our people, and the *verdomde* British just stood by and let it happen. More than 26,000 of our women and children died in the concentration camps. Does that answer your question?"

"You hate the British," Kezerian responded. "The British are fighting the Germans, so you're on the side of the Germans—there's an old Arab proverb: 'The enemy of my enemy is my friend.' Is that why you've come here today with those photographs?"

The soldier nodded.

The antiquities dealer went on. "You're wearing on your shoulders the red tabs of a South African volunteer. That is, you took the 'Africa Oath' and agreed to come and fight here. But if you're on the side of the Germans, why are you in Egypt fighting for the British?"

"There's a group of Afrikaner patriots, including Klaas van Deventer and myself, who believe that we can do much more damage to the British cause here in North Africa than at home in South Africa. And we're doing well. First, we gave you the photograph of the map of the defenses of part of the El Alamein line, and now these."

"But if you hate the British so strongly, Dan, why are you trying to sell me information that will inestimably help our German mutual friends?" Kezerian asked, a triumphant note starting to enter his voice. "Surely you should just ask me to send the photographs as well as everything else you know about the new anti-tank shells to the Afrika Korps as quickly as possible so that Field Marshal Rommel can take countermeasures?"

The South African looked at him quizzically. "*Meneer* Kezerian, what do you think I would do with 6,000 pounds sterling in used notes here in Alexandria? Do you really think that this money is for me?"

"Well, if it's not for you and your brother-in-law, who's it for then?"

"The *Stormjaers*."

"The what?" the dealer asked, utterly nonplussed for the second time. He had thought that he was starting to get the upper hand in the negotiations, but this new Afrikaans word threw him totally.

"It means the 'assault troops,'" the soldier explained. "It's a Nazi paramilitary organization back in South Africa. We engage in sabotage of all kinds: power stations, railroads, telephone lines and bridges. But we need money to buy guns and explosives. Your 100 pounds is already in Pretoria, and your 6,000 pounds should follow soon."

Stymied, Kezerian tried a new tactic. "Like you, I'm anti-British. We're on the same side. So why do you want me to pay for your anti-British sabotage?"

"You're a capitalist. We're national socialists, followers of Adolf Hitler, and we're all strongly opposed to communists, Jews and capitalists like yourself."

Again there was a long silence. Then Kezerian got up again. This time he walked over to his safe. Using his body to hide the combination from the eyes of the young soldier, he unlocked the safe and swung open the heavy steel door. He took out four wads of banknotes, each held together neatly by a strip of white paper, and handed two of the wads to the South African. "Here's 2,000 pounds sterling for the photographs." Then he locked the safe and resumed his seat.

The South African took the money and put it on the desk on the right side of the stack of photographs in front of him. He made no attempt to count the notes. Instead, he just pushed the pile of black-and-whites across the desk. Kezerian moved them to one side so that only the money in front of him lay on the desk between him and the soldier.

"Now," the dealer said, pushing the last two wads across, "here's another 2,000 pounds. Tell me about the new anti-tank shell."

The corporal placed the second installment on top of the first. He meticulously straightened the pile of money the same way he had straightened the pile of photographs, sliding the paper bands so that they were positioned exactly in line with one another. Only then did he respond.

"When my brother-in-law stood in front of the generals to take their photographs, they were absolutely silent. But when he crept up behind them, two of them were a little indiscreet and he overheard three things. In return for the 2,000 pounds you just gave me, here are two of the things he heard: "element 61" and "promethium.""

"And what do they mean?" Kezerian asked.

"Well, they meant nothing to my brother-in-law, either. But they mean a lot to me. That whole wall over there is just books. Do you happen to have an encyclopedia?"

"Of course I do."

"Fetch it and open it to the page that shows the periodic table of the elements."

Totally mystified, and starting to feel that he had just been swindled out of the second payment of 2,000 pounds, the antiquities dealer nevertheless did as he was asked. He walked over to the bookcases, opened one of the glass doors, and pulled out Volume 17, "P to PLAN," of the 14th edition of *Encyclopedia Britannica*. He closed the glass door and placed the heavy book on his desk. Then Kezerian opened the leather-bound encyclopedia and quickly found the relevant entry. He looked up expectantly at the soldier.

"Look at the bottom of the table," the soldier said. "There's a line of 15 boxes labeled 'Lanthanides.' The first box contains the number 57 and the last box has 71."

"Yes."

"The first box contains the number 57 and the symbol La. That tells us that the element lanthanum ('La' for short) is element number 57. Next to it is the box containing the number 58 and the symbol Ce for cerium."

"Yes, I see that. But what—"

"Just listen to me and don't interrupt. Now skip to the box two places to the right. It contains the number 60 and the symbol Nd for neodymium."

"Yes, I understand, but—"

"Look, if you want to hear about the new armor-piercing anti-tank shell, just shut up for a moment. Now, as I was saying, look at the next box. What does it contain?"

"I see the number 61, but the rest of the box is empty—there's no chemical symbol."

"Fine. Now, why is there no symbol in that box?" the corporal enquired.

"I don't have the faintest idea. Why?"

"Because at the time that your encyclopedia was published, scientists hadn't yet found any samples of element 61."

"Why not?"

"Well, the 15 Lanthanides are rare-earth elements. That is, there's very little of each of them on earth. On the other hand, the element carbon is found abundantly, in coal for example. There's even carbon in the air, in carbon dioxide. And many countries have deposits of iron. But I strongly suspect that you hadn't even heard of lanthanum, cerium, or neodymium until a few minutes ago."

"Yes, you're correct."

"And that's because they're so rare that only chemists, geologists and other scientists are even aware of their existence."

"I see," Aram Kezerian said.

"Scientists have been searching in vain for element 61 for decades. There've been a number of false sightings, and the name 'promethium' was put forward for one of those mistaken discoveries. So, when Klaas told me that the generals had mentioned 'element 61' and 'promethium' I realized what had happened: The Allies had found element 61 and were using it to make the new anti-tank shell."

Kezerian let out a deep sigh. "This is terrible news. I'm no general, but it seems to me that there's no way that Germany can find promethium and manufacture enough anti-tank shells in time for the coming battle in North Africa. The next clash here in Egypt will take place as soon as the Eighth Army has built up its forces—as everyone can see, reinforcements and supplies are pouring into Alexandria and Cairo. My guess is that the Allied attack will take place in about two months' time, far too soon for our side to do anything. But unless we do something, we're about to lose North Africa."

"Perhaps, perhaps not," the South African said. "But we need to look at the broader impact and the long-term picture. If our German friends can locate the promethium mine, they can do one of two things. They can capture it and manufacture their own anti-tank shells, to be used in other battles, perhaps on the Eastern Front where more major tank battles will undoubtedly take place. Or they can destroy the mine and prevent the Allies from acquiring any more promethium, thereby equalizing the balance again in future battles."

"Fine, but where's the mine?"

There was a long silence. Then the soldier looked meaningfully at the safe.

"Is the location of the mine the third thing that your brother-in-law overheard?" the dealer asked.

"*Ja.*"

"And is that information going to cost me another 2,000 pounds?"

"*Ja.*"

Kezerian slowly got out of his chair, reopened the safe and took out two more packages of banknotes. He meticulously locked the safe again and handed the money to the soldier. As he did so, he looked straight at the South African and again raised his left eyebrow questioningly. Then he resumed his seat.

The corporal placed the last two wads of banknotes on top of the other four and carefully aligned the pile of money, as before. Then he took a deep breath and slowly exhaled.

"So?" Kezerian asked.

"Klaas overheard one of the generals saying, 'New Zealand.'"

"But the general could have been saying something like, 'I say, old chap, the vintage cheddar we had last night in the officers' mess was absolutely scrumptious—that cheese must have come from New Zealand.'" Kezerian's imitation of an upper-class English accent was perfect.

"Yes, that's certainly possible," said the corporal, "but it wouldn't explain this photograph."

He reached into his blouse yet again and took out a single print, which he arrogantly flicked across the desk to the antiquities dealer. "There are two ammunition boxes shown in this picture. They're lying adjacent to one another on the sand next to the 6-pounder that fired the new anti-tank shell. You can tell that it's that 6-pounder, because you can see the 3,000-yard marker in the picture.

"One ammo box is open, showing five of the six shells it originally contained—the sixth shell was used in the trial. Now look at the box next to it. It looks identical to the first one, except that it's still closed. And look what's stenciled on the wood in addition to the usual markings. Two abbreviations. The first is 'Pm'—that's the chemical symbol for element 61, promethium. And the one in the bottom left-hand corner is 'NZ,' the abbreviation for New Zealand.

"Tell me, *Meneer* Kezerian," the corporal added, "do you really think this other box contains absolutely scrumptious New Zealand vintage cheddar?"

# CHAPTER TWO

*Garden City, Cairo, Egypt*
*Tuesday, August 25th, 1942*

The South African soldier knocked on the door marked "Room 26." On hearing Colonel Marlowe's gruff command to enter, the corporal turned the handle. As he came into the room, the scowl on his face disappeared, his slouched posture became ramrod-straight, and he snapped a precise salute that could have been given only by a British career officer trained at the Royal Military Academy Sandhurst.

"At ease, Captain Wright. Sit. I can see that you were in such a hurry to tell me what happened that you rushed from Alexandria straight here to my office and didn't even take the time to change out of the South African corporal's uniform that we obtained for you. Did that scoundrel of an Armenian antiquities dealer take the bait?"

"Hook, line and sinker, sir."

"Well done!"

"Here's the money, sir—six thousand pounds."

"Jolly good show, Wright! We'll change the money into Egyptian pounds and use it to pay our Arab informants. As you well know, we're always short of cash—for some reason, the powers that be chronically starve Security Intelligence Middle East of the funds we need. But tell me what happened. Did Kezerian suspect a trap?"

"At first he was exceedingly wary, sir, just as you'd predicted," Captain Wright answered. "But once he realized that I'd come to sell him a secret that'll change the course of the war, he threw all caution to the winds."

"Did you remember to speak a few words of Afrikaans?"

"I certainly did, sir."

"I trust that your Afrikaans accent was impeccable."

"It was, sir. The numerous bullies at Witvolstruishoogte Primary School saw to that. They made very sure that the *verdomde* British boy in their class at least could speak Afrikaans without a trace of an English accent. I wouldn't care to describe the years I spent as a youngster in a small country village in South Africa as particularly pleasant, but at least I acquired the skills to masquerade flawlessly as a Nazi Afrikaner and diehard fanatical member of the *Stormjaers.*"

"Did he ask you why you hated the British?"

"Yes, sir, he did, and I gave him the same answer that my 'brother-in-law' had given him when he sold him the photograph of the map of the defenses of part of the El Alamein line. This time Kezerian knew what was coming—he asked me if it was a consequence of the Boer War."

"I trust you gave him the 'Second War of Liberation' speech—all those Afrikaner patriots trot it out when you say the words 'Boer War.' It's like a red rag to a Boer."

"Very witty, sir." Wright felt obliged to smile politely at the excruciatingly bad pun before continuing.

"Yes, sir, I gave him the whole speech we'd prepared. Not that I needed to learn that part of the script—I heard it at least three times a day during the years my father was the doctor in Witvolstruishoogte."

"But back then you heard the whole story in Afrikaans, Wright. You needed to learn the English version."

"Quite right, sir."

"And how did the chemistry lesson go?"

"Surprisingly well, sir. Like almost all spies who reach the very top of their profession, Kezerian is highly intelligent. He quickly caught onto the fact that there's only one place on earth where promethium is mined, and that's in New Zealand."

"Excellent."

The colonel paused, thought for a few seconds and then went on.

"Wright, I assume that, now that you've delivered the photographs, you'll want to know what's going on."

"Indeed I would, sir."

"Of course, I can't tell you everything, Wright, but I'll go as far as I'm allowed. As you know, last month we finally managed to stop Field Marshal Rommel and his Afrika Korps. If he'd reached the Suez Canal, nothing could have prevented Hitler from getting his hands on the Middle Eastern and Persian oil fields. And that would unquestionably have meant a Nazi victory.

"At least we managed to stop Rommel at the El Alamein line. The battle ended after a month in a sort of stalemate, with both sides running perilously low on fuel, ammunition and tanks. Before we can achieve anything meaningful here in the Western Desert, we need major reinforcements. Not just men, but also supplies of all kinds, and especially more tanks. We desperately need to build up our forces, while sinking the Axis ships trying to cross the Mediterranean carrying supplies for Rommel and his Afrika Korps. Then we attack Rommel, break through the El Alamein line, and drive the Germans and the Italians from North Africa.

"After his visit here earlier this month, Mr. Churchill decided to appoint General Montgomery as Commander-in-Chief, Middle East Command. Monty took over about 10 days ago. His first order of business is obviously to rebuild morale and turn the Eighth Army into a fighting machine. He ordered us to put out the story that, soon after he arrived here, Monty remarked to a colleague, 'After having an easy war, things have now got much more difficult.' The colleague told Monty to cheer up, and Montgomery replied, 'I'm not talking about me, I'm talking about Rommel!'"

"Did that really happen, sir?"

"Probably not, Wright, probably not, but it's already done wonders for the men's fighting spirit. Did you know that Monty's making a point of visiting every single unit without exception and making himself known to the men? A few more weeks of the Montgomery treatment, plus a large influx of reinforcements, lots more tanks, ammunition, aeroplanes and fuel, and we'll be ready to drive Rommel out of North Africa. And that's where you came in."

Colonel Marlowe paused conspiratorially, then continued.

"Rommel is a superb tank general, and the coming battle will probably be the largest tank battle in history. We need to gain every advantage we can. If we can persuade Rommel that we have an anti-tank shell with twice the effective range and twice the destructive power, he'll be less aggressive than before—he'll order his Panzers to hold back when they see our anti-tank guns.

"And there's another vitally important aspect to all this. The Germans on the Eastern Front have just attacked Stalingrad. The Soviet Red Army has to hold the city at all costs—if the Germans manage to cross the Volga River, they'll get control of the Caucasus oilfields, and that will also mean a Nazi victory in this war. So Stalin will have to throw everything he has against the Germans. If he can stop them the way we held Rommel last month, he'll be able to counterattack the way Montgomery is about to counterattack—with hundreds of tanks. And again, if the Germans believe that the Allies have the promethium anti-tank shell, they'll hold back their tanks on the Eastern Front, just like Rommel is hopefully going to do here, and that'll give the Soviet commander the same advantage that we're trying to give General Montgomery in the desert."

"Sir, there's something I don't understand," Wright said. "You stated that if we can persuade Rommel that we have this anti-tank shell, he'll be more cautious in the coming battle. But why do we have to persuade him that we have the shell? On the contrary, surely we want him to be as aggressive as possible, so that his tanks will charge into our anti-tank guns and be destroyed before they can reach our lines? Surely my telling him about this shell was the worst possible thing we could do?"

There was a long pause. Colonel Marlowe cleared his throat and was about to speak, then thought better of it. Another pause followed, even longer than the first. Finally, Marlowe made up his mind.

"Wright, I'm going to trust you with a secret so important that, if you let the cat out of the bag, we may lose the war."

He paused again.

Wright said nothing.

"Captain Wright, let me ask you a question. Do you believe that we have an anti-tank shell made of promethium that's accurate over twice the current effective range and is twice as destructive?"

"Of course I do, sir. Before I went to see Kezerian, I carefully scrutinized the photographs I sold him. Not just the guns and the tanks, but the picture of all the generals, as well. And so, and so..." His voice petered out. Then he broke the silence. "Sir, do you mean to tell me that this is all an elaborate deception?"

"Well, Wright, have you ever seen one of these truly remarkable anti-tank shells?"

"Only the pictures of the five shells in the ammo box in that last photograph. I haven't seen the actual shells, of course, but I assume that this is all classified Top Secret, and that the men will be issued the new shells at the last minute, just before the battle commences."

"Yes, that is what you were supposed to assume in order to convince that blackguard of an antiquities dealer. And I have no doubt that he fell for it. But tell me, is it really likely that there's a mine somewhere in New Zealand where we've found an element that has eluded scientists for decades? And that our boffins somehow have discovered that, if you take this promethium and use it to make an anti-tank shell, the shell will travel twice as far and be twice as destructive as a standard shell? And that there's a factory somewhere, probably located near that mine in New Zealand—but perhaps in Australia—that's turning out these extraordinary armor-piercing shells? And that these miraculous shells have been shipped to us in Egypt in the greatest secrecy without anyone finding out about any of this?"

"But I've seen the photographs, sir."

"Really now, Wright, do you honestly and truly believe that the camera cannot lie? What if the second tank, the one supposedly hit by the promethium shell, was actually blown up with high explosives?"

The British captain's mouth dropped open, and he was unable to speak for several seconds.

Finally, he protested. "But sir, what about the photograph of the generals?"

"And what about that picture, Wright? Montgomery told his generals that he wanted some photographs of all of them together that he could use for morale purposes. They drove out to the training area in a bus, the combat photographers did their work, and a few minutes later the generals were on their way back to headquarters here in Cairo. The whole operation took about an hour, and while they were travelling in the bus, Montgomery discussed some of his plans with them—in order to avoid any time wasted. Once the generals were safely back in the bus and on their way to Cairo, an anti-tank gunner hit the first tank with a conventional shell, sappers blew up the second tank, and the photographers took the remaining pictures."

"But what about the abbreviations on the ammo box, sir? Why is there a 'Pm' on the second wooden box, together with the 'NZ' marking?"

"They're on that box because I ordered Sergeant Taubman, who spends most of the day sitting in Room 28 working extremely hard at decoding intercepted German messages, to get a set of stencils and a tin of black paint and put them on the box. I think he did an exceptionally neat job, don't you?"

Wright's eyes grew large but he did not say anything more. Then he blurted out, "Sir, how did you find out that Kezerian is a German agent?"

"The same way we've uncovered all the other spies we've caught," Colonel Marlowe said, "by sheer chance. A patrol in the Western Desert about 10 miles from El Alamein encountered a truck about to drive across a minefield we'd just laid. The driver was an Egyptian named Mahmud. On the seat next to him was a two-week old map of our minefields, and next to it was a map of the German minefields on their side of the El Alamein line. Under his seat we found a large envelope containing four of our Top Secret military documents. We staged a quick trial, sentenced him to death by hanging and then told him that if he divulged to us where he obtained the documents and worked for us, we'd overlook his traitorous behavior.

"He told us that he was a courier for an Alexandrian antiquities dealer named Aram Kezerian, ferrying documents across the desert from Kezerian to Field Marshal Rommel's headquarters behind the El Alamein line. We made enquiries and found that Kezerian inherited the shop from his father and grandfather before him, and was highly regarded by everyone for both his professional expertise and his scrupulous honesty."

"Did you say 'scrupulous honesty,' sir?"

"Yes. And that posed a problem for us. We didn't have any solid evidence against Kezerian, only the confession of a truck driver who'd say anything to save his miserable neck. And we couldn't question the dealer, because that would alert him that we're onto his nefarious activities. So instead we decided to utilize him to send disinformation to the Germans. As a first step, we prepared a map that purported to show the defenses of part of the El Alamein line, photographed it, and sent 'Klaas van Deventer' to sell the photo to Kezerian. I told your brother-in-law to ask for two hundred pounds but to accept whatever the dealer offered."

"But wasn't Kezerian highly suspicious, sir?" Captain Wright asked. "A soldier he's never seen before enters his shop with a picture of an item of military intelligence worth many thousands of pounds, but asks for only two hundred. Surely Kezerian realized that this was a trap?"

"You're looking at it the wrong way round. If Klaas van Deventer were an Allied agent, he'd know the true value of the map to an enemy spy. But our man wanted only two hundred pounds for it. To test him, Kezerian offered one hundred pounds, which van Deventer immediately accepted. No British agent would possibly do that."

"But why didn't you arrest the dealer after he paid for the photo?"

"For two good reasons. First, because he would've indignantly stated that a Top Secret map of the greatest military importance for which he'd just paid only one hundred pounds was unquestionably a forgery, and that he'd paid the soldier just to get rid of him and not cause a scene. Kezerian was well aware that there was no risk involved in buying the photograph from van Deventer. And second, Kezerian is the perfect conduit for sending disinformation to the Germans. His courier, Mahmud, is working for us. That's why we've done nothing about Kezerian—we have full control over what's passing between him and Rommel.

"But what if Mahmud conveniently 'forgets' to show us something?"

"That's a good question, Wright. But we've thought of that, too. When we gave him a current map showing a route through our minefields he could use to get to the German lines, we warned him that we'd be passing documents to Kezerian to check if Mahmud shows them to us on his way to Afrika Korps headquarters—the photograph of the defenses taken by your 'brother-in-law' was one of those test documents. As Mahmud handed over that day's delivery for Rommel to his British handler in Alexandria for checking, the intelligence officer said to him, 'Mahmud, there had better be a photograph of a map of part of the El Alamein line in this envelope.' Fortunately for Mahmud, the photo was there. But he got the message, and I doubt that he'll ever 'forget,' as you put it, to show us anything. After all, he's well aware that we can change our minds about the death sentence at any time."

"What's going to happen now, sir?"

"I have no doubt that tonight Mahmud is going to take your photographs to Rommel, together with a detailed report from the Germans' top spy in Egypt, your good friend Aram Kezerian. When we see his report, we'll know for sure whether you convinced Kezerian."

"So Rommel will know about the new promethium shell by late tonight?"

"I'm certain he will. And the *Abwehr* will find out about it soon thereafter. Fortunately, we think that the German Military Intelligence organization doesn't have an agent in New Zealand."

"Why 'fortunately,' sir?"

"Wright, surely you realize that we don't want the Germans to discover that there's no promethium mine in New Zealand, at least until we've won the two forthcoming tank battles I just mentioned to you? As I told you, our strategy is to make the Germans believe that we have the promethium anti-tank shell so that they'll hold back and fight defensively, giving us a clear advantage. It's true that they may have someone working for them in Australia, but he would have to travel from there to New Zealand, no easy task for a conscription-age man in wartime. Then he would have to scour New Zealand to try to find the promethium mine. In an atlas, the two main islands may look tiny, but together they're larger in area than the United Kingdom. However, if the Germans have an agent in place in New Zealand, he'll have the contacts to find out about all the mines in that country, and it wouldn't take long before he radios Berlin to tell them that the promethium story is a deceptive strategy designed to win future tank battles."

There was another pause.

"Any more questions, Wright?"

"No, sir. Thank you for taking me into your confidence, sir."

"Just remember to keep your mouth shut. Dismissed!"

Wright snapped to attention, saluted as smartly as before and left Colonel Marlowe's office.

Colonel Marlowe smiled. "Just enough truth to satisfy Wright's curiosity," he said to himself. "There's plenty of time before the battle starts to tell him what's really going on."

# CHAPTER THREE

*Coopers Island, New Zealand*
*Wednesday, August 26th, 1942*

The sun rose behind the thick bank of dark clouds as the blacked-out naval launch slid slowly up to the jetty where Major MacKenzie stood waiting. The soldiers lining the deck eagerly helped the seamen fasten the lines to the bollards. The first part of their trip, from Dunedin to Ruapuke Island, had been bad enough, with most of the 24 Home Guard soldiers aboard either feeling too nauseated to leave their sleeping bags or retching violently over the side as the ship rolled through over a hundred degrees of arc in the usual heavy swell. But when the ship entered Foveaux Strait, even the remarkable few who had managed to stay on their feet now succumbed to severe seasickness. With *terra firma* finally within reach, everyone wanted to assist in tying up the ship at Coopers Island as quickly as possible.

Under the orders of Major MacKenzie, the Home Guard soldiers unloaded the cargo onto the jetty. They carried the arms and ammunition from there to the ranger's house constructed some years before on the edge of the woods overlooking the wharf. When they had eventually organized everything to the Major's full satisfaction, the Major led the men from the house along the trail cut through the pristine temperate rainforest to the eastern side of the island, where the mine was located. He halted the column when the leading soldiers reached the small wooden guard hut. He then stood the men at ease, facing the mine. The old-growth forest rose behind them; the sea stretched into the far distance beyond the mine all the way to Chile.

"Former members of the First New Zealand Expeditionary Force," he began, "every one of you fought with extreme valor during the First World War. You distinguished yourselves at Gallipoli and in Palestine, during the Battle of the Somme, in the storming of Messines Ridge and at Passchendaele. You came home laden with honor. You are the finest soldiers that New Zealand has ever produced, heroes of the highest order. Small wonder that, when the British Empire declared war on Germany in September 1939, you all rushed to enlist in the Second New Zealand Expeditionary Force.

"And what happened?" Major MacKenzie asked. An indignant look appeared on his face and his white moustache bristled. "You were turned down on grounds of age and shunted into the Home Guard. It was a travesty, with New

Zealand's bravest and finest men being forced to stay home and guard our islands against a non-existent threat, while lesser men were allowed to fight in Greece and in North Africa."

The major paused again and gathered his thoughts. "But now, you have a chance to display your mettle once again. A genuine threat has arisen. Look at the mine in front of you. What do you see?"

A stocky man with gray wavy hair raised his hand. "Yes, Lance Corporal Lewin?"

"Sir, from here, the mine seems deserted. It doesn't look as if anyone has been inside it for months. On the other hand, the guard hut looks new—the wood hasn't yet been discolored by the weather."

"Very observant, Lewin. With your excellent eyesight you should once again be a front-line sniper, not a member of the Home Guard. Yes, the mine has been abandoned—for now. I shall explain.

"This mine contains deposits of a rare mineral. I cannot tell you its name, because it's a military secret. Actually, they haven't even told me what it's called, and that's a fact. But I've been informed that this mineral is essential for our war effort in Egypt. We've extracted as much of the ore as we're going to need to defeat Rommel and clear the Nazis out of North Africa. If we need any more for future campaigns, the miners will return and dig deeper into the earth. But in the meantime, we need to make sure that the enemy doesn't get its hands on this mine.

"I'm sure you've all been following the progress of the war. Everyone knows that the Japanese have reached the Solomon Islands. But Gaudalcanal is about 2,000 miles from Auckland and 3,000 miles from here. Furthermore, New Zealanders are fighting alongside our American allies in the Solomons and we're winning. So, there's certainly no imminent invasion threat of the conventional kind."

Major MacKenzie paused for the third time and gazed over the 24 men who were totally engrossed in what he had been saying. He resumed his briefing.

"Now, what if the Japanese learn about the deposits of the mineral inside the mine? They may well try to capture this island and hold it for a few days, just long enough to get their hands on a sufficiently large supply of the ore for them to use against us in the Pacific. Or they might give all or some of it to their German allies. As you can see, it's essential that we prevent the Japanese from getting their hands on the mineral.

"And that's where you men come in. The High Command in Wellington is concerned that the Japanese may mount an aircraft carrier-based paratroop raid, or perhaps they'll try to land commandos by submarine. Your task is to detect any invasion of any sort whatsoever, immediately radio accurate details to headquarters on the mainland, and then hold off the invaders until we can bring forces to bear from the mainland to fight alongside you.

"You'll be based in Cookville, the only village on Tudor Island. The jetty where you landed today on Coopers Island is only 200 yards from the Cookville jetty across Raphael Channel. Your billets will be in Cookville—24 of the islanders have kindly agreed to put you up in their homes. I'll divide you into three squads of eight men each. Each squad in turn will guard Coopers Island for eight hours. The boat bringing the next squad across from Tudor Island will take the previous squad back.

"Regarding Coopers Island: Most of the island is a nature reserve. As you've seen, it's a beautiful old-growth forest, totally unspoiled. The trees teem with birds of all kinds. Now listen carefully:

"There are three buildings on the island. First, there's the house overlooking the jetty where you've just stored your guns and ammunition. It was built so that the forest ranger who's responsible for the nature reserve can live on the island. We've taken over Coopers Island and barred all civilian visitors, so there's obviously no need for a ranger any more. The front room of the house, which overlooks the jetty where you came ashore, has a clear view across Raphael Channel of Tudor Island and its jetty. So I'm using that room as my office and my quarters. The other two rooms are for you men. One bedroom contains the weapons and ammunition that you just unloaded. The other is your Day Room. But you won't be spending much time there. When you're on duty, you'll patrol the island; when you're off duty, you'll return to Tudor Island. The islanders have set up the St. Barnabas Church Hall in Cookville as your Day Room there. It's also your mess.

"The second building on the island is the public toilet in the middle of the forest. The Ministry of Agriculture and Fisheries constructed it for the bird watchers who used to come here all the time—I'm sure you saw the signs pointing to the toilet as we passed that huge clump of silver ferns on your way here. The third building is the guard hut in front of you.

"Any questions?"

A tall soldier raised his hand. He had the build of an athlete and the tanned skin of a farmer.

"Sir," he asked, "what's the mineral used for?"

"Sergeant Clayton, even if I knew I wouldn't be allowed to tell you. But I genuinely don't know. I suggest that you ask General Freyberg that question when he comes here."

"The Commander-in-Chief is coming to Coopers Island?" a voice asked softly from the back rank.

"Never!" another nameless voice said. "The old bugger would get sea-sick."

Major MacKenzie knew better than to yell, "Silence in the ranks!" or, worse, "Sergeant, take those men's names!" Instead, he just smiled a mysterious smile and marched his men back to the jetty.

# CHAPTER FOUR

*Coopers Island, New Zealand*
*Saturday, August 29th, 1942*

Sergeant Clayton could not believe his eyes. He had patrolled the trail through the temperate rainforest that led from the ranger's house on the southern shore of Coopers Island to the beach on the northern edge. As he walked onto the pearly white sand, he saw two of the most beautiful young women he had ever seen in his whole life, and that included the unforgettable week he had spent in Paris before reluctantly boarding the ship that brought him home to New Zealand in January 1919 after the Great War had finally ended. The women sat on the sand directly in front of him, their arms and legs absorbing the rays of the winter sun; their shorts and tops were decidedly skimpy.

His orders were clear: He was to detect invaders, report their details accurately to headquarters, and then hold off the intruders until reinforcements from the mainland arrived at

Coopers Island. But every experienced soldier sometimes disobeys orders.

He knew how to speak sternly to young women; his own twin daughters, back on his Otago farm, were about the same age as the sunbathers. But as he approached the goddesses, the strict look on his face melted away. "What are you doing here?" he blurted.

"Why, sergeant, we always come here," the blonde said. "Mystic Beach is our favorite, favorite beach in all the world."

"Yes, miss, I can understand that. But don't you know that Coopers Island is out of bounds for all civilians?"

"Not the whole island, sergeant. We live in Cookville. You know Cookville—you've been billeted there since Wednesday. On perfect days like this, we row across the channel, tie up our boat at the jetty, walk through the forest and arrive at Mystic Beach. You walked through that beautiful forest to come here, didn't you? It's just dreamy, isn't it? Anyhow, we've been told that we can't use that jetty any more, so we just rowed around the island straight to Mystic Beach."

"Miss, the whole island is out of bounds to civilians. There are signs everywhere, including on that pole in the sand where you've tied up your boat."

"No, that sign doesn't apply to us," the brunette said. "We're locals; we've lived on Tudor Island all our lives."

"And another thing, miss, the jetty is on the south side of Coopers Island. Raphael Channel is narrow and relatively sheltered. But this beach is on the north side of Coopers Island. That's Foveaux Strait in front of you, one of the wildest waterways in the world. It makes the Straits of Magellan seem like a millpond. You say you're locals, so you must know that you took your lives into your hands when you left the north exit of Raphael Channel, turned eastward and entered Foveaux Strait in that small rowing boat."

Both women were silent. They knew only too well that Sergeant Clayton was right.

"Look. My orders are to arrest anyone who sets foot on Coopers Island."

"Arrest us?" The blonde fluttered her eyelids at Clayton.

"Yes, miss. That's my orders. But I'm a reasonable man. I'm prepared to let you go with a warning, provided you give me three promises."

The two women looked expectantly at Clayton.

"You must promise me that you will never, ever return to Coopers Island until the restrictions have been lifted. And that includes Mystic Beach and the forest. The entire island is positively out of bounds to all civilians at all times."

They nodded as the sergeant continued.

"You must give me your word that you will never again enter Foveaux Strait by yourselves."

He waited for them to nod again.

"And finally, you must promise to tell all your friends in Cookville that the entire island is out of bounds to everyone, including the locals."

The two young women solemnly promised.

"I know that forbidden fruit tastes the sweetest, and that you and your friends view visiting Coopers Island as a challenge. But all of us, myself included, are carrying guns loaded with live ammunition. And our orders are to shoot first and ask questions afterwards. You and I are on the same side; the Germans and the Japanese are our enemies. We could never forgive ourselves if we shot a fellow Kiwi.

"Now, there's no way on earth that I'm going to allow you to row back the way you came. Foveaux Strait is far too dangerous for that. The current is flowing strongly today, and you'll probably be washed out to sea.

"Instead, I'll escort you down the path through the forest to the jetty and explain the situation to Major MacKenzie. I'm sure he'll let you travel back with us to Cookville in the boat at the end of our eight hours of guard duty."

"But what about our rowing boat?" the blonde asked.

"That's up to Major MacKenzie. Hopefully he'll find some way to get it back to Tudor Island in due course. Now come with me to the jetty."

The two chastened young women rose and silently accompanied Sergeant Clayton.

When they reached the forest ranger's house, he told them to wait while he went inside and spoke to the Major.

"You can stay in our Day Room until the boat arrives," he said when he rejoined them. "It's the second door on the right as you go in."

As he watched them enter the house, he muttered a prayer under his breath for their safety and for the safety of all the young women of New Zealand, including his own twin daughters.

# CHAPTER FIVE

*Berlin, Germany*
*Wednesday, September 2nd, 1942*

"Gentlemen," said Admiral Canaris, head of the *Abwehr*, "I have called you here once again to come up with a good solution to an important problem. The *Führer* himself wants immediate action taken in New Zealand. Thanks to a comedy of errors, we actually have an agent in place there but, as you will learn, he's part of the problem, rather than part of the solution. We also have an agent in Australia but her situation, too, is somewhat problematic. Actually, it's considerably more than just somewhat problematic."

It was clear from the frown on the Admiral's elongated face that he was most unhappy with the situation. Under craggy white eyebrows, his steel blue eyes sent the message that he expected the members of his handpicked executive team to find a quick and effective solution to the problem. They were seated around the large wooden table in the conference room at *Abwehr* headquarters on the

Tirpitzufer, a tree-lined street situated adjacent to the Landwehr Canal in Berlin.

"First, I want to welcome Detective Chief Superintendent Horstmann and Major von Grauschild to our team. To ensure that they understand the problem that we're facing, I would like to ask Colonel Donndorf to give a brief summary of the information he gave us when we last met two days ago."

"Thank you, Admiral Canaris," Donndorf said. His manicured fingers adjusted the monocle in his right eye. "Gentlemen, you have in front of you a file containing a set of photographs plus a report from our top agent in Egypt, code name JULIUS. Up to now, we've found his information to be reliable. However, as you all know, the more reliable we consider an agent to be, the greater the risk that we'll be deceived if he passes on to us disinformation planted by the enemy. Accordingly, I was charged with contacting German's top scientists regarding the likelihood of the facts stated in the report from our agent.

"I telephoned a number of professors of geology and asked them three questions. First, I asked them if it was likely that the Allies had discovered element 61. They all told me that it was undoubtedly possible. Scientists have been actively searching for that element for decades now, so it's certainly conceivable that they've actually found the substance that they named promethium. Then I asked the professors if, given the geological structure of New Zealand, it was likely that promethium could be found there. They all said that this, too, was possible. In fact, they felt that promethium could have been discovered just about anywhere in that country. Finally, I asked them if it was likely that promethium could be found in sufficiently large quantities to make tens of thousands of anti-tank shells. Of course, I didn't put my question in those terms, but in effect, that was what I asked them. All the experts were emphatic that this was most unlikely. They informed me that rare earths are almost never found in deposits that are large enough to be economically exploitable, let alone in the vast quantities needed to make any sort of impact on the war. In short, the geological experts cast the strongest doubts on the information that our agent in Egypt passed on to us.

"Then I contacted four professors of metallurgy and also two chemistry professors. They were all extremely dubious that a shell made of element 61 would be superior in any way to a standard anti-tank shell made of steel. On the contrary, they stated that anything made from promethium was likely to be relatively soft. Again, for security reasons I didn't pose my question in precisely those words, but that was the implication of their responses to what I actually asked them. It quickly became clear that we were the targets of a disinformation campaign—for reasons still to be determined, the Allies want us to believe that they're in possession of a nonexistent superweapon.

"I'd nearly finished writing up my conclusions when one of the experts I'd consulted, Rainer Erzherzog, professor of metallurgy at the Kaiser Wilhelm Institute for Metals Research in Stuttgart, telephoned me back. Professor Erzherzog suggested that perhaps I'd been asking the wrong question. He pointed out that, when two elements are mixed, the resulting alloy can have properties that are vastly different to those of the two components separately. First, he gave as an example the fact that copper and tin are both soft metals, but their alloy, bronze, is hard. Then, he pointed out that we can considerably strengthen iron by adding another element, carbon, to yield steel.

"Finally, he gave a third example. He said that we can strengthen steel even further by adding other elements, such as silicon, manganese and chromium. Now, German anti-tank shells used to be made by adding nickel, chromium and molybdenum to steel, but because of the current shortage of molybdenum we now add silicon, manganese, and chromium, precisely the three elements mentioned in his 'example.' In short, it was clear that Professor Erzherzog had seen through my stratagem, and had realized that I'd actually been asking him about anti-tank shells. Then Erzherzog pointed out that it was certainly possible that adding a small amount of element 61 to the alloy that the British are currently using for their anti-tank shells would result in a shell with enhanced properties.

"I thanked the professor warmly and then contacted the same experts a second time. The geologists now all agreed that it was possible that a promethium mine in New Zealand could yield enough of the rare earth to enhance the strength and effective range of tens of thousands of anti-tank shells when added in small quantities. And all the metallurgists and the chemists also agreed that it was definitely possible that adding promethium to a standard steel alloy could yield a shell with considerably greater effective range and penetration power.

"In short, if we interpret the photographs and the report from our agent in Egypt as referring to 'anti-tank shells made of a steel alloy containing a relatively small amount of promethium' rather than 'anti-tank shells made solely from promethium,' then the report becomes scientifically credible."

"Thank you, Colonel," Admiral Canaris said. "Your conclusions lead directly to the problem that Germany is facing. If the facts stated in the report from agent JULIUS are true, then we have to locate that mine, and we need to do it quickly. Once we've found it, the High Command of the Armed Forces under Field Marshal Wilhelm Keitel will have to decide what action to take. It's likely that their plan will involve our Japanese allies who are now within striking distance of New Zealand. The Japanese Home Islands are surprisingly deficient in minerals, so Japanese metallurgists have become experts in discovering useful alloys made from the limited metals that they have. Accordingly, there's no question that Japanese metallurgy experts will closely scrutinize any request that the *Führer* may put to the Japanese Supreme Council for the Direction of the War. This makes it all the more vital that we determine with total certainty whether the report from Egypt is factually correct in all its details and, if so, precisely where in New Zealand the promethium mine is located."

This statement was met with nods from all the participants.

"So, gentlemen," Admiral Canaris continued, "our next move must be to find the mine, assuming that it exists. And that means sending an agent to New Zealand." He cleared his throat. As he started speaking again he opened the orange file, marked *Streng Geheim* (Top Secret), that was lying in front of him on the ornate wooden conference room table. "In 1937, we decided to send an *Abwehr* agent to Australia. We chose Siegfried Kleinfeldt. Kleinfeldt is a dedicated National Socialist; he joined the Nazi Party when he left school in 1930, three years before *Herr* Hitler became the German Chancellor. We trained him thoroughly, especially in codes and shortwave radio technology, because he was going to be the sole *Abwehr* agent Down Under. We sent him to London, and there he obtained a residence visa for Australia.

"Now, in July 1938, an international conference was held in Évian-les-Bains, in France, to try to find a solution to the issue of the increasing numbers of Jewish refugees fleeing from Germany.

At that conference, Australia was represented by Thomas Walter White, the Minister of Trade and Customs, who spoke out strongly against Jews coming to Australia. I have here in the file his actual words, namely, 'As we have no real racial problem, we are not desirous of importing one by encouraging any scheme of large-scale foreign migration.'

"Well, our agent arrived in Sydney just after White came out with that statement. The immigration officer there noted that our man had been born in Hamburg. He immediately concluded that the Aryan Siegfried Kleinfeldt was actually a Jew fleeing Nazi Germany and sent him straight back to England on the next boat."

Before Admiral Canaris had completed his sentence, Colonel Donndorf interrupted him. "Are Australian immigration officers really that stupid?"

"Apparently so," Canaris replied. "But the story gets worse. When Kleinfeldt arrived in England, the immigration authorities there sent Kleinfeldt straight back to Hamburg, because he'd been deported from Australia. And he's still sitting in Hamburg. Siegfried Kleinfeldt would've been the perfect agent for us in Australia. But for that idiotic Australian bureaucrat, we could send him a coded radio message instructing him to proceed to New Zealand immediately to investigate this mine.

"We were back to square one. Then, in September 1938 someone came up with the excellent idea of sending two agents to Australia. The first was Gretchen Konrad. She's an American woman, a member of the German American Bund, the American Nazi organization. Her personal details and three photographs are in the file in front of you. She's 35 years old and, as you can see, most attractive, with natural blonde hair and big blue eyes. Gretchen arrived in Chicago from Germany as a child of six, and accordingly speaks English with a perfect American accent. She's actually a veterinary nurse, but we provided her with forged papers stating that she's a qualified large-animal vet. After all, Australia is brimming with cattle and sheep, and we expected that an American-trained large-animal veterinarian would be welcomed with open arms."

Colonel Donndorf interrupted again. "Admiral, I appreciate that Gretchen was born in Germany to German parents, but for all practical purposes, she's an American. Can we trust a foreigner?"

"That's a good question. I'll tell you about her and then you can judge for yourself. Her father, Ludwig, became the European sales manager for an American airplane manufacturer. He made frequent trips back to Germany. On one such trip he met Hermann Göring, who introduced him to the *Führer*. Ludwig Konrad became a committed Nazi, joining the party in 1930. In 1933 he was a co-founder of the Chicago branch of The Friends of the New Germany, a forerunner of the German American Bund.

"Meanwhile, Gretchen qualified as a veterinary nurse and worked in a veterinary clinic in Chicago. She lived with her mother and father. Very occasionally men would invite her out, but most evenings she stayed home or went out with her parents. Her father kept trying to persuade her to join The Friends of the New Germany, but Gretchen reacted as any American child would— she did the exact opposite of what her father wanted.

"One day in September 1933, she packed a suitcase and left home without saying goodbye to her parents. She went to live with the owner of a dachshund she'd helped to treat, a member of the Central Committee of the Communist Party of the United States. Gretchen left the veterinary clinic and began to work full-time for the Communist Party. Her parents tried many times to contact her, but she spurned all their attempts.

"Four years later, she was in bed with the flu when she heard a radio broadcast by Father Coughlin. It was one of his typical attacks on President Roosevelt, capitalists and Jewish conspirators. Somehow Father Coughlin was able to awaken feelings in Gretchen that her father had been unable to arouse. Less than a week later, she was back home and working for the German American Bund."

"She seems unstable and unpredictable, and probably untrustworthy, as well," Colonel Donndorf said.

"True," Canaris replied, "but, as you well know, the same can be said for so many of our most successful agents. Well, in 1938, Gretchen announced that she wanted to return to her homeland and help build the New Germany. The Chicago leadership of the German American Bund, especially her father, persuaded her that she could be far more effective as an undercover agent. We arranged for *Abwehr* personnel stationed in America to train her in Chicago—we didn't want there to be any record of her travelling to or from Germany. In addition, there were a number of members of the German American Bund who instructed her in a variety of additional techniques, including handgun skills.

"When she had all the necessary expertise, we sent her by ship to Sydney, where she had no trouble finding immediate employment in Bathurst, a country town some five hours from Sydney by train—Bathurst is the center of a major wool production region."

"Isn't Bathurst also the first place in Australia where they found gold?" the colonel asked.

"Donndorf, gold doesn't enter into this—we're looking for a promethium mine, not a gold mine. Returning to the subject of Gretchen in Bathurst, we didn't provide her with a shortwave transceiver. The plan was that she would send messages to us via our second agent in Australia, just as soon as we could arrange for him to get there. In the meantime, we made the necessary arrangements for her to remain in contact with the people at the German Consulate-General in Sydney. They agreed to act as intermediaries, passing messages between Gretchen and us. Because she wasn't going to have a radio, we saw no reason to teach her coding techniques, let alone the absolute necessity to encode every single message she sent to us, without exception. And that was a bad mistake.

"About six months after she arrived, she sent us a lengthy radio message. She'd somehow managed to acquire a British-made transceiver, a Marconi I believe. We never found out how she obtained it or whether the way she acquired the set could've led to a security issue. The problem was that, because she knew nothing about codes, the message she transmitted to us was unencrypted—she'd had to send it in plaintext. She'd asked the radio operator at the German Consulate-General for wavelength information. Never dreaming that she mightn't encrypt her message, he gave her all the information she needed. So, one fine day, our radio station in Hamburg received an endless plaintext message in German that sent shockwaves through the *Abwehr*. We quickly transmitted a coded message to our Consul-General in Sydney to tell her to never send another message to us except in case of direst emergency, and even then to keep it as short as possible. We instructed her to tell us how she obtained the radio—but she never responded to that order via the Consulate-General. Finally, we also told her when and where to listen for messages for Berlin.

"And it's a good thing we did that, because I ordered a message to be sent to her this morning, in plaintext of course, telling her to go to Auckland right away because her brother is desperately ill. Sydney is the major city on the eastern seaboard of

Australia and the city closest to New Zealand, and Auckland is the capital of New Zealand, so there are plenty of ships she could take from one side of the Tasman Sea to the other. Of this, more later."

A hand shot up halfway down the table. "Yes, Major von Wilczek," Canaris said. "I know exactly what you're going to say. You're going to ask me if I took into account that my radio message that Gretchen received on Wednesday night at 10:30 p.m. Sydney time could result in her being arrested. And you know I'm going to reply that, if true, this promethium mine could change the course of the war, so I had to take the risk. Correct?"

"Not exactly," was the reply from a blond man wearing the Knight's Cross of the Iron Cross around his neck. "I was just going to respectfully point out that Auckland is the largest city in New Zealand, but Wellington is the capital."

His subordinates greatly respected Admiral Canaris, so the major's remark resulted in little or no reaction around the table. However, Canaris himself smiled broadly, enjoying the joke at his expense. He took a sip of water and then continued.

"Regarding our second agent in Australia, we decided to send him via New Zealand. Once he'd taken out New Zealand citizenship, he could move to Australia with no obstacles of any kind—we weren't going to have him sent back, too. We chose a German vet, Walter Benz. The reason we chose another vet is that he would be eminently employable in both Australia and New Zealand.

Ever since Captain Cook brought the first sheep to New Zealand in 1773, the sheep population has grown—today there are 20 sheep for each of the one and a half million New Zealanders.

"We changed his family name from Benz to Bennett; we couldn't have two agents in Australia with obviously German last names. We trained him as best we could in two months, gave him a Telefunken shortwave radio transceiver and sent him off to Auckland. But we made one mistake, unfortunately a big one: We didn't realize that the New Zealand electricity supply uses 230 volts, not 110 volts like here in Germany. We learned from a fellow passenger when he returned to Germany that Bennett arrived in Auckland and passed through immigration without any problems. But since then we've heard nothing from him, presumably because he blew his radio set when he switched it on the first time.

"So, we have a partially trained agent living not far from Sydney whom we can contact in plaintext, but who has been ordered not to transmit messages to us except in the case of dire emergency. And we have a half-trained agent, whom we believe is currently in Auckland—and we cannot contact him at all. And that, gentlemen, is why I said that our agents in New Zealand and Australia are part of the problem we're facing. Any questions or comments?"

A hand went up.

"Yes, Horstmann?"

Detective Chief Superintendent Horstmann was a nondescript man in all respects: average height, average build, receding brownish hair and a face that had no particular distinguishing features. Even his voice was unexceptional in every way. His suit was plain gray, his tie a darker shade of gray.

"Admiral, in your plaintext radio message transmitted to her today at her listening time, how was Gretchen Konrad instructed to contact Walter Bennett?"

"I simply told Gretchen to travel to Auckland because her brother, Walter Bennett, is desperately ill."

"I understand why Gretchen had to be given the family name of her brother in New Zealand, but surely the inclusion of 'Bennett' in the message might make anyone intercepting the transmission somewhat suspicious."

"Yes, of course. But I had no choice. The only way to get to New Zealand nowadays, other than sailing a small boat across the Pacific while praying that no aircraft or warship spots you, is by ship from Australia. And Australia and Germany are at war. To get a message to Gretchen I would first have to smuggle an agent from Berlin to, say, neutral Portugal, and then he would have to travel from there to Australia. That would take weeks, time that we just don't have. So I sent Gretchen a short message in plaintext. And it had to be in English—it would undoubtedly have set the cat among the pigeons if the Australian authorities had intercepted a plaintext transmission in German. How would you have handled it, Detective Chief Superintendent?"

"Admiral, I have no doubt that what you did was not just the best course of action under the circumstances, but also the only possible course of action. I asked the question because I think that, from now on, we need to be aware that both Gretchen Konrad and Walter Bennett may have been compromised, and the Allies may use one or both of them to feed disinformation to us. My work here in Berlin has taught me that the British in particular are experts at deception."

"I take your point, Horstmann. All of us are well aware of the many attempts that the British have made to deceive us. For all we know, the photographs that we have in front of us may be forgeries, too, and the new anti-tank shell may not even exist, let alone the mine in New Zealand."

"Another question, if I may?" Horstmann enquired.

"Yes, of course. Please go ahead."

"Let's suppose that the mine exists and that Gretchen finds it. How will she let us know what she's discovered?"

"I can only hope that she'll take her transceiver with her to New Zealand. Ideally, she'll locate Walter Bennett and give her radio to him, so that he can send encoded messages to us. But she may not realize that this would be the right way to go about it, or she may decide, for whatever reason, to leave her transceiver behind in Australia."

Donndorf interjected yet again. "Admiral, based on her past record, Gretchen is most unstable. Her behavior is unpredictable. And we know that she won't obey orders. In short, we cannot rely on her in any way. As far as I'm concerned, it's quite possible that she's now a member of the Communist Party of Australia, living with a member of the Central Committee there. Or she may be working for the Australian government. She may even have passed your message on to the Australian secret police."

"Donndorf," Canaris replied, "Earlier in the meeting you asked, 'Can we trust a foreigner?' In the case of Gretchen Konrad, we have no choice—we just have to. Everything is now in her hands. And when I say 'everything,' that may well include the outcome of the war."

# CHAPTER SIX

*Bathurst, Australia*
*Wednesday, September 2nd, 1942*

Gretchen Konrad took off her headphones and placed them on the kitchen table. Her hands were shaking. Finally, after three years of total silence, the *Abwehr* had sent her a radio message.

She had stolen the Marconi transceiver soon after she arrived in Bathurst, from a rural police station no less, and kept it hidden in a locked cabinet in her kitchen. One afternoon she had been called out to an outlying sheep farm to assist a prize merino ewe that was experiencing difficulties giving birth. She managed to save the lives of both the mother sheep and its lamb, earning the eternal gratitude of the farmer and his wife. It was now eleven o'clock, and they urged Gretchen to spend the night in their guest bedroom on the farm. But she insisted on returning to Bathurst in case someone needed her there in the morning to treat a sick animal.

On the long drive back through the darkness, she stopped at an isolated police station to use the restroom. The building was open, the lights were on, but no one was inside. On her way out, she noticed a radio transceiver on a table at the back of the charge office. On an impulse she darted behind the wooden counter, grabbed the radio and bundled it into the trunk of her car. She drove back to Bathurst quaking with fear, expecting every minute to hear a siren behind her, but she arrived back at her rented two-bedroom house without incident.

The way that Gretchen viewed the situation was that, for some unstated reason, her controllers in Berlin did not want her to have a radio. Accordingly, her training in Chicago had not included encryption, let alone Morse code. But she had managed to outsmart them all. Not only did she now have a transceiver, but she had also found a thin volume on Morse code in a second-hand bookstore in Bathurst.

She spent her lonely evenings learning all about dots and dashes. Once she understood the principles, she practiced assiduously. She perfected her technique by communicating on three occasions with a ham radio operator on an isolated sheep farm in Western Australia, more than 2,000 miles away, surely a safe distance from that rural police station. And when she was ready, she sent a long message in German to Berlin.

They were furious with her, so the Consul-General (and *Abwehr* representative) at the Sydney

Consulate told her when he telephoned her. He tried to explain the need for security and therefore encryption, but she cut him off and hung up the phone. Not wanting to lose her as an agent, he called back two days later and simply told her the day and time she was to listen each week for messages transmitted from Hamburg. Not long after that, war was declared, and all German diplomats in Australia had to immediately return to Germany.

Gretchen had the sense to realize that, during wartime, use of a radio to chat to lonely farmers posed a security hazard. From then on, every Wednesday night just before half past ten, she had taken out the set, placed it on the kitchen table, plugged it in, and listened in vain for a message in Morse sent from the *Abwehr* radio transmitters in a suburb of Hamburg. Other than that, the set remained safely locked away. It was hard for her to refrain from using it at other times, because on each occasion that she switched it on and donned the headphones, a thrill of triumph went through her body as she remembered what she had achieved behind the backs and against the wishes of her handlers. But her self-control was strong enough to keep her from transmitting and possibly being detected.

Week after week for three frustrating years she had listened for instructions from Berlin. All she heard in her earphones was static. But that night a message had arrived loud and clear. The operator in Hamburg had not known about Gretchen's expertise with Morse and had sent the message slowly, twice. She read the letters on the message pad yet again: "Your brother Walter Bennett in Auckland is seriously ill."

She immediately packed two suitcases. One contained the clothes she had brought with her from Chicago. Essentially living the life of a hermit in Bathurst, she had purchased only three items of clothing since her arrival in Australia. The first was a leather stockman's hat with a wide brim to protect her from the fierce Australian sun. Then she bought a water- and wind-proof Driza-Bone oilskin coat for outdoor work when the sun was not shining. Finally, two years after arriving in Bathurst, she took the opportunity to take out Australian citizenship, and she bought a new dress for the naturalization ceremony, held on Australia Day. The local Member of the Legislative Assembly had conducted the proceedings, and in his brief speech had directed warm words of welcome to the "American lady vet" who had immigrated to Australia to help the local sheep farmers.

After a few moments of thought, Gretchen put all three garments on top of her American clothes in her first suitcase. She had prepared the other suitcase two years before. On the outside she had stenciled the words "Veterinary Instruments" in white paint. Inside she had sewn straps to hold the radio in place. She had added pockets for the power cord, Morse key, aerial and other items.

Finally, she had purchased a lock and chain to ensure that no one would try to open the case.

Next she went to the second bedroom, which she used as an office. In her copy of the *Handbook of Veterinary Science* she had hidden nearly 500 pounds in banknotes, specifically for an emergency such as this. She took the Australian currency out of the book and placed it in her wallet, which she stuffed into her handbag, together with her Australian passport and her New South Wales veterinary license.

She managed to rouse the Bathurst telephone operator on duty that night, telling her that she (Gretchen) had to rush to the bedside of her sick sister in Melbourne and would be away for some time. Gretchen then wrote the same message on a sheet of paper from her prescription pad and fastened it to the front door of the house. Then she loaded her two suitcases into the trunk of her car and headed through the darkness to Sydney.

The first 40 miles along the Great Western Road were an easy drive. But once she reached Lithgow and entered the Blue Mountains, she had to concentrate on the road every inch of the way. She was relieved when she left the mountains at Penrith, but the strain of the winding road and her lack of sleep started to overwhelm her—she had been awake for more than 20 hours. She drove with the car windows open, in the hope that the night air would revive her, but it did not help much. She was able to keep going by thinking all the time of Nazi troops battling valiantly in the

Western Desert of North Africa and on the
Eastern Front in Russia, and hoping that her
mission in New Zealand would assist them in
achieving glorious victories.

Fighting her tiredness, she drove straight
toward the port, arriving as the sun rose. Being
wartime, she was closely questioned at the
inspection post by both a customs inspector and a
plainclothes police officer. Eventually they let her
pass after she had explained to them that she had
been summoned to New Zealand to try to contain
a virulent outbreak of Bluetongue disease that
threatened to cross the Tasman Sea and wipe out
every one of the 110 million sheep in Australia.

"Which is the next ship that's heading for New
Zealand?" she asked the customs inspector.

"The *Star of Adelaide* is sailing as soon as the last
of the cargo is aboard," he replied, "but you're
going to have to be extremely persuasive. Captain
Moffat is exceedingly reluctant to take female
passengers across the Tasman Sea."

"And why is that?"

"He says that the rough seas between Australia
and New Zealand are no place for the weaker sex."

"We'll see about that," she said grimly.

"By the way, you do know that it takes four
days to get there, don't you?" the customs
inspector asked.

"Four days?"

"Yes. These old cargo vessels aren't too fast, to
put it mildly. And ever since that attack by those
three Japanese midget submarines here in Sydney

Harbour three months ago, ships zigzag if they even suspect that there's a sub in the vicinity. That slows them down even more."

"I see."

"Well, best of luck, miss. Turn left over there, and Berth Seven is the third on the right.

Gretchen left her car in a parking place behind a warehouse. Then she took her handbag, lifted her heavy suitcases out of the trunk and carried them with difficulty over to the *Star of Adelaide*. A deckhand stood guard at the foot of the gangway.

"I'd like to see Captain Moffat, please," Gretchen said.

"Wait here," replied the seaman. He turned toward an upper deck of the ship and yelled to an unseen colleague, "Lady to see the Captain!"

About 10 minutes later, the captain appeared. His gray hair was extremely short, and this gave prominence to the two large ears that stuck out at right angles to his head. His badly creased navy blue shirt and blue trousers were stained with oil, and he looked angry.

"Yes?" he barked.

"I'm sorry to disturb you, Captain Moffat," she said sweetly, "I know how busy you are with the ship about to sail, but I have to reach New Zealand in a hurry."

"So why don't you fly, then?"

"Because there are no civilian flights in wartime. In any event, they won't take my veterinary equipment—it weighs too much."

"You're a vet?" Captain Moffat asked.

"Yes, I am."

"A lady vet?"

"That's right."

"There's no such thing."

She opened her handbag and showed the captain her veterinary license. "The New South Wales government says there is, and they want me to rush to New Zealand to help their government do something about this epidemic of Bluetongue disease. It's threatening to wipe out every last sheep in New Zealand and then cross the Tasman Sea and do the same thing to our sheep here. You know all about this outbreak of Bluetongue, of course."

Captain Moffat had never even heard of Bluetongue disease, and he certainly knew nothing about the 'epidemic' that existed only in Gretchen's fertile and creative imagination. But there was no way that he would admit his ignorance to any woman on any topic whatsoever, so he grunted affirmatively and then quickly changed the subject.

"What's all this talk about Australian and New Zealand governments? You sound like a Yank to me."

She opened her handbag again, this time taking out her Australian passport, which she showed him. "I'm proud to be an Aussie, same as you. Yes, I was an American. My government sent me to Australia to help with the war effort—the Allies desperately need Australian wool for military uniforms, and Australian lamb and mutton to feed the troops."

At the mention of "war effort," Captain Moffat changed his strategy and switched to Plan B.

"As a loyal Australian, I'll do anything I can to help the Allies achieve a speedy victory, but the stormy Tasman Sea is no place for a woman, not even a woman who's a lady vet."

Realizing the captain's Achilles' heel, Gretchen immediately brought the conversation straight back to the war.

"Captain Moffat, we all have to make unending sacrifices for this war. I'm prepared to face the rigors of the Tasman Sea in order to make sure that our troops get the wool and mutton they need."

Moffat jerked his right thumb over his shoulder. "Cabin Three. There'll be no charge for your passage, because it's for the war effort." Then he turned his back on Gretchen and quickly climbed up the gangway.

Gretchen turned to the deckhand. "Where can I find Cabin Three?"

Once again the deckhand communicated with his invisible comrade on an upper deck. "Passenger for Cabin Three!"

He turned to Gretchen. "He'll be waiting for you at the top of the gangplank, miss."

It was hard to clamber up the steps carrying her handbag and the two heavy suitcases, but there was no way she was going to ask anyone for help. A scruffy looking skinny man with long black hair was standing on the deck when she reached it. He pointed vaguely to his right. "Cabin Three is that way," he said, then left Gretchen to find it by herself. It was unambiguously clear to her that she was most unwelcome on the *Star of Adelaide*.

Gretchen struggled to open a heavy watertight door and found herself in the dining saloon. The two tables were laid for breakfast. She noticed a few food particles on the cutlery, and quickly realized that cleanliness was not a top priority of the chef or the steward. She wondered to herself about the possibility of contracting food poisoning en route to New Zealand.

On the other side of the saloon was a door leading to a corridor with a number of cabins on each side. The first door was labeled "Men." She was not in the least surprised to find that there was no corresponding door labeled for the use of members of the other gender.

"Well, they'll have to share their facilities with me," she said to herself. "It's just another sacrifice that has to be made for the war effort."

Two doors down she found Cabin Three. She had not slept for more than 24 hours, and that together with the long drive through the mountains in the pitch dark, the weight of the two suitcases she had carried, and the mental stress she was under since receiving the radio message from Germany had all taken their toll. She was exhausted. So she simply put her suitcases down and climbed into the lower bunk. A few minutes later she was asleep.

\*\*\*

Gretchen was awakened by the sound of her suitcases sliding around and slamming into a bulkhead. Groggily she got up from the bunk to solve the problem, and found herself thrown to the floor of the cabin as the ship pitched, yawed and rolled in the high seas.

The four days of the crossing from Sydney to Auckland were the four longest days of her life. The chance of food poisoning never arose, because just thinking about food made her feel even worse.

When the ship finally rounded North Head and sailed into the calm waters of Waitemata Harbour to dock, Gretchen ventured on deck for the first time. The sun on the eastern horizon had just started to climb into the intense blue sky, the water was an even deeper shade of blue, and a few wisps of white cloud scudded high overhead. Seagulls floated above, arrogantly screeching as they defied the law of gravity. In the distance she saw hundreds of yachts moored in a bay like a forest of bare tree trunks.

Gretchen suddenly felt that all was right with the world and with herself in particular. She went back to her cabin, picked up her unopened suitcases and headed for the gangway. As she entered the dining saloon for only the second time on the voyage, the deckhand who had stood at the foot of the gangway stopped her.

"Sorry, miss," he said, "but no one can leave the ship until it's been cleared by customs, immigration and the health authorities. Sit here, they'll soon come into the saloon. You can leave your suitcases in that corner."

Gretchen now noticed that one of the two tables had been cleared, and a large shallow wooden box lay there. It was filled with passports, identity cards of various sorts and a sheaf of papers. She took a seat at the other table, which was once again laid for breakfast. Was it only four days since she had so nonchalantly embarked on the *Star of Adelaide*?

The watertight door opened and four men entered, all carrying briefcases. An army major accompanied the three officials listed by the deckhand. It was immediately obvious to Gretchen that all the men were surprised to see her there—Captain Moffat's misogyny was apparently widely known. They nodded politely as they entered, but otherwise ignored her as they went through the various items in the box. They worked methodically and did not talk at all, but the customs officer hummed tunelessly to himself under his breath.

After about 15 minutes, the immigration official spoke to Gretchen. "Could I see your passport, please?"

As she got up and handed it to him, the captain entered the dining saloon. Ignoring Gretchen, he asked the men, "I assume that everything is in order, as usual. Have you cleared the ship?"

"Why is your manifest incomplete?" asked the major. "All it says here is 'Female passenger for Auckland.' This is inadequate at the best of times, and totally unacceptable in wartime. For all we know, this lady might be a German spy." All four men seated at the table guffawed loudly, and Gretchen contributed a ladylike laugh to the general merriment. Captain Moffat had a distinct "We are not amused" look on his face, and his large protruding ears reddened.

Having opened her passport by this time, the immigration official said, "As soon as we've examined Miss, er, Konrad, we'll clear the ship, Captain."

Moffat stomped out of the dining saloon. The immigration official turned to Gretchen and said, "Please take a seat. This won't take long. I see you're an Australian citizen. But you were born in Bremen, in Germany, so I have to ask you a few questions."

Gretchen nodded her understanding.

"What is the purpose of your visit?"

The presence of the health official had made her wary of using the Bluetongue yarn yet again. Instead, she came out with the story that she had constructed while waiting for the four men to plough through the many documents in front of them.

"I received a letter from a colleague in Auckland. He's currently overwhelmed with work. He knew that I had a month's leave coming from my veterinary practice in Bathurst, and he asked me to come here and assist him. I've never been to your beautiful country, and I thought that a working holiday would provide an excellent way of visiting New Zealand, while helping a friend out."

"You're a vet, then?" asked the major.

"Yes, I am."

"I didn't know that Australian vet schools admitted women," he continued.

"They do. But I got my degree in Veterinary Medicine at the University of Tennessee in Knoxville, in the United States."

The major went on. "How did you end up in Bathurst?"

"I've always wanted to see the world, so I answered an advertisement for a job in Sydney. Unfortunately, it had been taken by the time my letter arrived there, but I was offered the job in Bathurst instead."

The immigration official interrupted. "I don't think we need to keep you any longer, Miss, er, Doctor Konrad. Please give this card to the official at the exit to the docks. Enjoy your stay!"

He stamped her passport with an unnecessary flourish, and then pointed in the direction of the gangway. Gretchen looked at the yellow card she had been given. It bore her name, an official stamp, a signature and the date. She put it inside her passport, which she carefully inserted inside her handbag.

She left the saloon with her suitcases and struggled unsteadily down the gangway. Following directions given by a passing stevedore, Gretchen made her way to the exit of the cargo docks where she encountered a customs official and a uniformed police inspector. She handed them her passport together with the yellow card she had been given. The police officer checked both documents carefully and then waved her through. Gretchen went up to the customs official and asked, "Where can I get a meal?"

"You just came from Australia, didn't you?" he asked with a friendly grin.

"How did you know?" she replied.

"They say that there are only two possible crossings of the Tasman Sea: really bad and much worse. It's an exaggeration, of course—occasionally the sea is calm. Ironically, even though Abel Tasman was the first European to discover New Zealand after a nightmare journey sailing across what is now called the Tasman Sea, he never actually set foot in our country because he was too seasick! Anyhow, ravenous passengers can get a hearty meal at the Seafarers Café across the street over there. They'll even take Australian money—they know that new arrivals are so desperate for food after four days of starvation that they simply can't wait to go to a bank to change their money. And after breakfast, you might want to take a room at the Captain Cook Hotel—it's one block from the café."

# CHAPTER SEVEN

*Auckland, New Zealand*
*Monday, September 7th, 1942*

A delicious aroma met Gretchen when she entered the café. She made her way to an empty table in the corner, and a waitress approached. She was plump and pretty, and her starched white apron and cap gleamed.

"Good morning, miss," she said. "You look tired. Have you just arrived from Australia?"

"Good morning. Yes, on the *Star of Adelaide.*"

"Well, it's breakfast time, miss, so you'll be wanting a plate of chops, eggs and chips."

And without waiting for an answer she headed off to the kitchen. Gretchen wasn't sure if the waitress had said "chips" or "chups" but decided against calling her back—the young woman apparently knew what was appropriate for breakfast.

While she waited, Gretchen glanced round the café. Almost all the tables were taken, and the room was filled with happy chatter. The clock mounted on the wall opposite her showed that it was just after nine, and she immediately adjusted her watch to New Zealand time.

Ten minutes later the waitress returned with a white oval plate containing three large lamb chops, well done; two fried eggs with intensely yellow yolks, cooked sunny side up; and a mountain of crisp fried potatoes, the "chups." Gretchen suddenly realized that the New Zealand accent was totally different from the Australian dialect of English spoken back in Bathurst, which at that instant seemed to be part of another universe.

"I'll bring your tea and toast right away," the waitress said, and bustled back to the kitchen.

Gretchen could not decide if the food tasted so wonderful because she had not eaten for four days, or whether the chef at the Seafarer Café was a culinary genius. She ate every mouthful, wiping the remaining drops of the rich egg yolk from her plate with the last of her toast. She was strongly tempted to ask for a second plate, but wisely just asked for her bill.

"Please pay the cashier," the waitress said, tore a paper off her order pad, laid it on the table and hurried off for the third time. It was clear from her manner that she did not expect a tip, and she probably would have politely refused if Gretchen had been unwise enough to offer one. Just as back in Australia, tips apparently were not customary here.

Gretchen was amazed to see how little she had been charged, even allowing for the fact that the

New Zealand pound had been devalued to only 16 shillings sterling. She paid with Australian money, and the smiling cashier handed her New Zealand coins as change.

"Thank you, miss, and please come again."

Gretchen was about to thank the cashier, when suddenly she found herself yawning uncontrollably.

"You must be tired, miss, after crossing the Tasman Sea and all. The Captain Cook Hotel is only a block away, up the street. It's a most respectable hotel, reasonably priced, and you'll be comfortable there."

Gretchen thanked her and headed in the direction indicated. As she reached the front door of the hotel, an elderly porter stepped out, took her luggage from her hands and held the door open for her. At the reception desk an older, immaculately coiffed woman greeted her with a sympathetic smile.

"Did you just arrive from Australia? My dear, you must be exhausted after that four-day nightmare. Porter! Take the luggage up to Room 16, please."

And turning again to Gretchen, she added, "Don't worry about signing the register now—you can do all that after you've had a good sleep."

Still wearing the clothes she had on when the brief message from Germany arrived, she flopped onto the bed and immediately fell into a deep slumber.

She dreamed that her father appeared and repeatedly badgered her with the same four questions in the same order: Why are you in New Zealand? Who is Walter Bennett? How will you make contact with him? How will you recognize him?

Gretchen woke in a sweat, her heart thumping in her chest. Eventually she managed to calm down and get back to sleep, but the dream kept recurring.

# CHAPTER EIGHT

*Auckland, New Zealand*
*Tuesday, September 8th, 1942*

After breakfast the following day at the Seafarers Café, Gretchen asked the cashier where she could find a public phone.

"There's a red telephone box a few blocks up this street. It's quite similar to the ones you have in Australia. If you give me back that shilling I just gave you in your change, I can give you the pennies you'll need to pay for your calls."

"And where can I find a bank to change some money?"

"Unfortunately, the nearest bank is a good 10 to 15 minutes from here. From the phone box you continue up this street until you reach St. Columba's, that's the large stone Presbyterian Church. Then you turn left. Keep going, and you'll find it on the right."

Gretchen thanked her and headed for the public telephone box. She found it easily. Looking at her watch, she saw that it was nearly eight. She could catch Walter before he left for work.

The telephone directory was badly tattered. She noticed that it bore the date 1939—to conserve paper, no new directory had been printed during the three years since the war had started. There were two entries for "Bennett W." She dialed the first number.

"I'm so sorry to bother you," she said.

"No worries," replied the friendly voice at the other end.

"I'm trying to contact Walter Bennett."

"Sorry, there's no Walter Bennett here. I'm Wilfred Bennett."

She thanked the man, apologized again for disturbing him, and hung up. Then she dialed the other number. This time a woman answered after only one ring. "Fancy you asking for Walter Bennett—someone else phoned me last week with the same question. Yes, Walter used to have this telephone number, but he's moved to Wellington. I hope you find him."

Checking that she had sufficient coins for the long-distance call, she asked the operator to connect her to Walter Bennett in Wellington. She deposited the requested two shillings in the slot. A minute later she heard a male voice with a heavy Teutonic accent saying, "This is Walter Bennett."

She immediately switched to German.

"*Herr* Bennett, my name is Gretchen Konrad. I've been sent to meet with you."

The man stuck to English. "My name is Bennett. Who are you? What do you want? And who sent you to meet with me?"

Still speaking German, she replied, "My name is Gretchen Konrad. I was sent by the organization we both work for."

"I work for the Ministry of Agriculture and Fisheries."

"No, I was referring the organization that sent you to New Zealand."

There was a long silence, interrupted by the operator asking for more money. Gretchen hastily deposited the additional coins, and then spoke urgently in German. "*Herr* Bennett, I'm in Auckland. I must meet with you urgently. I'll take the next train to Wellington. Where can I find you this evening?

"29 Captain Cook Terrace," he said before hanging up.

As she left the public telephone box and started walking in the direction of the bank, Gretchen asked herself why Bennett was so frightened. Then she wondered about the address he had given her. She was staying at the Captain Cook Hotel, and Bennett claimed that his home was on Captain Cook Terrace. Obviously, this was this just a coincidence—she hadn't told him the name of her hotel in Auckland. But did Bennett actually live there, or had he just given her the first street name that came into his mind? And was there any significance to the number 29?

After walking briskly for a quarter of an hour she found the bank easily enough, but she had to wait outside in the queue until it opened at nine. When her turn came, she asked the teller to exchange three hundred Australian pounds into New Zealand currency. The teller asked to see her passport. Then he asked her for her address in New Zealand, and how long she intended to stay. He seemed strangely reluctant to change her money, but he finally provided her with the currency she requested.

Gretchen immediately hurried back to her hotel, repacked the few items that she had taken out of her suitcase, paid her bill, and asked the porter to fetch her luggage and summon a taxi to take her to the railway station. After a short ride, the driver dropped her in front of a vast beaux-arts brick edifice.

There was nearly a half-hour wait for the 10:15 train. Gretchen used the time to buy a newspaper and two magazines for the 10-hour journey. However, she never had the need to open them because she was so captivated by the ever-changing views from the train window. She saw white beaches and rugged coastlines, mountains and volcanoes, and endless varieties of thick bush and forest. Even when she went to the dining car for her meals, she continued to stare out the window at the glorious vista, never the same from moment to moment.

As the sky began to darken, the train pulled into Wellington railway station. Despite the fuel shortage, Gretchen had no trouble finding a taxi to take her to Captain Cook Terrace. Number 29 proved to be a single-story detached house built in the art deco style.

She rang the bell and a man came to the door. The two agents looked at one another. They were remarkably similar in appearance. Both were about 35 years old, of medium height, slender, with fair hair and blue eyes. Gretchen's hair was long, with a parting on the left side. Walter's hair was of military length, but with a parting on the same side as Gretchen's. Neither wore glasses or jewelry of any kind. But an outside observer would have noticed one big difference: Gretchen looked confident, whereas Walter was clearly afraid.

"May I come in?" Gretchen asked in English. She saw how frightened he was, and remembered his reluctance to speak German.

"Yes. Come inside and sit." His English had become stilted and Germanic.

"Thank you."

He ushered her into the kitchen. She placed her two suitcases on the linoleum floor against the wall and sat on one of the two wooden chairs. The walls of the kitchen were bare; there was not even a calendar.

Walter sat opposite Gretchen. It seemed to her that he was extremely tense, almost fearful.

"Who are you and why have you come here?" he demanded to know.

"I received a message from our employer, telling me to come to Auckland and meet you. I tried to phone you in Auckland, but I was told that you now live in Wellington. And here I am."

"But why were you sent to see me?"

"I don't know, but we can find out why."

"Are you crazy? What do you mean, you don't know why you're here but we can find out?"

Gretchen realized that it was now or never. She would have to reveal herself and face the consequences if this was the wrong Walter Bennett. The name was correct, and he clearly understood German and spoke English with a German accent that was heavy at times, notwithstanding his last name. There was no possible alternative course of action. She took a deep breath and crossed the Rubicon.

"I have a radio transceiver in that suitcase."

There was a long silence.

"I said, I have a radio transceiver in that suitcase."

"Yes, I heard you the first time. Does it work?"

"Of course."

She put the suitcase on the table. Then she took a key out of her handbag and unlocked the chain. She opened the suitcase and showed him the contents. His mouth dropped open.

"Are you sure it works in New Zealand? The one they gave me was for the wrong voltage. I turned it on and it blew up."

Gretchen smiled to herself. She had found the right Walter Bennett. A wave of relief passed through her body and she shuddered slightly.

"Yes, it works. That's how I received the message in Australia to contact you."

"You came here from Australia?"

"Yes, I live in Bathurst, a town not too far from Sydney. And they sent me a message to come and visit my brother, Walter Bennett, in Auckland."

"I don't understand. Why didn't they tell you what you are to do here?"

"I know Morse code well, but they didn't teach me anything about encryption. So the *Abwehr* people were forced to send me the message unencrypted. That meant that they had to say as little as possible."

"They sent you a message in plaintext?" Bennett asked with a note of rising panic in his voice.

Knowing nothing about encryption, Gretchen had not heard the word "plaintext" before. But she quickly realized that it was a technical term meaning "unencrypted" and nodded her assent.

"They sent out my name in plaintext?" he asked again. The man was visibly more terrified than before.

"Yes, but there's no harm in that."

"No harm? No harm? How on earth can you say such a thing? Now the New Zealand police know that I'm an *Abwehr* agent."

"Not at all. The radio message said: 'Your brother Walter Bennett in Auckland is seriously ill.' Now how does that message tell the New Zealand police, or anyone else for that matter, that you're an *Abwehr* agent? No one knows who sent it, who they sent it to, where that person lives, or anything else. It was a short radio message sent into the ionosphere, and that's all."

Bennett thought for a minute. "The message said that your brother in Auckland is seriously ill. But I'm not seriously ill, and I live in Wellington, not Auckland."

"Precisely. And in addition, you're not my brother. In the highly unlikely event that someone somewhere in the world picked up the transmission and decided for some unfathomable reason that the message is sinister in some way, they would quickly discover that there's no Walter Bennett in Auckland, and that would be the end of that."

"But there is a Walter Bennett in Wellington. You're talking to him."

"But you're not seriously ill, and you don't have a sister. So the trail leads nowhere. But there's no trail in the first place. Someone sent out a radio message that mentioned your name. It was one of millions transmitted that day. You have absolutely nothing to worry about."

Bennett seemed to calm down slightly. But he was clearly still fearful. Gretchen realized that there was nothing she could do to assuage his fears. Instead, she decided to try to move forward.

"I have to send a message in code to Berlin to find out why they sent me here and what I'm supposed to do. Could you encrypt it for me?"

There was a long pause while Walter thought about her request. He realized that, if he did not agree to help her, she might send a message in plaintext, which would be utterly disastrous for his safety. The only way he could stay safe, he decided, was to co-operate with this woman who had come from Australia to imperil him by tying him to his past as a former *Abwehr* agent.

"Yes, I can do that. When is your connection time?" Walter asked. And then he realized that he could stay out of trouble with the New Zealand police if he did nothing more than encrypt and decrypt Gretchen's messages. His fears started to abate somewhat.

"I'm scheduled to receive every Wednesday night at 10:30 p.m. Australian Eastern Standard Time. That's 12:30 a.m. on Thursday morning, New Zealand Standard Time. My transmission time is 10:30 p.m. every Thursday night."

Walter corrected her. "In their emergency regulations last year, the government extended our half-hour daylight savings to cover the whole year and not just from the first Sunday in September, which was two days ago. So, here you receive on Thursday morning at 1 a.m. and transmit on Friday morning at 1 a.m., New Zealand Summer Time.

"With the current time regulations, my window is now every Monday night at 10:30 p.m.," he continued. "I was told to receive at that time and to transmit exactly 24 hours later, on Tuesday night at 10:30 p.m." Walter informed her. "Tonight is Tuesday night. So that gives you more than two hours to compose a message, for me to encrypt it, and then for you to transmit it tonight. You'll tell them to send the reply to us during your reception window."

"Fine." Gretchen said. "You said that they gave you a transceiver, but for the wrong voltage. So how have you communicated with them?"

"I haven't. I've been here for four years with no means of communication, neither sending nor receiving. They'll be most surprised to hear from me after all these years."

"Yes, I expect so," Gretchen said. "Now, I think I need to get started putting my message together. We have to make the transmission deadline."

Gretchen nervously drafted and redrafted her message. After half an hour of hard work, she handed it to Walter.

"Excellent!" he proclaimed in a patronizing manner. "Short, but you've included everything they need to know. You've told them you're in Wellington with me, you state that you've brought your transceiver along with you, and you ask them what they want you to do here. Then you tell them when to reply. Perfect. It'll take me less than an hour to encrypt it."

Walter sat at the kitchen table and encrypted the message. Gretchen sat in the front room and read the magazines she had bought for the train trip. Walter joined her just before ten.

"As I thought, it took me less than hour to encrypt," he said. "But then I checked each word, just to be safe. Everything is perfect—it's ready to be sent. Let's set up the radio on the kitchen table.

The aerial can go from there into the front room—
that should work well."

"While we're waiting," Gretchen said, "may I
ask you a few questions?"

"Certainly."

"Can I stay here?"

"Of course. Where else would you stay? By the
way, who knows you're here?"

"Just the taxi driver who brought me to your
house straight from the railway station."

"Well, stay indoors. After work at the Ministry
tomorrow I'll buy extra food—the only food items
that are rationed here are sugar and tea."

"Do you have a spare bedroom, or should I
sleep on the couch?"

"I have three bedrooms, and you can sleep in
the back one. The bed is quite comfortable. Now,
after you've sent the message, what should we do
with the radio?"

"In Bathurst I keep it hidden in a locked
cabinet in my kitchen."

"I have a locked closet in my bedroom. Let's
store it there when it's not in use."

Gretchen noticed that not only did Walter seem
to have lost his fears, but also he had switched to
German. She smiled to herself.

And now it was the time for her to send their
message to Germany. She turned on the set and
put on her headphones.

***

The next day Gretchen made a conscious effort to relax and recover from her tense drive through the night and her ordeal on the *Star of Adelaide*. However, the eagerly awaited response from Berlin was uppermost in her mind. She kept asking herself why the *Abwehr* had sent her to New Zealand.

That evening, Walter arrived home laden with food. Gretchen helped him cook their dinner. After the meal, they sat in the front room. Gretchen turned to Walter and asked, "Could you explain the encryption process to me? I've heard of the Playfair code—is that the sort of thing you use?"

"Not at all," Walter replied with a superior expression on his face. "I use this codebook that they gave me. It's just a dictionary together with a reverse dictionary. Suppose I want to send the message 'Germany is winning the war.' I first look up 'Germany' in the dictionary, and I get the five-letter group AUUWX."

"But what does AUUWX mean?"

"It doesn't mean anything. It's just a random set of five letters. Similarly, 'is' is encrypted as AYLWI. The whole message would read AUUWX AYLWI PJTJM KORLH IROQE."

"I understand," Gretchen said. "But how does the recipient decrypt the message?"

"You use the reverse dictionary. All the 50,000 or so words in the dictionary are listed in alphabetical order. So if I look up AUUWX in the reverse dictionary, it tells me that the word is 'Germany.'"

"Are there really 50,000 words in the dictionary?"

"Yes. They went through thousands and thousands of messages and constructed entries in the code dictionary for all the words they found."

"But suppose the message you want to encrypt is 'Gretchen is here in Wellington.' Surely you won't find 'Gretchen' or 'Wellington' in your dictionary?"

"No, you're quite right. You won't. But the letters of the alphabet are all there. I would simply spell out your name as 'Letter G,' 'Letter R,' and so on. Of course, sometimes you can use clever tricks. For example, if I want to send the message 'Winston Churchill,' I can write the message as 'win stone church hill' and then use the codebook to encrypt those four words. Another trick is to use a synonym. For example, to save having to spell out 'transceiver' letter-by-letter in the message you transmitted last night, I just substituted the word 'radio.' Encryption is not hard at all."

"In that case, can I encrypt the next message we send to Germany?"

"No, I think it would be better if I did it, and then you can check my work by decrypting the message back to plaintext."

# CHAPTER NINE

*Wellington, New Zealand*
*Thursday, September 10th, 1942*

It was two o'clock on Thursday morning. From the time that Walter had arrived home on Wednesday evening, they had waited with increasing tension for 1 a.m. to arrive. Fueled by fear, the pressure grew until Gretchen finally excused herself and went to sit and read in her bedroom until a quarter to one. Then she went into the kitchen and found that Walter had already set up the transceiver and aerial as before.

The radio operator in Hamburg transmitted the lengthy message from *Abwehr* headquarters in Berlin precisely on time. Gretchen wrote down the groups of five letters, and then handed the lengthy message to Walter to decrypt using his codebook.

Admiral Canaris himself had signed the message to them. He began by congratulating both agents on their achievements. He informed them about the promethium anti-tank shell, and explained in detail why their mission was of critical importance to Germany. He then instructed them to locate the promethium mine in New Zealand and report back to him as soon as possible. He went on to point out that the Allies would surely guard a mine of such vital significance to their war effort, so if Gretchen and Walter saw a mine that anyone could freely access, they could probably scratch it off the list. Conversely, if a mine was well protected and had a relatively new boundary fence, they should definitely investigate it further. Furthermore, there had to be a way of transporting ore from the mine to a factory. Unless there was some means of achieving this, the mine could probably be disregarded. Canaris also pointed out that promethium was a newly discovered element, and the mine might therefore be unusual in some respects. He concluded by reminding them that this was an extremely urgent matter, and the Third Reich needed accurate information regarding the promethium mine as soon as possible. Accordingly, he informed Walter that his transmission window was now every evening at 10:30 p.m., and instructed him to listen 30 minutes later for transmissions from Berlin. Nowhere in his communication did Canaris even hint at the possibility that the mine might not exist.

Walter read the message aloud to Gretchen and then Gretchen asked him to read it again. She was like a child in a chocolate factory. She did not notice that Walter was markedly less enthusiastic than she was. Also, she still had not realized that, as far as he was concerned, his contribution to the German war effort began and ended with code matters. For Walter, all other aspects of the mission were solely Gretchen's responsibility.

But then an idea suddenly came to him. A smirk flitted across his face.

"I know how you can do what Admiral Canaris wants," he said. "The only thing you need is a list of all the mines in New Zealand."

"But surely that's classified information during wartime," Gretchen said.

"Of course it is, but I'm very high up at my job—I report directly to the Permanent Secretary for Agriculture and Fisheries. Max Malone, one of my friends, has a similar position in the Department of Lands and Survey, and he would certainly have such a list."

"But why would he give the list to you?"

"Suppose I tell him that we've received a report of sheep dying from eating bushes poisoned by minerals from mines, and that my Minister wants me to organize an inspection of every mine in New Zealand."

"Will he fall for that?"

"I think he will—he's brilliant, but he's totally devoid of commonsense. Anyhow, let's turn in now. I have to go to work tomorrow."

***

That evening, Walter came home with a smug look on his face. Gretchen could see that he was extremely pleased about something.

"I think you got the list of mines from your friend," she said with a smile.

"Yes, the stupid fool fell for it. I went to his office first thing in the morning and asked him for the list. Max seemed extremely dubious about the whole matter. He wouldn't even give me a definite answer. But just before I left for home, he came to my office and handed the list to me."

"Well, let's go through it together."

There was a long pause. Then he said, "Let's first sit down and talk about this."

"What's there to talk about?" Gretchen asked. "The only question is whether we should celebrate your triumph before or after working through the list."

"No, there's something we need to discuss first. Sit down."

They sat on the wooden chairs in the kitchen as on the first night. He paused again.

"Look, Gretchen," he finally said, "I've been in New Zealand for more than four years now and all that time I haven't been with a woman."

"So?" Gretchen asked. "What does that have to do with the list?"

"Everything. If you want the pleasure of having the list, you're first going to have to give me some pleasure."

"Are you saying what I think you're saying? That I have to sleep with you in order to get the list?"

"In a word, yes."

"Are you crazy?"

"Yes. More than four years without a woman has driven me crazy."

"Why don't you sleep with a prostitute?"

This remark shocked him even more than his demand had shocked her. "Don't be stupid. Prostitutes carry all sorts of foul diseases. And in any case, it's morally wrong to pay for sex."

"Morally wrong? *Morally wrong?* Isn't it much more morally wrong for you to blackmail me into sleeping with you?"

"It's not blackmail at all. I'm not threatening you with anything. I'm simply saying that, unless you give me a really good time in bed this evening, I'm not going to give you the list of the mines."

"But you've read the message from Admiral Canaris. The future of the Third Reich depends critically on the mineral in this mine. We have to locate it, and quickly."

"You still don't seem to understand, do you? I'll spell it all out for you in words of one syllable. I don't give a tinker's damn about the Third Reich. They sent me here with a radio set that was built for the wrong voltage. Until you arrived here this week with your transceiver, I was totally cut off from the Third Reich and its bumbling idiots who don't even know about electricity. Once I realized how incompetent those stupid Nazi blockheads are, I decided that I wanted nothing more to do with them. All I'm prepared to do for those morons at the *Abwehr* is to encrypt and decrypt your messages.

"If you want that list of mines so that you can go off by yourself and look for the promethium, that's fine with me. But first there's a price you'll have to pay. Remember, nothing in life is free."

While he was at work she had prepared a delicious dinner. They ate it in chilly silence. After dinner he read the morning newspaper from cover to cover, then announced that he was going to bed. "And if you want that list," he reminded her, "I suggest that you join me there in a few minutes—if not sooner."

During the meal, she had suddenly realized that one way of acquiring the list was to kill Walter. But how would she dispose of his body? Her mission was to find the promethium mine, and being arrested for murder would prevent her carrying this out.

Eventually she came to the conclusion that she had no alternative. As a loyal servant of the Third Reich, she needed to obtain the list of mines from Walter, and the end definitely justified the means. So, when she heard his bed creaking, she went to her room, took off all her clothes and put on her robe. She walked into his bedroom, which was now in darkness, dropped the robe and climbed into his bed.

It was all over in less than three minutes. He rolled off her and onto his back, and almost instantly started snoring. Gretchen fled to the bathroom, where she endlessly tried to wash away the shame of what had happened.

She stayed in bed the next morning until Walter had left for work. The list of mines was lying on the table in the kitchen. Gretchen picked up the sheets of paper, glanced quickly through them, folded them, went to her room and put them into her handbag. She dressed mechanically. Next she took a screwdriver that she had noticed in a drawer in the kitchen, prised open the locked bedroom closet, and took her transceiver and the codebook. She then packed both suitcases, chaining and locking the one that again held her radio and now the codebook as well. She phoned for a taxi and, when it arrived, she left the house taking all her belongings with her.

"Would you please take me to a hotel near the station?" she asked the driver.

"How about the Masonic Hotel?" he suggested.

"Anything but the Captain Cook Hotel," she responded. "Is there a Captain Cook Hotel near Wellington Station?"

"No, I'm afraid there isn't."

"Excellent. I want nothing more to do with Captain Cook. Ever."

# CHAPER TEN

*Wellington, New Zealand*
*Friday, September 11th, 1942*

Walter returned home from work on Friday evening to a quiet house. He deduced that, contrary to his explicit instructions, Gretchen had gone out for a walk. His conclusion was soon bolstered by a knock on the door—after all, he had not given her a latchkey.

He walked purposefully to the front door, intending to inform Gretchen in no uncertain terms that this would be the last time that she would go outside like this. He was dumbfounded when he opened it to find two men standing there. One man was tall and thin, black haired, with a widow's peak. His eyebrows arched down on both sides, framing his brown eyes. His nose and his lips were thin, and he had a pronounced five o'clock shadow, especially near the jaw line. The other man was also thin, but shorter than his companion. His copper-colored hair was curly. He was fair skinned, with a light sunburn on his cheeks and forehead. A band of freckles spread across his snub nose, extending an inch or so on each side. His eyes were blue-green, and a half-smile hovered on his face.

"Walter Bennett?" the taller man said in a deep voice.

"Yes. Who are you?"

"I'm Detective Chief Superintendent Jennings of the New Zealand Police Force and this is Detective Superintendent Mudge of the New South Wales Police Force. May we come in?"

Walter just stood there, so Jennings took him by the arm and led him into the front room. Mudge closed the door behind them and followed the other two men.

"Sit down, Mr. Bennett," Jennings instructed him.

"Wh-why are you here?" he stuttered.

"Where's Gretchen Konrad and, more importantly, where's her radio set and your codebook?"

"I have no idea what you mean."

"Yes, you do. Miss Konrad arrived here on Tuesday night, with a Marconi transceiver in her second suitcase—the one with the lock and chain. That night she sent a brief encrypted message to Berlin asking for instructions. No, I'm not smart enough to be able to decrypt the message—you carelessly left the piece of paper with both the plaintext and the encrypted version in the wastepaper basket in your bedroom, torn into four pieces. And we found the reply from Admiral

Canaris in the bedroom closet where you kept the radio, both the five-letter groups and the plaintext."

"How dare you come into my house when I'm not here? And that closet is locked."

"Here's a search warrant that gave us the right to enter your premises this morning, soon after Miss Konrad left, taking her radio set and your codebook with her. And, no, we didn't jimmy open your locked closet—your colleague did that," Jennings said.

There was a lengthy silence while Walter tried, unsuccessfully, to collect his thoughts. Then Detective Superintendent Mudge began to speak. The half-smile stayed on his face as he did so.

"We want that radio set, Mr. Bennett. We've been following it ever since your fellow spy stole it, and we want to know where it is."

"She stole it? Gretchen stole the transceiver?" he asked.

"Yes. From a police station."

"I don't believe you."

"You'd better believe us, Mr. Bennett. We need to know where Gretchen is and where the radio and the codebook are. And we need to know *right now*." There was an unmistakable underlying threat in Mudge's voice.

"You're making all this up. How can anyone steal a radio from a police station?"

"Walter, we have more than enough evidence against you to hang you three times over as a German spy. If you want to save your life, you'd better answer all our questions fully and truthfully. *Immediately. Or else.*" Now the threat was out in the open.

"You're talking nonsense. I'm not a spy. I've done nothing wrong. I'm a civil servant. I work for the Ministry of Agriculture and Fisheries. What makes you say that I'm a spy?"

"Walter, I'll tell you the full story, to convince you that we know everything. And then you'll tell us what we want to know. Or you'll hang as a spy."

"I'm not a spy," Bennett insisted.

Mudge laughed mockingly. "Oh yes, you are. And I'll prove it. We know everything. One night in 1939, before the war, a Senior Constable was alone on duty in a small rural police station in the Bathurst district of New South Wales. Just before midnight, his daughter phoned him to tell him that his wife had suddenly been taken seriously ill. He was understandably distraught and raced out of the police station, leaving the lights on and forgetting to lock the door behind him. He rushed his wife to Bathurst hospital. When he returned to the police station at about 7 a.m., he discovered that the radio set had been stolen.

"Once everyone had stopped laughing at the idea of an item being pinched from a police station, I put together a squad to investigate the matter. I didn't view it as petty theft. Rather, with war in Europe looming, I wondered if it could be a national security problem. My superior officer in Bathurst thought that I was crazy, but he gave me a week to solve the case.

"This was clearly an opportunistic crime—the thief couldn't possibly have known in advance that the police station would be unlocked and unmanned. But who would've been out in that area of the country after midnight? And why would they go into the police station? We phoned a few farmers in the district, but no one had any information that could help us.

"After work, I decided to have a beer at the pub around the corner from where I live. And there I overheard a sheep farmer telling his friends all the minute details of the miracle that the new vet had performed on his farm. She'd saved the life of his prize merino and her lamb.

"I quickly put two and two together. I went over to him, introduced myself, and asked him what time the vet had come to his farm and when she'd left to return to Bathurst. Everything fitted. I went to the local magistrate and informed him that the new vet in town, an American national born in Bremen, had the opportunity to steal the radio set. He immediately signed the search warrant.

"We watched Dr. Konrad for a day or two, and when she left for a veterinary emergency on a farm some 50 miles from Bathurst, we unlocked the back door of her house with one of our skeleton keys and searched the premises thoroughly. Only one cupboard was locked, a kitchen cabinet. And inside the cabinet we found the radio set. We made a note of the transmission wavelength, relocked the kitchen cabinet and left the house.

"My superior officer now agreed with me that this was indeed a national security matter. But we don't have a security organization in Australia, so I was put in charge of the case. Despite what they say in books or Hollywood films, catching spies is just like catching any other gang of criminals. You don't arrest just one—instead you use him or her to find the other members of the gang. But I had no experience of spy rings. So I asked the powers that be if I could consult MI5. After several lengthy telephone calls between Bathurst and London, I was able to put together a plan of action.

"I'm not an expert on radio and the like, so I visited a professor at Sydney University. I won't bore you with the technical details, but we set up a listening post in Bathurst. A clever boffin doctored the stolen radio so that we knew whenever she turned the set on and when she turned it off. The first thing we heard was Gretchen chatting to an isolated merino sheep farmer on a ranch beyond the black stump in Western Australia; his nearest neighbor was a hundred miles away in Coolgardie. Of course, she wasn't actually talking to him, they were communicating in Morse code.

"She pretended to be a male farmer from just outside Orange, a town not too far from Bathurst, probably because she knew that any sandgroper worth his salt would immediately travel more than 2,000 miles from his farm in Western Australia to meet a sheila in person in New South Wales if she were unwise enough to initiate a ham radio conversation with him. Heck, if he was lonely enough, he'd walk the whole distance.

"Finally we had a breakthrough. Just before the outbreak of war, we intercepted a lengthy message that Gretchen sent in German plaintext to the *Abwehr* in Berlin. We couldn't believe our luck. Now we knew with absolute certainty that Gretchen Konrad was a German agent, and we wanted her to lead us to the rest of the spy ring.

"But then—silence. For three long years, she transmitted nothing at all. Furthermore, every Wednesday night at 10:30 p.m. she tuned to the frequency she'd been given, but nothing was sent to her. We occasionally entered her home while she was out and looked at the receiver, but the reception frequency was unchanged—she didn't even take the elementary precaution of changing the setting before turning her transceiver off.

"And then nine days ago, on Wednesday night, 2nd September, at 10:30 p.m., a message came through in English plaintext. It was transmitted slowly, as if the sender thought that Gretchen was a grossly inexpert Morse practitioner. The plaintext message was then transmitted a second time, again at the same slow speed. I don't need to tell you the message, Walter, your fellow spy must have told you about it."

Walter seemed to be in another world. It was unclear to the two policemen whether he had even been listening to what Detective Superintendent Mudge was saying.

But then Walter spoke. "Remind me what the message said." His voice came out in an expressionless monotone. His German accent was heavier than ever.

"The message," Mudge said, "was: 'Your brother Walter Bennett in Auckland is seriously ill.' Gretchen doesn't have a brother named Walter Bennett. And if she had a brother, she wouldn't need to know his last name, so she correctly understood that the purpose of the transmission was to instruct her to come to Auckland and contact someone called Walter Bennett.

"I'm telling you the whole story, Walter. I'm telling you everything in detail so that you realize that you cannot hide anything from us. You're a filthy spy, Walter. And to save your dirty little neck from the hangman's rope you're going tell us what we want to know. Now."

Mudge stared Bennett in the eye with loathing. Then he continued. "The woman on duty at the listening post phoned me to come at once. As I drove past Gretchen's house, I saw that all the lights were on. When I reached the listening post, I parked the car and crept back to her house. Through a crack in the curtains I saw her packing.

"I immediately contacted the higher-ups in Sydney. They advised me not to follow her, because she would see my car lights behind her as she drove through the dark night on the unlit Great Western Road. There were only two ways she could get to Auckland: by air or by sea. So they arranged for cars to be waiting to follow her if she approached Sydney Airport in Mascot or Sydney Harbour.

"We saw her board the *Star of Adelaide*, and arranged with our Kiwi counterparts to have her followed when she arrived in Auckland. More precisely, a number of high-level telephone conversations took place. It was vital to fully brief the New Zealand government regarding the German spy ring in Australia because it seemed that there was at least one secret agent in New Zealand who was part of the organization, with a second one about to visit him. We even communicated with MI5 in London. It appeared that something major was about to happen.

"I flew to Wellington, in order to arrive in New Zealand ahead of Gretchen and, more importantly, to liaise with various New Zealand authorities. The *Star of Adelaide* docked in Auckland, and a team of experts in surveillance followed Gretchen day and night. I'll ask Detective Chief Superintendent Jennings to tell you what happened next."

The tall thin man with the widow's peak took over the narrative immediately so as not to give Walter a chance to try and find a way out of the situation.

"Actually, Walter, I need to go back to two or three days before the ship arrived. We knew that Gretchen was due to arrive in Auckland on Monday, 7th September, and that she would try to find someone named Walter Bennett. A careful search of all the records showed that there's only one person in New Zealand with that name, and that he lives in Wellington, not Auckland. Furthermore, no Walter Bennett has ever had a telephone registered in his name in Auckland.

"Fortunately, there are two 'Bennett W' entries in the Auckland telephone directory. One belongs to a man named Wilfred Bennett. The other entry is the home number of Emily Bennett, the widow of William Bennett, who died in March 1940. I went to visit Emily. She turned out to be a jovial retired schoolteacher who was only too delighted to assist the police to catch a criminal, even though I cautioned her that she could never tell a soul about her role in the plan. I told her that, if anyone phoned for Walter Bennett, she was to say that he previously had had that number, but that he was now living in Wellington. Then I asked her if she minded if we put a tap on her line for a few days. She laughed and replied that a tap would only add to the fun. In fact, when Gretchen phoned her on Tuesday, Emily embellished the story a little and said that someone else had phoned a week before, also asking for Walter Bennett. Fortunately, her unauthorized attempt at being creative did no harm at all.

"We had a tap on your phone, too, of course, so we knew to expect Gretchen here on Tuesday night. Sure enough, a taxi picked her up at the station and dropped her at your home. And we know that she's been in this house until she left this morning, because we had watchers at both the front and the back of your house, Walter.

"On Wednesday night," Jennings continued, "she sent a message to Berlin. It was encrypted. We know that you did the encryption, because Gretchen doesn't know the first thing about codes. That's why that long message in German that she sent to Berlin three years ago was in plaintext. I'm right, Walter, aren't I?"

Bennett nodded warily.

"You see, Walter, we know everything. All the details. And we know you're a spy."

Jennings went on. "Then, an encrypted message arrived from Berlin at 1 a.m. The five-letter groups written on the paper that we found in your clothes closet are in Gretchen Konrad's handwriting. But you wrote the corresponding plaintext words next to each group. So we know that you were responsible for decrypting it. You admit it, don't you?"

This time Walter did not move.

"Now, Walter, it should be obvious that, as Detective Inspector Mudge told you, we have more than enough evidence to convict you as a spy. If you want to save your miserable life, you'd better answer our all questions fully and truthfully."

Walter shifted his position in the chair. "Go ahead," he said. "Ask your questions."

"Let's start at the very beginning. You were trained as an *Abwehr* spy in Berlin and sent to New Zealand in 1938."

"Not exactly. I was supposed to go to Australia. In order to avoid problems with the Australian authorities, I was sent to New Zealand to acquire New Zealand citizenship as quickly as possible, and then use that citizenship to get into Australia without any problems."

"I see," Jennings said. "But you've been a New Zealand citizen for quite a while now. Why are you still here?"

"I was sent to Auckland with a Telefunken radio set built for 110 volts mains. Here in New Zealand, the mains voltage is 230 volts. As soon as I'd checked into a hotel, I turned on my transceiver to inform the *Abwehr* that I'd arrived. The set blew up. From that moment on, I was no longer an *Abwehr* agent—I was not prepared to work with an organization that didn't even know the mains voltage here. So all this talk of hanging is nonsense, I'm afraid. I've never ever done anything in this country that could even remotely brand me as a spy."

"Really? Is that so? Didn't you encrypt a message to be sent to an enemy country, Germany, and decrypt the reply? Didn't you knowingly collaborate with an enemy agent, one Gretchen Konrad? And if you were no longer an *Abwehr* agent but rather a loyal New Zealand citizen, why didn't you just send her away or, better still, call the police?"

There was another long silence. Then, with obvious reluctance, Walter spoke.

"I helped her on condition that she sleep with me."

"I see," Jennings said again. "So you betrayed your adopted country, New Zealand, for sexual purposes. You're not just a Nazi spy and a traitor to New Zealand, you're a pervert, too."

More silence.

"Bennett, you're in even bigger trouble than you were before. I strongly advise you to tell us everything."

"I *am* telling you everything. What am I holding back? What lies have I told you?"

"Let's go back to the beginning again. You were sent to Auckland by the *Abwehr* essentially to take out New Zealand citizenship. How did you end up here in Wellington?"

"When I arrived in Auckland, I immediately tried to find a job as a vet. I found an advertisement in the *Auckland Star* on that first day—it was for a position at the Ministry of Agriculture and Fisheries. At the interview they told me that I was overqualified for the job and that I would be of much greater use advising the Ministry in Wellington, the capital. So the day after my interview in Auckland I took the train to Wellington. I was quickly promoted to a senior position in MAF. I've lived here in Wellington ever since."

"Yesterday," Jennings said, "you asked Max Malone for a list of all the mines in New Zealand. In the light of the message from Admiral Canaris asking you to find a mine for him, wasn't that also an act of treason, or did you do that just for sexual reasons?"

Walter Bennett said nothing.

"Well, which was it: treason or sex?"

"I told Gretchen I wouldn't give the list to her unless she slept with me."

"So it was for sex then. But somehow I doubt if the judge will see the subtle difference when he sentences you to death for treason."

"I am *not* a traitor."

"Well, your good friend Max Malone seems to think that you're one. In his opinion, only an enemy agent would ask for a complete list of mines during wartime. So as soon as you left his office, he rushed off to see the Permanent Secretary for Lands and Surveys, who immediately called us in. We decided to provide you with a list, and that was why Max came into your office just as you were leaving, and gave it to you."

Bennett remained quiet.

"Now, Walter," Jennings demanded, "where's Gretchen? And where's that radio set?"

"How should I know? Weren't you having her tailed?"

"We followed her to the Masonic Hotel. We watched her carrying her bags into the building. But we later learned that she walked right through the lobby and out the back door. Since then, she's disappeared. Do you know where she is?"

"No, I don't. Clever woman, isn't she, picking up the tail? I'd no idea that I was even under surveillance, but Gretchen manages to elude you just like that. Well, well, well."

"You're coming with us, Bennett," Detective Chief Superintendent Jennings declared. "And you'd better be able to tell us where to find her. And her radio set. And your codebook."

# CHAPTER ELEVEN

*Wellington, New Zealand*
*Friday, September 11th, 1942*

Gretchen sat on her bed in her room in the Arthur Hotel trying to make some sense of the mining data she had taken with her from Walter's house. There were 46 mining properties listed in the document prepared by the Department of Lands and Surveys. The location of each property was given in terms of the longitude and latitude of the mine. The type of work—surface, open pit, or underground—was also specified. The sheets of paper in front of her stated explicitly what was mined at each property. The names coal, silver, iron, limestone, copper, chromium and molybdenum cropped up fairly often. She had no idea what molybdenum was, but it seemed that it was mined at five different properties, so it obviously could not be another name for the mysterious and rare promethium mentioned in the radio message from Admiral Canaris.

Then she noticed that, for four of the mines, the word "Various" appeared in the column listing the products extracted from the ground at that mining property. This was surprising, because there were enumerations of up to 10 different minerals that were mined at some of the other properties. The only explanation, as far as she was concerned, was that the output from those four mines was secret for some reason.

The latitude and longitude of those four mining properties meant nothing to her. She would have to buy a map of New Zealand, perhaps at the stationery shop she had noticed as she walked from the Masonic Hotel to the Arthur Hotel where she was now staying, and use the map to determine the exact location of each of the four mines.

She felt sick in the stomach at the mere thought of the Masonic Hotel. The taxi driver had dropped her in front of the hotel and parked there to wait for other customers. As she walked into the Masonic, she was assailed by a strong smell of boiled cabbage, an odor that was utterly repugnant to her ever since she was a little girl growing up in Germany. She did not want the taxi driver to see her rushing out of the hotel he had so kindly recommended, so she walked as fast as she could through the lobby, in the hope that the hotel had a back door. Luckily for her, she found that she was able to leave the Masonic Hotel via that route. Diagonally across the street she saw a sign reading "Arthur Hotel." The exterior of the building looked well maintained and her suitcases were heavy; proximity, appearance and cabbage had decided the accommodation issue for her.

At the stationery shop near the Arthur Hotel, Gretchen had no problems buying a large map that showed the lines of latitude and longitude; unlike both wartime Britain and Nazi Germany, there were no restrictions on the sale of maps in New Zealand. In order to pinpoint the mines accurately, she also purchased an extra-long wooden ruler, two pencils, a pocket pencil sharpener and an eraser. As an afterthought she added a smaller touring map of the country that she could use as she travelled from mine to mine.

Returning to her room, she looked through the sheets of paper for the first mine with "Various" in the relevant column. And then she noticed something that she had missed before. The list that Walter had obtained from Max was neither an original nor a carbon copy. It appeared to have been made from stencils and run off on a mimeograph machine, probably a Gestetner. She knew that if a typist made a mistake while cutting a stencil, she could paint over the wrong letters with sticky pink fluid. Once the fluid had dried completely, filling in the grooves of the wrong letters, she could retype over that area of the stencil. But if she noticed a mistake only after the complete page had been typed, she would have to put the page back into her typewriter and carefully align the stencil to ensure that the new letters would be typed exactly over the old.

Using her new ruler to check the alignment, she saw that each incidence of the word "Various" was slightly misaligned with the rest of the line. Three were retyped a little too high; the fourth was a bit too low. And all four were positioned slightly to the left of the correct position. There was no doubt in her mind—the entries had been changed before the list was run off on the mimeograph machine to hide the real products of those four mines. And that meant that the promethium mine was one of the four.

With her confidence buoyed by her deduction, she tried to plot each of the four mines on her map of New Zealand. But the scale of the map was still too small. One mine appeared to be located in the water off the south coast of the South Island. Another seemed to be placed in the middle of a large town on the North Island, which was equally implausible. She marked the approximate positions of the four mines on her touring map, and returned to the stationer.

"I want to hike in the regions of New Zealand I've marked here," she told the shop assistant. "Do you have more detailed maps in stock?"

"Yes, certainly, madam. The New Zealand government strongly encourages hiking in our beautiful countryside, so the Department of Lands and Survey has produced really excellent maps at a scale of one inch to the mile. They're like the Ordnance Survey maps in the United Kingdom, but here we call them NZMS 1 maps. They show the topography, so you can choose the trail that's right for you. Let me have a closer look at your touring map and I'll get you the maps you need—I hope they're all available. There are supposed to be 191 topographical maps in all, but they haven't issued them yet for some parts of New Zealand, including large areas of Fiordland, the most beautiful part of our country."

She returned a few minutes later. "I've got everything you'll need here, except for the islands on the south coast of the South Island—I don't think those maps have been published yet. I assume that the cross here in the water refers to Tudor Island."

"Yes, of course. My intention is to hike, not to swim!"

"Nevertheless, madam, I suggest you take your bathing costume with you when you go to Tudor Island. And I'll explain why I said that. Look at this other map. The scale isn't as large as the NZMS 1 maps for the area will be when we get them, but it's the most detailed one we have of the area. I suggest you take it as a substitute. Here's Tudor Island. Can you see Raphael Channel? It's this L-shaped waterway here on the northeast corner of Tudor Island. The channel separates Tudor Island from Coopers Island. You really should take a boat from Cookville on Tudor Island to visit Coopers Island—it's absolutely gorgeous there. It's all pristine temperate rainforest, the loveliest forest you've ever seen. And here on the north coast of Coopers Island is Mystic Beach, one of the loveliest beaches in the world. You can even land a boat on the sand. It'll be a trip you'll never forget!"

"Thank you for the advice. By the way, do you know where I can buy a rucksack?"

"Yes, I do. There's a camping shop about three blocks from here. Turn left as you leave the shop, and you'll find it on this side of the road, just before you get to the traffic lights. Before the war, they had almost everything you could possibly need for hiking. But I'm not sure how their stocks are at the moment—these days all the factories obviously give preference to the needs of the Army."

Gretchen paid for the maps, thanked the helpful and informative sales assistant, walked straight to the camping shop where she made several purchases, and then returned to her hotel room. Now that she had her detailed maps, she was quickly able to determine the precise locations of the four mines. But in what order should she investigate them? Two were on the North Island, two on the South Island. She was currently in Wellington, on the southernmost tip of the North Island. So, two of the mines were to her north and the other two were located south of where she now was. If she could find the promethium mine on the first or even the second attempt, she could inform Canaris a lot sooner than if she had to traipse all over both islands before reporting to him. And that might save thousands of German lives and affect the outcome of the war.

Gretchen carefully reread the data on each of the four mines, but no additional ideas came to mind. Then she had another look at her touring map. The narrow body of water linking the North Island with the South Island was labeled "Cook Strait." And Gretchen wanted nothing further to do with Captain James Cook. So she immediately decided to visit the two mines on the North Island first. Only if both proved disappointing would she be prepared to venture across Cook Strait and investigate the other two mines.

The first mine was located in the Bay of Plenty area near Tauranga. The second was in the volcanic Rotorua area, not too far from the first mine. Using her touring map, she discovered that Tauranga and Rotorua were both accessible by rail. The only question was: Which of the two North Island mines should she visit first? She tried to recall something she had learned at school in Chicago during a civics lesson. Her teacher had quoted something about luck that Thomas Jefferson, the third president of the United States, had said. How did it go again? Suddenly, it jumped into her mind: "I'm a great believer in luck, and I find the harder I work, the more I have of it." Although that was not what Jefferson meant, Gretchen decided to toss a coin to decide. "Heads Tauranga, tails Rotorua," she said aloud.

She emptied the coins in her purse onto the bed. She noticed that most of the money had the head of King George V on the obverse or "heads" side; two displayed his successor, the current king,

George VI. It was terribly important to her to choose the correct coin—should she select a shiny copper penny with a tui bird on the tails side, or a two-shilling piece featuring the kiwi, the national bird? Then she saw that the silver shilling depicted a Maori warrior carrying some sort of weapon, a staff of some sort, perhaps a spear. New Zealand was at war with Germany, and she was engaged in a hunt to find a metal that was used in a weapon.

That decided it for her. She picked up one of the shillings and tossed it into the air. It came down heads.

***

The porter was able to provide Gretchen with a railway timetable, but before she could leave Wellington the next day for Tauranga, there was one further essential item on her agenda. She wrote a message to Canaris and encrypted it using the codebook she had taken from her erstwhile colleague's locked bedroom closet. She set up her radio set, draping the aerial around the room. At 10:30 p.m. she transmitted her encrypted message to Berlin.

She informed Canaris that she had received a list of all the mines in New Zealand from Walter, who had obtained it from a colleague in the Department of Lands and Survey. She stated that four mines were specially indicated on the list. She strongly believed that the promethium was being mined at one of those four sites, and gave the precise location of each. She also told Canaris that she was leaving by train for Tauranga the next day after which, if necessary, she would travel to Rotorua. After transmitting her message she heard the standard brief acknowledgement of receipt. Then she waited until 11:00 p.m. for a possible reply from Berlin. All she heard was static. Satisfied that she had done her duty, she coiled up the aerial neatly and put her radio back into its suitcase.

She undressed and climbed into bed. For the past 24 hours she had managed to function by actively suppressing all memories of the humiliation that Walter had inflicted on her. But now, with a new phase of her mission about to start, Gretchen was no longer able to stifle her emotions. She found herself replaying those ghastly three minutes over and over in her mind, perhaps in the hope that growing familiarity would eventually make the whole incident seem commonplace and ordinary. Unfortunately, each iteration was more cruel and hurtful than the last.

# CHAPTER TWELVE

*Wellington, New Zealand*
*Saturday, September 12th, 1942*

"How on earth," Detective Chief Superintendent Warren Jennings of the New Zealand Police Force asked in a gloomy voice, "are we supposed to entice Gretchen Konrad into visiting the mine on Coopers Island in about 10 days' time, when we still haven't managed to discover where she is now, at five o'clock in the morning? And when we do find her again, following her is going to be three times harder than before, now that she's aware that we're shadowing her. We both know that you need three times as many people when the subject knows that she's being tailed, but we just don't have the personnel—so many of the younger men understandably have volunteered to fight."

"It's not quite that bad," Detective Superintendent Peter Mudge of the New South Wales Police Force replied. "We know that she transmitted a message to Berlin last night at half past ten, and your direction finders were able to

123

determine that she was still somewhere in Wellington, probably within half a mile of the Masonic Hotel. If we had enough people we could've searched every building in the area—an enemy agent whose skills are so superlative that she can elude experienced watchers with such ease isn't going to be stupid enough to stay in a hotel or a boarding house. But with so few men left at our disposal, it was hopeless to try."

"Don't talk to me about the Masonic Hotel," Warren said despondently. "It seems that the two men tailing her followed her inside. There was no sign of her, and the lobby was deserted. They rang the bell on the reception desk. The receptionist came out of the office and said she hadn't seen anyone enter the lobby. Neither of the detectives knew that there's a back door to the lobby, so they ran back into the street. They asked passersby if they'd seen Gretchen. A newspaper seller volunteered that a woman with two suitcases had hailed a taxi and he'd heard her tell the driver to take her to the station. So our men rushed to the railway station and searched it thoroughly, but found nothing. They contacted the taxi companies and asked them to find out if any of their drivers picked up a woman with two suitcases from the Masonic Hotel and where they'd dropped her off. Three hours later we found out about the back door of the Masonic Hotel. So the detectives phoned the taxi companies again, this time asking about a woman with two suitcases at the back door of the Masonic Hotel. We haven't heard anything yet, and I don't think we will."

"You're much too pessimistic," Jennings said. "Look on the bright side. Some of the five-letter groups in last night's message are the same as five-letter groups in the other two messages, so surely we have a reasonable idea of what she said."

"Unfortunately, we don't know very much," his Australian colleague replied. "We've had two mathematics professors and a professor of German from the Victoria University of Wellington battling away the whole night through trying to decrypt the message that Gretchen just sent. The trouble is that the three men can't communicate with one another. The sole language that two of them speak is higher calculus and the third one knows only German.

"And why on earth," Peter asked sarcastically, "were those two encrypted messages written in German? Can't the Nazis speak English, like civilized people? Gretchen has lived in our neck of the woods for years. She's even taken out Australian citizenship. And Walter is a naturalized New Zealander. Yet, when it comes to sending spy messages to Admiral Canaris in Berlin, for some reason that is completely incomprehensible to me, they both absolutely insist on sending them in German. The sun will be up in an hour or so. I'm tired way beyond the point of total exhaustion. And so far the three stooges haven't produced a single sensible word of English. Warren, it's completely beyond my understanding why you

Kiwis didn't have the sense to hire a German-speaking professor of mathematics."

"Actually, Peter, we do have a German-speaking professor of mathematics at the Victoria University of Wellington."

"So why in the name of Sir Robert Peel aren't you using him, instead of this chaotic all-night decryption triad that's going nowhere fast?"

"Because he's safely locked up in an internment camp as an enemy alien. He's a Nazi through and through, and I wouldn't trust that Kraut bastard to do anything for us."

"Okay, so under the circumstances maybe we're doing the best we can to decrypt the message. But what I wouldn't give for a copy of the codebook," Peter Mudge said wistfully.

"Gretchen's obviously got it with her," Warren responded. "If we can find her, we can lay our hands on the codebook and discover what she said in last night's message. Our first priority is getting our hands on that blonde vet. We know she's in Wellington—or at least we're sure that she was here at 10:30 p.m. So there are two likely possibilities, and only two. First, she might take a train in the direction of Auckland. So let's put one of our men on the northbound platform at the railway station and see if she shows up. Or, she might take the ferry from Wellington to Picton on the South Island and then a train to Christchurch or Dunedin or somewhere else south of Picton. So I'll put a second watcher at the ferry terminal."

"And what are the unlikely possibilities?" Mudge asked nervously.

"I can think of three. She might already have left Wellington late last night on a midnight train, assuming we still run them during wartime. Or, she might stay on in Wellington. Now that's highly unlikely—she's trying to find the mine and she must know by now that it's not in this city. So there's no point in our sending the one or two available men to search Wellington—the bird will have long since flown the coop. Finally, she might try something unexpected."

"Such as?"

"I cannot possibly even begin to think what she might take into her head to do," Warren responded. "Anyone who's smart enough to elude a tail the way she did is capable of almost anything. As far as we know she's never been to Wellington before and she's never been inside the Masonic Hotel in her entire life, yet she tells a taxi driver to take her there so that she can lose us by going out the back door. I ask you, how did she know that there's a back door to the lobby of the Masonic Hotel when none of my men did? It's enough to drive me to drink."

"C'mon Warren, it's not even half past five. Your pubs don't open until ten or eleven. I've heard that you Kiwis are hard drinkers, but this is ridiculous."

"And I'm in no mood for feeble Aussie attempts at humor at this ungodly hour. I'm going to organize watchers at the station and the ferry terminal. And then I'm going home to bed for a few hours of sleep. We've both been up all night, so I suggest you go back to your hotel and do the same."

"Fine. And tell your three clowns at the Victoria University to get some shut-eye, too. I think I know why they're not getting anywhere. But I'm too tired to explain it to them, and they're definitely too tired to understand what I want to tell them."

*** 

The telephone next to his bed woke Peter Mudge from a sound sleep. Still semi comatose, he picked up the receiver to hear a voice saying, "We've found her, but she's ditched the radio."

"Who's this?" Peter asked, slurring his words.

"It's Warren, of course. Who did you think it was? I sent Senior Sergeant Hastings to the railway station in civvies. He ignored my orders to wait on the northbound platform and hung around the ticket office instead. Gretchen turned up in hiking clothes and bought a ticket to Tauranga, changing trains at Hamilton. I've arranged for a plainclothes policeman at Hamilton to board the Tauranga train when he spots Gretchen. She can't have seen him before, so hopefully she won't realize he's tailing her. Although with her, you never know. What a woman!"

"What was all that about the radio?" Peter asked. "What did you mean by 'she's ditched it?' How's she going to tell Berlin where the mine is?"

"Hastings said that she's got a rucksack on her back. There was no sign of her two suitcases—he tried the left luggage office just before he returned from the railway station, but they're not there. So, she doesn't have the radio with her, and we don't know where it is. If she wants to contact her Nazi friends, she's going to have to pick up her radio from wherever she's hidden it—presumably it's still in one of her suitcases. If we follow her, we should be able to locate it eventually. But if she starts pulling that back door stunt again, we haven't a hope."

"Talking about following her," Peter asked, "what did you mean about Hastings going to the left luggage office before leaving the railway station? Why didn't he follow her to Hamilton?"

"There was no reason for him to do so. He knew that she's headed for Tauranga, where one of the four mines is located. Also, that train doesn't stop anywhere between here and Hamilton. So, unless she pulls the cord of the emergency brake and jumps off, she's on her way to Hamilton and from there to Tauranga. Hastings waited on the platform until she boarded the train and he saw it pulling out of the station. Then he phoned me. At home. While I was trying to catch up on my sleep."

"Tell me more about the radio—I'm really concerned about it, for obvious reasons."

"Hastings reported that Gretchen was dressed for hiking: boots, rucksack and all," Jennings said. "She's even wearing a beanie—you know, one of those knitted woolen caps with a pom-pom on the top. Hastings is adamant that there's no possible way there could be a transceiver in her rucksack, and I know he's right—we saw that transceiver in Bathurst, and it just fits into a large suitcase. It can't possibly be in her rucksack. She's hidden her two suitcases, presumably somewhere in Wellington. She must know that we just don't have the manpower for a house-to-house search to find the radio and the codebook."

"I'm looking at my watch. Have I really been sleeping for only 20 minutes?"

"Yes. And I didn't even get a chance to close my eyes before Hastings phoned."

"What time does Gretchen get to Tauranga?" Mudge asked.

"Around 7 p.m. if both trains are on time, which is possible but highly unlikely."

"Fine. That gives us lots of time. I'm going to sleep until noon, and I suggest you do the same. Let's meet at police headquarters. We'll go from there to see the three professors when they're all awake and back at the university."

# CHAPTER THIRTEEN

*Wellington, New Zealand*
*Saturday, September 12th, 1942*

"Peter, this is Professor Brodsky."

"How do you do?" Brodsky said. "I'm delighted to meet you, Detective Superintendent Mudge."

"And this is Professor Blackwell."

"We're fellow countrymen, Detective Superintendent. I was born in Melbourne, but I've been living here in Wellington for more than 30 years."

Mudge looked at the two mathematicians. Brodsky was considerably shorter than most men. He wore round glasses with thick lenses. His black hair was neatly combed. His suit, shirt and tie were impeccable. In contrast, Blackwell was tall with a large unkempt bushy beard. The beard, like the few wisps of hair on his head, was a ruddy brown. Mudge noticed that Blackwell had piercing dark brown eyes, as if he was looking right through the Australian detective.

At that moment a third man entered the seminar room in the Department of Mathematics at Victoria University. Warren Jennings introduced him. "Professor Hallerstein, this is Detective Superintendent Mudge, who's working with me on this case."

Professor Hallerstein shook hands with Mudge. "I'm delighted to make your acquaintance, Detective Superintendent." Hallerstein's English was pedantic, as if he had learned it by reading a textbook. His heavy Teutonic accent made it difficult for Mudge to discern his words. Hallerstein's suit had a distinctly foreign cut. Mudge guessed that he had fled Germany not long before the outbreak of war.

Mudge suggested that they all sit down at the large table in the seminar room.

"Gentlemen, first and foremost thank you very much for your time and effort in helping us try to decrypt this message. I particularly appreciate the way that you worked all through last night. I hope that you got some rest this morning.

"Let me state at the outset that I barely passed Year 11 mathematics and that was the last time I studied the subject, much to the relief of all concerned, myself included. Professor Hallerstein, I'm not ashamed to admit that my knowledge of German is nonexistent. Nevertheless, I think I may be able to help the three of you with the decryption.

"First, however, I need you to sign a stronger version of the Official Secrets Act than the one you signed last night. Please read all three pages carefully before you put your initials at the bottom of the first two pages and sign your name at the bottom of the last page. In brief, the document says that everything that transpires in this room is Top Secret, and if you divulge anything to anyone at any time, you'll be sent to prison for a lengthy stay."

The three professors each read their copy of the document word by word. Then they all signed. Mudge noticed that the two mathematicians had utterly indecipherable signatures, scrawls of the wildest kind, whereas Hallerstein's signature was a work of art that displayed his full name, Andreas Nepomuk Hallerstein, in an immaculate copperplate script.

"Thank you, gentlemen. Now, I can give you some Top Secret information that may help you to decrypt the message. The first thing that you need to know is that there's an *Abwehr* spy ring operating in New Zealand."

Professor Blackwell raised his hand. "What's '*Abwehr*'?" he asked.

Hallerstein answered before Mudge or Jennings could open their mouths. "*Amt Ausland/Abwehr im Oberkommando der Wehrmacht,* or *Abwehr* for short, is the German military intelligence information-gathering organization. In English, the name means Foreign Affairs/Defense Office of the High Command of the Armed Forces. The head of the *Abwehr* is Admiral Wilhelm Canaris. He reports directly to the *Oberkommando der Wehrmacht* or High

Command of the Armed Forces, currently under Field Marshal Wilhelm Keitel. The headquarters of the *Abwehr* are in Berlin, right next to the offices of the *Oberkommando der Wehrmacht.*"

Both police officers immediately understood why the three professors had made so little progress the previous night. Mudge swiftly interjected before Hallerstein could say anything more.

"Last night you were given two plaintext messages in German and their encrypted counterparts. You were also given a third encrypted message, and asked to reconstruct the German plaintext. You made every effort to decrypt the third message. I suspect that the reason that you didn't make much progress was that, for reasons of national security, we didn't give you the full context of the messages.

"That was a truly stupid mistake on our part, for which we sincerely apologize. From now on we'll provide you with maximum information, and answer all your questions to the very best of our ability.

"I've just told you," Peter continued, "that there's a Nazi spy ring operating in New Zealand. We know of two members: a man called Walter Bennett, who is currently under arrest, and a woman named Gretchen Konrad."

"Is that Konrad with a K or Conrad with a C?" Hallerstein asked.

"Konrad with a K."

"Thank you."

"You're most welcome," Mudge replied, trying his hardest not to grit his teeth or roll his eyes. "Gretchen Konrad," he continued, "is still at large. She has the radio that she used to send and receive the three encrypted messages. She also has a copy of the codebook that she employed for encryption and decryption. As you know only too well, each German word in the codebook is represented by a group of five arbitrary letters. And where a word isn't listed in the codebook, it has to be spelled out—the codebook contains a unique five-letter group for each letter of the alphabet, as well as each of the 10 digits.

"As you learned from the second message, Gretchen travelled to New Zealand from Australia in order to locate a mine. She's in possession of a document that lists a number of mines. We strongly suspect that she's narrowed her search down to four possible locations: near Tauranga; not far from Rotorua; in the vicinity of Akaroa; and on Coopers Island."

"The document I mentioned gives the exact latitude and longitude, in degrees, minutes, and seconds of arc, of the four mines. Here's a copy of the information she has about those mines. I strongly suspect that the message you are endeavoring to decrypt contains the locations of the four mines, both the coordinates and the nearest large town."

All three professors were silent, but the eyes of the two mathematicians lit up. Then Brodsky spoke. "And the clue that you've just given us is to look for repeated letters. Right?"

Professor Blackwell nodded enthusiastically. "Yes, and possibly repeated numbers, too."

"Yes, indeed," Professor Brodsky said.

Professor Hallerstein, however, looked utterly bewildered. It was clear that his numerate colleagues were once again talking a language he did not understand. Mudge quickly jumped in before Hallerstein could ask an endless question, or before either of the mathematicians could give an incomprehensible explanation.

"Professor Hallerstein, the names Tauranga, Rotorua, Akaroa, and Coopers could not possibly be in the codebook. They would have to be spelled out letter by letter. The name TAURANGA has three A's: the second letter, the fifth letter, and the eighth letter. So, you three professors need to look through the encrypted message looking for a five-letter group that occurs in this pattern."

Peter Mudge got up from his seat and walked over the blackboard mounted on one wall. He picked up a piece of white chalk and wrote "- A - - A - - A."

"Each dash denotes some other five-letter group. If you can find that pattern, you may have the name TAURANGA."

Professors Brodsky and Blackwell nodded and smiled broadly.

"When you think you've identified the letter A, you look for AKAROA. Its pattern is 'A - A - - A.' If you can find that pattern, too, then you've probably identified the letter A correctly. You now also have the patterns for T, U, R, N, and G from TAURANGA, and for K and O from AKAROA.

"Then, look for the name ROTORUA. You already have the five-letter groups for R, O, T, and A. If you can find the pattern 'R O T O R - A,' that gives you five-letter group for the letter U.

"And then, because you know the five-letter group for the letters O and R, you should be able to find the name COOPERS."

"And the digits are similar," Blackwell said, jumping up and joining Peter Mudge at the blackboard and absentmindedly taking the chalk from his hand. "The latitude of New Zealand is roughly between about 35 degrees and 45 degrees South, so you'd expect the latitude of the four mines to have the pattern '3 - DEGREES' or '4 - DEGREES.' And when you have that, you have the five-letter group for the word 'degrees' as well as the number 3 and the number 4."

"And the longitude in New Zealand," Brodsky added, joining the other two at the blackboard and taking the chalk from Blackwell, "is approximately between about 165 degrees and 180 degrees—I think. So, the longitude pattern would always be '1 - - DEGREES.'"

"Right," Mudge said. "So, could you three experts please look for patterns? That should give you lots of information. In addition, you know the meaning of some of the five-letter groups already, because they correspond to words that occur in the two earlier messages."

Brodsky immediately put the piece of chalk in his hand onto the shelf under the bottom edge of the blackboard and rushed over to the table. Blackwell followed him, and the two started looking for patterns. Professor Hallerstein looked dazed and totally mystified.

Jennings took Mudge aside. "Don't worry, they'll involve their Germanic colleague as soon as they need a translation. For now, let's just leave them to it."

*** 

An hour or so later the phone rang at police headquarters. Warren Jennings picked it up. He listened for a few seconds, then put his hand over the mouthpiece and said quietly to his Australian colleague, "They've cracked it. They're sure about all but a handful of words."

Jennings sat at his desk writing out the decrypted message. Then Peter Mudge heard him say, "You've done your country a great service. Please thank the other two professors, as well."

He hung up the receiver and turned to Mudge. "That was Brodsky. They successfully decrypted almost the whole message half an hour after we left, but Hallerstein insisted that they check every single detail before reporting to us. Brodsky and Blackwell are going off to celebrate while Hallerstein checks everything yet again, for some reason that I don't pretend to understand. I was going to ask Professor Brodsky how mathematicians celebrate, but I wasn't sure that I really want to know."

"Very wise of you. So, what does the message say?"

"Your hunch was correct. Gretchen informed Canaris that the promethium mine is at one of four locations. For each mine, she specified both the exact coordinates and the nearest town or the name of the island. Finally, she said she was going to Tauranga today, which we already knew from Senior Sergeant Hastings, and then on to Rotorua, which we could have guessed."

"In other words," Detective Superintendent Peter Mudge said, "in all probability she's going to be at the mine on Coopers Island in about 10 days. How about that?"

# CHAPTER FOURTEEN

*Hamilton Railway Station, New Zealand
Saturday, September 12th, 1942*

"There's no hurry, miss," the kindly train conductor said. "You don't have to run over to Platform Three. Even though it's past the departure time, the train for Tauranga won't leave until everyone from this train who's changing for Tauranga is aboard."

But with the course of the war at stake, Gretchen was not going to take any chances. She rushed up the stairs to the overhead bridge to cross to the next platform. When she ran down the stairs to Platform Three, she found that, as the conductor had promised, there was no indication at all that the Tauranga train was about to depart. She chose a carriage at random, and sat on the first seat with her back to the engine.

She found that she was sweating as a consequence of her sprint to change trains, so she got up and went to the lavatory at the other end of the coach to wash her face. When she returned to her seat, she found a man of about 25 sitting opposite her. She greeted him politely, and then took out a magazine to read on the journey. Unfortunately, it slipped out of her fingers onto the legs of the man across from her.

She apologized profusely. As she did so, she noticed that he was extraordinarily handsome, with the looks of a film star. She had an urge to run her fingers through his disheveled hair until it looked as perfect as his face. Other than his fair hair, he strongly reminded her of Dana Andrews, whom she had just seen starring in *The Westerner.* She simply could not take her eyes off his hair.

To make up for her carelessness in dropping the magazine, Gretchen felt that she should strike up a brief polite conversation with her travelling companion.

"Are you travelling all the way to Tauranga today, or just to Morrinsville?" she asked.

"Tauranga. And you?"

"Yes, I'm also going there."

There was silence for a few seconds. Then the train pulled out with a jerk.

"We're off," she said. "Only 15 minutes late. Can we make up the time en route?"

"I don't think so. This train is almost always late."

"Oh, do you take it often?"

"Yes, I have a friend with a bach at Omokoroa Beach, and he lets me stay there when I have a few days off."

"What's a bach?"

"You certainly don't sound as if you come from these parts. Are you an American?"

"I was, but I'm an Australian now."

"Well, a bach is a New Zealand word for a shack on a beach. It's the first syllable of 'bachelor pad,' because most baches are quite small. This one has one bedroom, and a front room with a couch, and that's about it."

"Do you lie on the beach all day?"

"Well, the beach is fantastic. But I love to fish. My friend has a tinny, that's a small open boat made of some metal, aluminum I think. I go out on Tauranga Harbour—it's a huge tidal estuary. The fishing there is fantastic."

There was a long pause.

"My name is Wesley. My friends call me Wes," he added.

"And I'm Gretchen."

"That's a pretty name."

"Thank you." She smiled at the compliment.

"Are you visiting family in Tauranga?"

"No, I'm on holiday in New Zealand. I live in Australia. I've selected a few places where I'd like to hike. One of them is the area around Omanawa Falls near Tauranga. Do you know that part of the world?"

"No, I don't, but you certainly look as if you could hike that area with ease."

As he complimented her again, Gretchen was surprised to experience a rush of warm feelings towards him. Spending time with Wes on Omokoroa Beach and going fishing with him in his friend's tinny seemed very inviting. She was shocked and bewildered by these emotions—after her horrific experience with Walter she had thought that she would never again want to go near a man. Was this her subconscious mind urging her to prove to herself that she was a desirable woman and not just a receptacle for a vile sexual predator like Walter Bennett?

\*\*\*

By this time, Detective Constable Wesley McFee was feeling extremely uncomfortable. Earlier that day, his station commander had given him a physical description of Gretchen, and he knew the clothes that she was wearing. His instructions were to go to Hamilton train station in hiking clothes and wait on the Tauranga platform until Gretchen arrived from the Wellington train. He was to observe which carriage she chose and take a seat where he could circumspectly observe her. If she took a taxi when the train arrived in Tauranga, he was to write down the number of the vehicle she took, and later find out her destination from the driver. If she took a bus, he should take the same bus as inconspicuously as possible. And if she started to hike purposefully in the direction of the backpacker hostel in McClaren Falls Park, he was appropriately dressed for the 15-mile pursuit. But no matter what happened, under no circumstances was she even to suspect that he might be following her.

He had entered the train carriage that Gretchen had chosen, but he found it deserted. He assumed that she had gone into that carriage with the intention of moving into a different carriage to mislead the watchers. So he took the first seat facing the engine, and waited for the train to depart. Once the journey had started, he reasoned, he would ask the conductor to search the train for her, and he would then move discreetly to the carriage she had chosen. Hopefully she would not notice that he had moved, and she would think that he had been there all the time.

To his utter surprise, Gretchen left the lavatory and sat opposite him. He suddenly noticed the rucksack stowed under her seat, but by now it was too late. He was trapped. Worse, she had started a conversation with him. He started to panic. What would he say if she asked him what he did? And what was the purpose of his trip to Tauranga? Fortunately, he had stayed a few times at his uncle's bach, and he knew where the key was kept, so he could carry off that part of his story if necessary. But why would it be necessary? His job was to follow her without being detected. Once he had found out where she was staying, his orders were to immediately report to Inspector Urquhart at police headquarters in Tauranga for further instructions and then sleep in a room in the bachelor quarters behind the police station. If for some reason he could not come to the police station that night, he would spend the night at the bach, and go and meet Urquhart at nine the next morning.

But then the same worrying thought came to him again: What would he say if she asked him what he did? Conscription had been introduced in June 1940, and every man in New Zealand aged between 18 and 46 became liable to be called up by ballot. Was there a way in which he could convince her that his number had not come up for more than two years? Unlikely. And anyway, why hadn't he already volunteered to join the Second New Zealand Expeditionary Force? He obviously could not inform her that, as a policeman, he was exempt from military service.

He was about to break out in a cold sweat when an idea struck him. He would tell her that he was a serviceman on leave, spending a few days on Omokoroa Beach.

***

The train stopped for two minutes at Morrinsville, then continued on its way to Tauranga. Gretchen was unable to suppress her growing feelings of attraction to Wes. She had to make her move now.

"Wes, what do you do for a living?"

"I used to work as a mechanic in a garage, but as soon as war was declared I joined up. I've been given a week's leave. I have no family, so I'm spending the time at the beach."

"A week on that beautiful beach, catching your meals in your tinny—that sounds fabulous."

She took a deep breath and went on. "Wes, your description of Omokoroa Beach has made me want to stay there. You mentioned that the bach has one bedroom, plus a couch in the front room. I know you'll think that this is an awful cheek on my part, but do you think that your friend would mind if I slept on the couch? In return, I'd pay for all the food and drink."

"Well, the fish are free—I'll just catch as many as we need," he said, cursing himself as he did so. He had responded to the free food and drink offer, not her request to sleep on the couch in the bach. And now there was no way to get out of it. On the one hand, he would certainly be able tell his superiors the next morning exactly where she had spent the night. But he was fully aware that he was now in serious trouble. They had not specifically mentioned it at the Royal New Zealand Police College at Trentham Military Camp, but he knew instinctively that you must never share a bach on a beach with someone you are following. And he could see no possible way out of the mess in which he now found himself.

# CHAPTER FIFTEEN

*Tauranga, New Zealand*
*Saturday, September 12th, 1942*

The train pulled into Tauranga some 45 minutes late. As they left the station, it started to rain.

"Let's grab some fish and chips," Wes suggested, "and then we can take the last bus to Omokoroa Beach."

"That sounds like a good idea," Gretchen said. "It's too late and too dark for you to go fishing for our meal tonight."

As they started to eat their food, a bus drove past.

"Damn," Wes said, "I'd forgotten that the train was late. That was the last bus—I hope you're in the mood for a 15-mile walk."

"In this rain? As they say in New York City, fuggedaboudit! I see a Station Hotel across the road. Let's get rooms there. We'll take the first bus to the beach tomorrow morning. And don't worry, I'll pay for the rooms. It's all part of the deal."

Wes reasoned to himself that staying in separate rooms in the same hotel was fractionally less reprehensible than sharing an isolated bach with the person he was supposed to be following without being observed. So he just nodded. When they had finished their meal, they crossed the road to the hotel. Brushing the rainwater off their clothes, they approached the middle-aged receptionist behind the desk.

"Two single rooms for tonight, please," Gretchen said.

"I'm so sorry, madam, but there's a big wedding in the town tonight. Such a lovely couple—the daughter of one of our town councilors is marrying the oldest son of our high school principal. There's not a room to be had within a five-mile radius. And it's started to rain, too. I don't know what to suggest. But let me just check something."

She went into the office behind the reception desk, and came out a few minutes later carrying a letter. "The Shepstones of Frostingale Farm have reserved a room for tonight, but they haven't arrived yet, and it's nearly eight o'clock. They're such nice people. They would definitely have let me know if they weren't coming, so something must have happened—I do hope that nothing's seriously wrong. Our policy is to keep rooms only until six o'clock, so I can let you have theirs. It's a double room with an en suite bathroom. But now that I come to think of it, the room has a couch as well as a double bed. Would that suit you?"

"No," Wes said, but at the same time, Gretchen said, "Yes."

The receptionist laughed girlishly. "Usually it's the lady who's concerned for the proprieties, not the gentleman. Sir, the lady seems happy with your sleeping on the couch. If you look out the window, you'll see that it's raining harder than ever now, and it doesn't look as if it's going to let up for hours. And you certainly won't find any other accommodation tonight. Won't you consider taking the room?"

"Of course, he'll take it," Gretchen insisted. "Thank you so much for your help. I'll sign the register, to show that everything's completely above board."

The receptionist smiled. "In that case, the matter is settled. Room 12, up one flight, turn left, and it's at the end of the corridor. Sunday breakfast is served from eight to nine. I hope you both have a pleasant stay."

They walked to the room in silence. It was a large room, with a double bed on the right side and an ugly green couch against the left-hand wall.

"I'll take the couch, of course," Gretchen said. "That's what we agreed on the train, and that's what we're going to do."

"No, I'm used to roughing it. You take the bed."

"Wes, a deal is a deal. I would hate to think that an honorable person like you might break an agreement."

Yet again Wes found that, to his great surprise, Gretchen had outmaneuvered him. The women in his world almost invariably went along with the man's suggestions, except when it came to courtship—New Zealand society was puritanical in the extreme. Despite his film star good looks, Wes had made love with only two young women, both of them as inexperienced as he was. Neither occasion had been particularly enjoyable for him or for either of them. For Wes, sex was a greatly overrated activity.

"It's getting late. Let's go to sleep. You can have the bathroom first."

Wes was about to say, "Ladies first," when he realized that he would probably lose that argument, too. So he meekly complied with Gretchen's suggestion.

When Gretchen came out of the bathroom, Wes was lying on the far side of the double bed with his back to her. She switched off the light and then climbed into the near side of the bed. Wes was so taken aback that he couldn't think of anything to say. She shifted toward him. With her left hand she started playing with his hair, something she had wanted to do ever since meeting him. Her right hand started stroking his bare chest.

Wes finally reacted by saying, "No," as firmly as he could without being rude.

"Why not?"

He thought quickly. "Because I'm a queer."

Her right hand moved lower down. "Well, if you're a queer, how do you explain this?"

There was silence. Gretchen's right hand continued to stroke.

"That isn't the reason, is it? What's the real reason?"

He tried a new tack. "I don't have a condom. You might get pregnant."

She laughed. "No, that's not possible at this time of the month."

He had no idea what she meant, but made a third attempt.

"Gretchen, I'm most inexperienced in these matters and I'm worried that you'll be disappointed."

She laughed again, a kindly laugh. "Don't you worry about that. Just lie back and enjoy every minute."

Gretchen's right hand mysteriously stroked away all further objections—during the four years Gretchen spent with her communist lover, she had acquired great skill in the erotic arts. Wes totally surrendered himself to her. As they finally climaxed together, she grabbed him tightly—she was not going to let him roll off and go to sleep. She waited until he was ready once more, and then started to make love to him again. This time Wes was eager to be a full participant from the start. When it was over, she kissed him and let him fall asleep on his side of the bed.

\*\*\*

A second storm woke her in the middle of the night. She looked at the Adonis sleeping next to her, and gently started kissing him. It took her a few minutes to rouse him, but once he was fully awake, he was an equal partner in what followed.

As the sun rose, Gretchen awoke again. Wes was breathing heavily, dead to the world. Gretchen thought to herself that the forthcoming week with him at the beach house was going to be the most wonderful time of her whole life. Then her strong sense of duty interrupted her reveries. The fate of tens of millions of her fellow countrymen depended on her finding the promethium mine, and quickly.

# CHAPTER SIXTEEN

*Tauranga, New Zealand*
*Sunday, September 13th, 1942*

She woke Wes at eight o'clock. "Get up, sleepyhead, it's time for breakfast."

"Not yet, come snuggle up with me," he pleaded as he reached for her.

"The storm has passed, we're going to walk to Omanawa Falls. It's only 15 miles. And when we get there…"

"Yes?"

"…if you've been a good boy, you'll get a reward."

"What kind of reward?"

"Well, if you don't get dressed and go down for breakfast right now, you'll never find out."

After a country breakfast they returned to their room. In view of what had happened the previous night, Wes had only one thing on his mind, and it certainly was not the fact that he was supposed to report to Inspector Urquhart at Tauranga police headquarters in five minutes' time.

"Now seems a good time for a repeat performance," Wes said hopefully.

Gretchen ignored the remark. "Pack your things into your rucksack. We're leaving."

"Why don't we leave our rucksacks here and pick them up on our way back from the waterfall to the bach?" he asked.

"No, we're taking everything with us. Come on now."

Wes didn't even stop to wonder why she insisted on their taking all their belongings along and just meekly followed her down the stairs. She paid for their accommodation and food, took the packed lunches she had ordered at breakfast, thanked the receptionist for her kindness and helpfulness when they had checked in, and left the hotel with Wes in tow.

Gretchen continued to lead the way, NZMS 1 map in hand. She turned left at the corner. The imposing police headquarters building dominated the next block. Gretchen's mind was on the mine next to Omanawa Falls, so she took no notice of the large stone structure. But her companion was suddenly shocked back to reality. He instantly realized that, if he left Gretchen and reported for duty, she would immediately be aware of the true situation, which was totally contrary to his instructions. On the other hand, if he just walked on past the police station where he was supposed to have reported to Inspector Urquhart 10 minutes earlier, that would unquestionably constitute gross dereliction of duty.

A sudden idea came to him. He called out to Gretchen, who was striding out some five or six yards ahead of him. "I've got an old school friend who works in the police station here. I'm just going to pop in to see him for a minute. I'll be back in just a jiffy."

"No dramas," she said. "I'll come along. I want to meet your friends."

Now, Wes was in a horrible bind. He knew most of the members of the Tauranga police force, and they would surely greet him as a colleague as he walked in, instantly giving away the game to Gretchen. He thought of stooping to retie a bootlace as he walked in, so the man behind the counter would see Gretchen first. But the moment he straightened up, it would be all over.

Finally, he thought of a stratagem. He waited for Gretchen to backtrack and catch up with him. He took her by the arm and walked next to her through the double doors into the police station. Behind the counter stood Constable John Wilkins. Wes had known him for years—they had been together at the Royal New Zealand Police College. Before Wilkins could say a word, Wes asked loudly, "Constable, is Denis Cummings around this morning?"

Wilkins immediately realized that Wes was warning him not to say anything. First, Wes had addressed him as "Constable," rather than by his first name. But more importantly, every policeman in New Zealand was familiar with the name of the

Police Commissioner—Denis Cummings was loved and feared in equal measures.

"No, sir, he's not in yet. Can I give him a message?" John asked.

"Yes, please. Could you tell him that Wes came to see him with Gretchen? We're about to hike to Omanawa Falls."

"Yes, sir, I'll let him know the moment he gets in."

"Thank you, Constable."

Wes escorted Gretchen out of the police station.

*** 

As soon as the two had left police headquarters, John Wilkins rang Inspector Urquhart's office.

"Sir, something most peculiar is going on. Wes McFee was here a moment ago arm-in-arm with a beautiful blonde. He pretended not to know me. He asked for Denis Cummings and—"

"Did you just say that Wes asked to see Denis Cummings?"

"Yes, sir. And when I told him that Denis Cummings wasn't in yet, he left a strange message. He said, 'Tell Denis that Wes came to see him with Gretchen, and—"

"John, did you say Gretchen?"

"Yes, sir, Gretchen. That was the name he said. And he said that he and Gretchen were hiking to Omanawa Falls."

"Did you let on in any way at all that Wes is a detective, Constable?"

"No, sir. He walked in with the blonde, and I was about to greet him, but when he called me Constable and asked for the Commissioner, I treated him respectfully as a member of the public."

"You did well, John. Write up the incident in detail, quoting precisely what you and Wes said, word-for-word. I'm going to make a phone call to Wellington, and then I'll drive in my own car in the direction of Omanawa Falls. Oh, what are they wearing?"

"They're both in hiking clothes, sir."

"Good. Then they should be easy to spot. If Wes comes back here, continue to pretend you don't know him."

"And if the blonde comes back, sir?"

"Just say something like, 'Weren't you here earlier today, miss?' and then take your cue from what she says."

\*\*\*

Inspector Urquhart immediately placed a long-distance call to Detective Chief Superintendent Jennings in Wellington. When the trunk operator finally connected him, he told Jennings what had happened at Tauranga police station a few minutes earlier.

"Jock," Warren Jennings said, "what do you propose to do?"

"There's only one road to Omanawa Falls, and it's going to take them about four hours to get there. It's virtually a straight route for about 15 miles, so they can't get there any faster by taking shortcuts across fields or through forests. I was thinking of going home, changing into civvies and then driving up to the falls. When I see them, I'll offer them a lift."

"No, that's not a good idea at all. Gretchen will immediately catch on. She's sharp as a tack and she'll very quickly realize that you weren't really intending to go to the falls. Also, she'll want to locate the mine, and your presence will hamper her. After all, she can't tell you what she's up to. No, you stay away until you're sure that they're on their way back. Then you can offer her a lift to wherever she's going, presumably the railway station.

"What I don't understand," he continued, "is how young McFee features in all this. I personally instructed him unambiguously and in words of one syllable that Gretchen was not to discover that he was following her. According to what your constable told you, he's not following her, instead he's walking arm-in-arm with her. It's probably some new-fangled technique that they're teaching the incoming recruits at the Police College—the best way to be sure that you don't lose a suspect is to walk hand-in-hand with her. I wonder what McFee does when he's told to tail a male subject surreptitiously?"

Jock Urquhart decided that the safest response was just to ignore the question. Instead he said, "I've had an idea. Suppose Gretchen caught him staring at her in the train. He's extremely good looking, so he could get away with saying that he was struck by her beauty, or some such hackneyed line. Next thing you know, they're walking hand-in-hand into my police station."

"But aren't police absolutely forbidden to fraternize with criminals?"

"Did you tell him that she's a criminal?" Jock asked.

"No, not exactly."

"Just how 'not exactly,' Warren?"

"I didn't tell him that she's unquestionably a Nazi spy. I just told him to follow her. Surely he knows that we only follow suspects?"

"Actually," Jock said, "I think that what he's done is nothing short of brilliant. Gretchen Konrad must know that no policeman would walk hand-in-hand with her, let alone try to pick her up in a train carriage. We need to arrange some sort of medal for him. By the way, where do you think they were last night? The train came in even later than usual, so they couldn't have taken a bus to the bach where Wes told us he was going to stay. He was scheduled to take the first bus back into town this morning. That's why he was supposed to meet with me at nine o'clock, instead of the usual eight o'clock."

"If they couldn't take a bus, what about a taxi? Could you contact the local taxis and find out what happened?"

"Certainly. I'll phone around and get back to you."

\*\*\*

An hour later, Jock Urquhart phoned Jennings back.

"Warren, you're not going to believe this. As I told you, the train was really late so they missed the bus to the beach. Instead they spent the night in a double room at the Station Hotel here in Tauranga."

"Are you serious?"

"Deadly serious. I've spoken to the receptionist, Carol Bentley. Carol's a cousin of my wife, so I've known her for maybe 15 or 20 years. She told me that Gretchen came in with our boy in tow and asked Carol for two single rooms. Carol explained that the hotel was full because of a wedding. She added that there wasn't a room to be had in the vicinity. Then Carol found she had this room available with a double bed and a couch, which she offered to them. Gretchen said 'yes.' Wes said 'no.' But Gretchen overruled him, and they spent the night in the same room. I can only assume that he slept on the couch while she occupied the bed."

"Did you ask to inspect the room?"

"There was no need. Gretchen signed the hotel register in her own name and gave her Bathurst address. She obviously wouldn't do that if she were up to some sort of hanky-panky."

"Back up a minute. Did you just say that Gretchen signed the register? And that she did so in her real name?"

"Yes, that's what Carol told me."

"So, Gretchen's a Nazi spy on the run from the police. She eludes us in Wellington using great skill and heads for the Tauranga mine. And then she registers in a hotel under her own name? And gives her actual address? That makes no sense at all to me. Someone with one-hundredth of her intelligence would have told Wes to sign the register. Or she could have made up a name and an address."

There was a long pause while both men tried to come up with a plausible explanation. Then Warren changed the subject.

"Jock," he asked, "have you ever worked with the vice squad?"

"Never."

"Pity. Even so, I think you'll be able to successfully carry out the next part of this investigation. Phone Carol and tell her not to let anyone into the room. Then get over there and determine who slept where."

"Are you saying what I think you're saying?"

"Yes, I certainly am. Phone me back when you have the answer."

\*\*\*

"Warren, it's Jock."

"Hold on a minute, Jock. I'm going to ask Detective Superintendent Peter Mudge to join in this conversation on the extension. He's our Australian contact, working with me on this case. I've shared with him everything you've told me today."

"Good morning, Peter," Jock said. "Pleased to meet you."

"Likewise," Mudge replied. "And what did you discover at the Station Hotel?"

"There's no question that they both slept in the double bed. And there's undeniable evidence of extensive sexual activity. I've impounded the sheets, much to Carol's horror."

Warren Jennings chuckled lewdly. "We'll make a vice-squad cop out of you yet, Jock! More seriously though, the case has taken a disturbing turn. Unless he has an extremely good explanation, Wes will be looking for new employment tomorrow. His behavior, though unacceptable and inexcusable, is understandable: he's young and he's handsome, and she's extremely pretty. What I cannot fathom is what Gretchen is up to. She did three things in Tauranga that I find almost impossible to understand.

"First, she's a Nazi spy trying to find a mine as quickly as possible. Rudyard Kipling put it best: 'He travels the fastest who travels alone.' Nevertheless, she picks up a young man in the train and spends a night of passion with him.

"Then, she takes him along with her while she goes looking for a mine. I could possibly understand her asking a local to accompany her as a guide, but Wes comes from Hamilton. He can't help her, and he certainly can hinder her by asking her what she's up to and other questions that she won't want to answer.

"And finally, she knows that we're after her—the proof of that is her escape through the back door of the Masonic Hotel. But then she signs the register at the Station Hotel when she so easily could've told Wes to do it. And she registers in her own name and gives her address in Bathurst."

"You're right; it's very strange," Detective Superintendent Mudge said. "But she could've picked Wes up as cover. Yes, he's about 10 years younger than she is, but maybe he was the only possible male on the train from Hamilton—we all know there's a war on. But if that's what happened, she would've told Wes to sign the hotel register."

"What if he picked her up?" Warren asked.

"Has he ever done anything like that before?" Peter Mudge enquired.

"Do you mean: Has he ever initiated a sexual liaison?" Warren asked. "I've no idea. Probably. Most young men have these days. But I'm sure that he's never done anything like this with a suspect—and there's no way he could stay on in the police force with that on his record. The rules here in New Zealand are the same as in your country and, I should imagine, everywhere else in the world."

"So, we have truly strange behavior on the part of both Wes and Gretchen," Jock said. "That makes even less sense than before."

"I agree," Jennings said. "But we need to discuss what to do next."

"Well," Peter pointed out, "we've got to let her find the Tauranga mine, and then we have to ensure that she gets to Rotorua for the next mine."

"Is this some sort of treasure hunt?" Jock asked.

"Sorry, mate, we can't tell you everything about this case—the national security people would have our guts for garters. But I can tell you this. We have to ensure that Gretchen Konrad has the opportunity to find the mine near your Omanawa Falls. And after that, she has to find another mine, this one near Rotorua."

"Why?" Jock asked.

"I'm sorry, but we're not allowed tell you that either. But I can inform you officially that this matter is of the very highest importance. I've been told that the outcome of the war could depend on the outcome of this case."

"I see. Well, she's here in Tauranga. What do you want me to do?"

"Help her to get to Rotorua after she's visited your mine."

"There's just one tiny little problem with that," Jock said.

"Oh?"

"There's no mine anywhere near Omanawa Falls."

"According to a document that Gretchen has, there is," Warren said. "And I can tell you exactly where it is."

"Warren," Jock said, "I was born on a farm near the falls. I grew up in those hills. I managed to get posted here as a policeman, and I was the investigating officer for various thefts of copper wire from the hydroelectric plants on the area's rivers. In short, I know every inch of that part of the world like the back of my hand, and I can tell you categorically that there's no mine within a 10-mile radius of the falls."

"Jock, you must have a large-scale map of the area in your police station."

"Of course."

"I'm going to give you the coordinates of the mine. Take this down." Warren gave Jock the latitude and longitude figures from a copy of the document that Walter had obtained for Gretchen.

"Fine, I'll check it out right now. Hold the line, I'll be back in a minute or three."

Warren and Peter heard the usual long-distance hiss for a while, and then they heard footsteps walking toward the phone, accompanied by loud laughter.

"Are you two still there?" asked Jock. He was having difficulty controlling his amusement.

"We're here."

"As you approach it, it does look like a mine. And the closer you get, the more it seems like a mine. But it isn't a mine."

"So, what is it then?"

# CHAPTER SEVENTEEN

*Tauranga, New Zealand*
*Sunday, September 13th, 1942*

They had been walking for nearly four hours now, stopping only to admire the incomparable vistas as Omanawa Road gradually climbed upward into the high hills behind Tauranga. It was a typical cool New Zealand spring day and Gretchen and Wes were both fit, so neither was breathing faster than usual as they neared a sign that read "Omanawa Falls."

"Here's where we turn off the road," Gretchen said. "According to the map, we're about half a mile from the mine."

"Gretchen, you've been talking about this mine since last night. But every time I've asked you about it, you've changed the subject. Now that we're almost there, will you please tell what this is all about?"

"Patience is a virtue, Wes. But I promise you that it won't be much longer now."

They started walking down a well-travelled gravel road lined on both sides by dense woods. Gretchen did not recognize any of the trees, so she concluded that they must be walking in an old-growth forest. The downward gradient began to steepen. They came to an area where wild flowers in a wide variety of bright colors thickly bordered the route on either side. Then the road turned to the right, and they saw a concrete support for an aerial tramway ahead.

Gretchen pointed to the support. "They must use the tramway to transport ore from the mine to this point. Then they probably drop the ore from the buckets into trucks that transport the ore to Tauranga Harbour. Judging from the severe inclination of the road, those trucks had better have four-wheel drive."

Wes looked dubious. "The aerial tramway is considerably rusted. It doesn't look as if it's been used for many years. I can see the stationary cable that supports the buckets, but where's the wire that pulls the buckets along? And I don't see any buckets, either. Come to think of it, there doesn't seem to be a motor anywhere."

"It must be at the other end. It makes more sense that way—they would want the buckets to move along only when they've filled one, and they do the filling at the mine end of the tramway, not here."

Gretchen said nothing as they passed a second support with the cable still caked with thick red rust. They walked another 20 yards and finally heard the sound of a waterfall. A few yards more, and the trees on the left parted. They saw that they were high up on one side of a deep valley, which was thickly lined on both sides with trees and large bushes. Two hundred yards below them, a large pool filled the valley floor. The water was an intense shade of turquoise, quite unlike anything Gretchen had ever seen before.

"Where's the waterfall?" Wes asked.

"It sounds like it's somewhere to the right, but the trees are blocking our view. Maybe there's another gap farther on."

Much to their disappointment, the lush foliage grew even denser as they continued. Finally the trees cleared, and they could see a river on the other side of the valley. It flowed directly toward them then plunged in a thick white column over a cliff into the pool below. The base of cliff behind the waterfall had eroded away over the centuries, so there was a large hemispherical cavity behind the torrent. Even Gretchen, whose thoughts had been focused on the mine all day, was totally entranced by the scene in front of and below her.

They could not tear themselves away from the view. Eventually Gretchen said quietly, "We have to go on."

"Why?"

"This place is truly gorgeous, but we're here to find a mine."

"Let's sit here and eat our lunch," Wes suggested.

They ate their sandwiches in silence. Wes wolfed down his food; Gretchen ate slowly and thoughtfully. When she finished, she started walking again in the same direction as before.

They came around another corner and encountered a flight of moss-covered stairs leading downward; a rocky mountain lay directly ahead of them. The steps led down to a stout metal door in the mountainside.

"Ah, the mine!" Gretchen began the descent. In her haste she slipped on the lichens, but quickly recovered her footing. At the bottom of the stairs she reached triumphantly for the door.

"Locked!" she announced in dismay.

Wes joined her. "Is this the mine you're looking for?"

"Yes, it must be. Look at the map. We're at the end of this track, and that's where the mine is located—I've marked it with an 'X.' The river is here on the map, and there's the waterfall. We're definitely at the right place. Any ideas?"

Before Wes could say anything, they heard footsteps and a powerfully built man of about 45 appeared behind them at the top of the stairs. He, too, was in hiking clothes, and carried a walking pole in his right hand.

"Good afternoon!" called Gretchen.

The man responded in kind, adding, "I'm coming down to join you."

"The door to the mine is locked," Gretchen said.

"Mine? What mine?"

"According to my map, this tunnel leads to a mine."

"Then your map is wrong," the man said. "The door leads to the first hydroelectric power station in the southern hemisphere."

"A power station?" Gretchen asked, her voice betraying her frustration on learning that there was no mine. "But why is it inside the mountain?"

"In 1914," the man replied, "an engineer named Lloyd Mandeno applied for permission to take water from the Omanawa River to generate electricity for Tauranga. The initial reaction was outrage. The very idea that someone might destroy the natural beauty of this place was anathema to the Public Works Department, let alone the people of the district. But Mandeno explained to the authorities that all of the powerhouse would be located inside the mountain. Nothing would be visible from outside, other than the power lines carrying the electricity to the town and the aerial tramway used to transport the generator and other machinery into the tunnel that he blasted out of the solid mountain. So, technically I suppose, this *is* a mine—an excavation made in the earth to extract rock. But the rocks weren't removed for their ore content, but rather to create a space for a powerhouse hidden inside the mountain."

In spite of her intense disappointment, Gretchen was interested in what the man had to say. "And what happened?"

"The Public Works Department agreed to the scheme. It took Mandeno only a year to complete the whole project. A few years later they enlarged the power station and installed a bigger generator to provide more power—the town of Tauranga was starting to grow. The power station runs fine. You can't hear the hum of the generator from up here because of the roar of the falls. And the reason that the door is locked is for safety reasons—you can't have people wandering in and out of a hydroelectric power station."

"But why is the aerial tramway all rusted up?" she asked.

"There's been no need to use it for nearly 20 years. If they ever need to replace the generator again, they'll first have to repair the tramway. But my history lesson has gone on long enough. Are you two hiking through this region?"

Wes, who had recognized Inspector Jock Urquhart from the beginning, had wisely kept out of the conversation. He continued to be a spectator as Gretchen responded to the question.

"Not really. Wes here is a soldier on a week's leave, which he's spending at a bach at Omokoroa Beach. He kindly agreed to keep me company today. I'm interested in mines, and I'm hiking through New Zealand looking at a few in particular."

"That's an unusual hobby. What sparked your interest in mines?"

Gretchen thought quickly.

"My grandfather was a geologist," she said. "When he died, he left me his collection of rare rock samples. That's how it all started."

"What sorts of mines interest you?" Jock asked.

"Unusual mines, excluding mines that actually are power stations," she said with a forced laugh.

"And where are you off to next?" he asked.

"Rotorua."

"And how were you planning to get there?"

"By train."

"You could do that, but then you'd have to catch the last train tonight to Morrinsville, spend the night there, and take the train to Rotorua tomorrow morning. I reckon you'll be sitting in trains for at least six hours. But Rotorua is only 40 miles due south of here on Pyes Pa Road. Why don't you take the bus? It'll take you only about an hour and a half. My car is parked not far from here, and I'll drop you at the bus stop on my way back home in Tauranga—you'll be in Rotorua by four o'clock, I reckon. By the way, Wes, I live quite close to Omokoroa Beach, so I'd be delighted to take you there."

"That would be very nice. Thank you," Wes said.

"My name is Jock."

"And I'm Gretchen."

They walked together back up to Omanawa Road in silence. Urquhart didn't want to start an unnecessary conversation in case he accidentally let slip that he was a policeman, and he wanted Wes to stay quiet for the same reason. Gretchen was too disappointed to say anything. Perhaps unreasonably, she had pinned her hopes on Tauranga, and was most unhappy that the first mine she had managed to locate had turned out not to be the one that the *Abwehr* had sent her to New Zealand to find.

But there was also a more compelling reason for her silence—Gretchen had to think hard. Circumstances were pulling her in two directions. She wanted with all her heart to be with Wes for the remainder of his seven days of leave. However, she had told Jock that Wes was spending his leave at the bach on Omokoroa Beach, so how could she let Jock see her take Wes with her to Rotorua? But she could not stay in Tauranga with Wes—victory depended on her locating the promethium mine.

They reached the road. Jock's car was parked a few yards away, in the shade of a large pohutukawa tree. During the 30-minute drive back to town, Jock Urquhart twice pointed out an exceptionally beautiful view, but other than that he continued to say nothing.

Wes used the time to try to decide what to say to Jock when they got back to the police station. As they neared the town, he decided that he would give a detailed truthful account of everything that had happened from the time he saw Gretchen at Hamilton railway station, but he would take care to omit to mention anything about the previous night's sleeping arrangements.

Finally they reached the bus terminus. Jock spoke up. "There's the stop. The bus will be here in 10 minutes."

All through the car trip Gretchen's emotions had swung like a pendulum between her need for healing after what Walter had done to her and her duty to the Third Reich. At the bus stop, duty won. She thanked Jock formally. She then turned round to Wes who was sitting in the back seat and told him warmly how much she'd enjoyed his company. She got out of the car with her rucksack and took a seat on the bench inside the bus shelter.

Jock waved to Gretchen, then drove around the corner and parked where Gretchen could not see the car. "Wes," he said, "go with her to Rotorua."

"What?"

"Get out, walk round the corner, and tell her you want to go with her to Rotorua."

"What reason should I give?

"After last night's activities, you should have no trouble at all in coming up with an exceptionally convincing reason."

Wes blushed beetroot. "How did you find out? And why should she agree to take me along?"

"Regarding your last question, I have no doubt that she'll agree. But even if she doesn't, she can't stop you taking the bus and then giving a report to the station commander at the police station when you arrive in Rotorua. I'm about to phone Wellington to update them, and they'll tell Rotorua what's happening. The bus leaves in five minutes. Now go!"

Wes climbed out of the back seat, grabbed his rucksack and hurried toward the bus stop.

Gretchen caught sight of him as he rounded the corner. "What are you doing here?" she asked.

"I'm coming with you to Rotorua."

"But what will Jock think? I told him you were spending the rest of your leave at your bach."

"Jock be damned! I'm coming with you. I'm nuts about you and I want to spend the rest of my life with you."

# CHAPTER EIGHTEEN

*Tauranga, New Zealand*
*Sunday, September 13th, 1942*

As soon as he got back to Tauranga police headquarters, Urquhart put a telephone call through to Detective Chief Superintendent Jennings in Wellington. For once, the long-distance operator was prompt.

"Warren, please put Peter on the line. There've just been some new developments that you both need to know about."

There was a click as Peter picked up the extension.

"Warren and Peter, in about ninety minutes' time, Gretchen and Wes will arrive in Rotorua on the bus from here in Tauranga."

Without giving them a chance to ask any questions Jock went on. "Nearly four hours after they left the police station, I drove up Omanawa Road. I passed them in my car when they were still about half a mile on this side of the road to the waterfall. I drove past the turnoff and parked in the bushes. I waited for a while and then followed them as quietly as I could. I caught up with the pair just as they encountered that metal door I told you about.

"I learned from Gretchen that she's visiting 'unusual' mines. She informed me that Wes is a soldier on a week's leave, staying at a bach at Omokoroa Beach."

"And what did Wes say in response to that?"

"Wes kept quiet from beginning to end. The only time he spoke was after I dropped Gretchen at the bus stop for Rotorua, parked around the corner, and ordered him to accompany her. He asked me, 'What reason can I give her?' I told him that, after what had happened in the double bed the previous night, it would be easy for him to come up with a reason. He had the good manners to blush. So, gentlemen, Gretchen has been to her first mine and she's on a bus on the way to Rotorua, the site of the second mine."

"Will she take Wes with her to the mine?" Warren asked.

"I have no idea. This morning you pointed out that she's behaving most strangely for a Nazi spy on the run. I agree that her behavior is bizarre in the extreme. When I dropped her at the bus stop, she thanked Wes fondly for his company and left. Clearly she didn't want me to find out that they're considerably more than just casual acquaintances, but the fact is that she didn't even kiss him goodbye—I tell you, that came as a bit of surprise to me. Was that play-acting or was it real? I simply cannot predict what she'll do or not do."

"What's your best guess?"

"All I'm prepared to say is that I'm sure that Wes will do everything he can to share her bed tonight. Will she tell him to get lost when they arrive in Rotorua? Or is she also eagerly anticipating more romance? I just have no idea."

"The reason I asked you," Warren said, "is that I need to know what to tell Rotorua."

"Tell them to have someone in civvies to meet the bus," Jock suggested. "If Gretchen and Wes are all lovey-dovey when they arrive there, Wes will eventually be able to give us an update that should enable us to keep following her. If not, your man in Rotorua will have to tail her."

"You'd better tell Rotorua to send an unmarried man to meet the bus," Warren said. "It's quite possible that Gretchen is going to try to sleep with every good-looking policeman in sight. Which leads to a fascinating question: How come she didn't try to seduce you, Jock?"

Urquhart snorted and put down the phone.

\*\*\*

When the bus to Rotorua drew up at the Tauranga stop, Gretchen and Wes allowed a family with a curly-haired little girl to board first. Then Gretchen climbed on, with Wes following close behind. She whispered to Wes, "Sit a few seats away from me," then made for the back row of the bus.

Her directive puzzled Wes, but once again he obeyed her unquestioningly.

Gretchen wanted to think without distraction. On the one hand, she reasoned, Jock was right; technically, there was a mine next to Omanawa Falls. But for most people, she thought, a mine is a hole in the ground dug for the specific purpose of extracting minerals. In fact, she suddenly realized, the word "mineral" was probably derived from the word "mine." But there never was any intention to get minerals out of the Omanawa cavity in the mountain. By no stretch of the imagination could anyone consider hydroelectric electricity to be a mineral. No wonder that, on her list of mines, the product of the Omanawa mine was stipulated as "Various." Now she was having second thoughts about locating the other three mines that she had previously identified. Back in the Arthur Hotel in Wellington she had decided that the entries for the mines with "Various" products had been changed to disguise what actually came out of those mines. If the promethium mine was indeed one of the four, then the actual product would have been changed to "Various" for reasons of military secrecy. But what if there were other reasons? For example, she knew that Rotorua was a region of intense geothermal activity—what if the second mine was just a geothermal power station? That 'mine' might simply be a hole in the ground from which superheated steam emanated from deep down in the earth's crust to drive a generator. In fact, what if all four "Various" mines were just power stations that used renewable energy sources?

Then she thought more carefully for a moment. What about Coopers Island in the far south? There was no geothermal activity there, as far as she knew. And no waterfalls, either. But then she recalled that for years the Canadian government had been discussing the feasibility of harnessing the huge tides in the Bay of Fundy in Nova Scotia to generate electricity. What if the Coopers Island mine was just a tidal generating plant? And what about Akaroa? All she could remember about the town was that French settlers had founded it. She could think of no way that Akaroa could produce electricity from renewable energy.

She decided to start again from the very beginning. She had orders from Admiral Canaris to find the exact location of the promethium mine in New Zealand. Her former colleague Walter Bennett had managed to obtain a list of every mine in New Zealand for her. None of the mines mentioned promethium as a product, so she had assumed that one of the four "Various" mines was the mine that she sought. But what if she were wrong? What if the promethium mine was so secret that it did not appear on any list of the Department of Lands and Survey? What if the military, fully aware that the outcome of the war hinged on the rare-earth metal, had decreed that there was to be no mention whatsoever of the mine anywhere other than deep in their Most Secret files?

Max Malone had served as a top-level conduit to the Department of Lands and Survey. What she needed now was someone with access to the highest levels of the military establishment. She thought of Mata Hari, who had affairs with high-ranking military officers to obtain information for her German spymasters, Major Röpell and Captain Hoffmann. Gretchen's sole point of contact with the military was Wes, who had told her that he was on seven days' leave from the Army. He did not mention his rank, but she assumed that Wes was probably a private, or a sergeant at best. She asked herself if her burgeoning passion for Wes would allow her to try to use him to obtain the information she sought—probably not, she decided. Then she thought again about Mata Hari, and wondered if she had enjoyed sleeping with Allied staff officers as much as she (Gretchen) was looking forward to spending the night with Wes. She got up from her seat, walked to where Wes was sitting, tapped him on the shoulder, and indicated with a come-hither motion of her right-hand index finger that he should now join her at the rear of the bus. As she walked back with him, she thought of Mata Hari for the third and last time. This time Gretchen recalled that Mata Hari had been executed by a French firing squad in 1917.

# CHAPTER NINETEEN

*Rotorua, New Zealand*
*Sunday, September 13th, 1942*

The bus from Tauranga arrived at Rotorua at precisely the scheduled time. Sergeant Neil Evans watched as discreetly as he was able from a nearby bus shelter. Evans was a happily married man with five children. However, all the single policemen stationed at Rotorua had volunteered for military duty and were now in Egypt with the New Zealand 5th Infantry Brigade, so Evans had been deputed to follow Gretchen. He saw a family of three leave the bus, followed by a blonde woman hand-in-hand with a handsome young man who looked like Dana Andrews. Both had rucksacks on their backs.

Gretchen and Wes walked idly around the town center until they spied the Lake Hotel. Gretchen led the way in, and Wes closely followed. She asked the receptionist for a double room. The receptionist looked pointedly at the ring finger on Gretchen's left hand. She immediately realized that the woman behind the counter was exceedingly uncomfortable with the idea of an unmarried couple sharing a room. On the other hand, the receptionist appeared to be acutely aware of the fact that the owner of the hotel was standing behind her.

After a long silence, the receptionist said, "I can let you have Room 11, a double room, for 18 shillings and sixpence. The rate includes breakfast, served between seven and nine o'clock. Would you please fill in your details here?"

She pushed the book toward Wes. Gretchen reached across and pulled the hotel register toward her and supplied her name, address and signature. The receptionist tried to manifest her distaste for the whole situation without the owner noticing, but her body language gave her away. The owner, a gray-haired man in an old but well-cut suit, immediately came forward. "Welcome to the Lake Hotel," he said in a cultured English accent. "I hope that you'll both have a pleasant stay."

"Thank you," Gretchen said. "By the way, tomorrow morning we want to visit the geothermal site at Waiotapu. What's the best way to get there?"

"There's a bus every hour on the hour. Did you arrive here by bus or by train?"

"We came by bus from Tauranga."

"Very good. Your bus stop for tomorrow morning is about 50 yards farther down the street from where you got off the Tauranga bus this afternoon—the sign on the pole says 'Waiotapu.' Will you be wanting a packed lunch?"

"Yes, please."

"Two lunches will be waiting for you on your breakfast table tomorrow morning. Once again, I do hope you'll enjoy your stay."

Wes and Gretchen went upstairs to their room. Sergeant Evans was standing across the road, trying unsuccessfully to blend into the landscape. He waited a few minutes, and then walked into the hotel. The owner spied him.

"Good afternoon, Sergeant Evans," he said. "How can I help you?"

"I'm here on duty, Mr. Kaplan."

"But you're in civvies."

"After 22 years in uniform, 10 of them as a sergeant, Chief Inspector Higgins apparently wants me to try out as a detective."

"I see. I assume you've come here in disguise to check on the six o'clock swill?" the owner said, with a broad smile on his face. "Well, it's Sunday, so the hotel bar is closed. There's not going to be that last minute rush before closing time."

"You will have your little jokes, Mr. Kaplan, but I'm actually here for a different reason. May I please see your register?"

"Of course, Sergeant. Here's the book. What are you looking for?"

"It's this last entry here: Gretchen Konrad."

Sergeant Evans took out his notebook and pencil, licked the pencil point in the approved manner, and laboriously copied the details onto the next empty page of his notebook.

"May I ask what this is all about?"

"Of course you may, sir, but I have no idea. No idea at all. You might want to ask Chief Inspector Higgins. He refuses to tell me anything, but you may be luckier."

"Top Secret, eh? Well, I won't say a word about this to Miss Konrad or her friend. Did you know I was in military intelligence in the last war?"

"No, sir, I did not. But I'm glad to hear that you're a master of discretion."

Kaplan decided that he would ask Higgins a few questions next time he dropped into the hotel bar for a Speight's Gold Medal Ale on his way home.

As Evans left the premises, Kaplan remarked to himself that the Sergeant looked exactly like a police sergeant in civvies trying his level best not to look like a police sergeant in civvies, and failing dismally in the attempt.

*** 

"Detective Chief Superintendent Jennings? It's Tom Higgins in Rotorua. We spoke a few hours ago."

"Yes, indeed. Would you please hold the line for a minute? I'd like my Australian colleague, Detective Superintendent Peter Mudge, to also hear first hand what you have to tell us."

"Peter Mudge here, Tom. What have you learned?"

"Well, my sergeant saw McFee and Konrad walking hand-in-hand as they left the bus from Tauranga. He followed them as they strolled around the town, apparently without a care in the world. Then they entered the Lake Hotel, where they're registered in Room 11. More precisely, Konrad signed the register."

"Did she give an address in Bathurst, New South Wales?" Jennings asked.

"Yes, she did. And after examining the hotel register, my man returned to the station as instructed. We're awaiting a visit from Detective Constable McFee in due course, probably some time tomorrow. I will, of course, contact you as soon as he comes here to report."

"Tom, this is important: Was your man careful to ensure that he wasn't detected as he followed the pair around?"

"He claims that he was discretion itself—I have my doubts, however. Unfortunately, he was the only man available this afternoon. If it weren't for the war, he definitely would *not* have been my first choice for surveillance duty, to put it mildly. In fact, this was the first time that we've ever told him to tail a subject, for good reason. However, you'll be pleased to know that Sergeant Evans told me that McFee and Konrad are apparently so besotted with one another that they wouldn't have noticed if he'd followed right behind them dressed as a female Great Spotted Kiwi and banging a big bass drum. I've known Neil Evans for nearly 20 years now, and I'm inclined to believe him when he says things like that."

\*\*\*

"Curiouser and curiouser," Peter said to Warren. "She's once again infatuated with Wes."

"Her attitude toward him in front of Jock Urquhart may just have been play-acting," Warren said. "Or, more likely, she didn't want to embarrass Wes. The rest of the time she's displayed a consistent fascination for him. In fact, I think she's falling in love with him."

"Could it be the other way round?" Peter mused.

"Meaning what exactly?"

"Could her attitude when they were with Jock have been her true feelings? Her passionate feelings for Wes as observed at the Tauranga police station and in Rotorua might have been feigned."

"If you're right," Warren replied, "she must have pretended to be thoroughly smitten with him the whole of last night. That would mean that she's a superb actress in bed. And tomorrow morning, Higgins will be able to tell us if there was an encore performance. No, I think that she's as utterly enraptured with him as he is with her."

"There's another thing, though," Peter remarked. "A spy on the run doesn't allow herself to get intimately involved with the enemy. And whoever heard of a secret agent registering at two hotels in a row in her own name and giving her home address? Also, she exhibited the highest skill level when she eluded us at the Masonic Hotel, but she's allowed two different policemen to accompany her, namely Wes and Jock. And she apparently didn't notice that she was being followed by a clumsy middle-aged police sergeant on his first tailing assignment."

"So?" Warren asked.

"So we may be making a huge mistake. Gretchen Konrad may no longer be a Nazi secret agent."

"What precisely are you saying?"

"First let's think back to what we know about Walter Bennett," Peter said. "By his own admission, he was sent here by the *Abwehr*. But he told us that, after the mix-up with the voltage of the radio set, he decided that he didn't want to be a Nazi spy any more.

"Turning now to Gretchen, the evidence is overwhelming that she was loyal to Adolf Hitler and his regime from the time she arrived in Bathurst until Walter forced her to sleep with him. Is it possible that the next morning, utterly disgusted by what had happened, she took her radio and Walter's codebook and disposed of them somehow? She evaded our surveillance using the skills that she'd been taught, not because she feared that we might interfere with her finding the mine, but because she wanted to reinvent herself as an honest citizen. That would explain why she registered at both hotels in her own name and why she's allowed herself to become intimately involved with Wes."

"Do you really believe what you're saying?"

"It fits all the facts," Mudge replied.

"Actually, it doesn't. If she were a dinky-di Aussie, devoted and true to your country, Peter, she'd either visit the usual tourist sites of New Zealand or go straight back to her home in Bathurst. Instead, she's travelling from mine to mine. Why would that be?"

After some thought, Peter replied, "You're right and I'm wrong. She's still an active *Abwehr* agent. But what I just said can be modified to explain her behavior."

"Oh?"

"She's pretending that she's no longer a Nazi spy to throw us off her scent. As we both agree, no secret agent would possibly act the way she's been behaving. She's doing all this to convince us that she's an honest citizen, so that we'll stop tracking her movements and let her find the promethium mine unhindered."

"There's a much simpler explanation that also explains everything," Warren Jennings said.

"And what's that?"

"She's a woman who's totally infatuated."

"Are you saying that she's in love with Wes?"

"I doubt it. She's known him for less than two days. But she certainly seems to be smitten."

\*\*\*

Wes and Gretchen walked hand-in-hand to the huge park that borders Lake Rotorua, the second largest lake on the North Island. After admiring the view, they ambled through the town. They passed a café that was advertising steak, eggs and chips for one shilling and sixpence. This seemed to Gretchen to be too good to be true.

"Do they really charge so little?" she asked.

"Yes, that's the usual price in New Zealand," Wes said. "We're at war, and the government controls the prices of essential items, such as food. Fortunately, there's almost no rationing."

After they finished their tender steaks, the friendly waitress suggested that they might like to have a dish of ice cream, but they both had other delights on their minds.

# CHAPTER TWENTY

*Rotorua, New Zealand*
*Monday, September 14th, 1942*

The bus dropped them at the entrance to Waiotapu.

"Before we go inside," Wes insisted, "we need to walk to the Lady Knox Geyser."

"Why?"

"It's one of the great mysteries of nature—we learned all about it at school. The geyser erupts at precisely 10:15 a.m. every day. How can a geyser tell the time like that?"

"The whole thing's a flimflam," Gretchen said. "I read all about it in *The National Geographic Magazine* on the coffee table in the hotel lounge. Around 1900 they opened some sort of open prison in this vicinity. The prisoners utilized the hot water of the geyser to wash their clothes. Then one day, they used soap, as well, and the geyser erupted. It wasn't long before they put two and two together: Soap makes that geyser erupt.

"Soon the tourist industry got into the act. They laid carefully selected heavy rocks around the opening to decrease the size of the orifice—the jet of water now shoots more than 50 feet into the air. Then someone came up with the clever idea of adding soap from a hidden pipe at precisely the same time every day, to create the illusion that the geyser knows when it's 10:15 a.m. The Lady Knox Geyser is just a tourist trap. Anyhow, we're here to see a mine, not a geyser. Let's have a look at the map."

Wes was visibly disappointed by her decision, but he said nothing. The previous night had been even more wonderful for him than before, and Wes had no intention of getting on the wrong side of Gretchen by arguing with her. Instead, he obediently glanced at the NZMS 1 map.

"Here's where we are, at the entrance," Gretchen said. "The mine appears to be inside the geothermal site, which is strange. How do they get the ore out? There's no road or rail track here, not even an aerial tramway."

"Maybe it's another power station," Wes suggested. "But there are no power lines here. Perhaps they go off in the other direction."

"Let's ask at the ticket office."

The woman selling tickets knew nothing about a mine. "Here's a map that shows the various points of interest inside—it'll take you about an hour and a half to see everything if you follow the indicated route. Why don't you go inside and look around? By the time you return here, Mrs.

Johanssen will be back. Her family owns the whole place. If there really is a mine here, she'll know all about it, I'm sure."

Gretchen bought tickets, and they entered through the turnstile. For Gretchen, this visit to Waiotapu was merely a way to pass the time until the owner came back and could point them in the direction of the mine. After all, Gretchen had visited Yellowstone National Park in Wyoming, the greatest geothermal wonderland in the world. She was sure that Waiotapu would prove to be just some sort of rinky-dink cheap imitation.

Nearly two hours later she stumbled out of the site in a daze of wonderment. Waiotapu had put Yellowstone to shame. The natural features were superlative and extraordinary. The sulfur-rich Artist's Palette gleamed with an intense yellow hue. Carbon dioxide bubbles rose in the Champagne Pool hot spring, which was surrounded by bright orange deposits stained with antimony. The mud pools boiled angrily. And the colors and shapes of the Primrose Terrace defied description. Best of all, the marvels of nature that she saw were situated right next to one another, unlike Yellowstone where there were many miles between the attractions.

Mrs. Johanssen was waiting for them when they returned to the entrance.

"I understand you're looking for the mine," she said.

"Yes, that's why we came here," Gretchen said. "But we had no idea of the richness of the glories of nature that we've just encountered. This place is one of the seven wonders of the natural world. It puts Yellowstone in the shade."

Mrs. Johanssen smiled. "Yes, it's truly magnificent. But returning to your question, the mine is right here. You're standing on it."

Wes and Gretchen looked startled.

"There's a sulfur mine right underneath us," Mrs. Johanssen said.

"But there's nothing to be seen," Gretchen replied.

"That's because of the volcano. In 1886 Mount Talawera erupted, destroying some of the most beautiful features of the area, such as the Pink and White Terraces. The eruption also destroyed the mine."

"Was no attempt made to reopen it?" Gretchen asked.

"No. People were understandably now too scared to go underground in this area. In any event, the sulfur mine on White Island is adequate to meet New Zealand's needs. No investor has been foolhardy enough to try to reopen a mine that might well prove to be economically unviable as well as a deathtrap."

Gretchen was again stunned by the turn of events. But she pulled herself together, politely thanked Mrs. Johanssen, and walked swiftly back to the bus stop with Wes following closely behind her.

"Where's the next mine?" Wes asked.

"We're going back to Wellington," Gretchen said. "I've got to rethink things."

"Even if we can catch a bus back to Rotorua right now," Wes said, "it's still going to arrive too late for us to be able to catch a connecting train to Wellington tonight. So, do you want to spend the night in Rotorua or in Hamilton?"

"It's really lovely in Rotorua. Let's go back to the Lake Hotel and take the first train out tomorrow morning."

\*\*\*

"Sergeant Evans? It's Joe Kaplan here, from the Lake Hotel. Yes, I'm fine, thank you. The reason I'm phoning you is that I thought you might want to know that Gretchen Konrad and that young man are back here again. I've put them in the same room as before, Room 11. No, there's no need for you to put on your civvies and come back here— the register entry is the same as yesterday's. Yes, same name, same address, same signature. Oh, there's one other thing. She mentioned that tomorrow morning they're taking the seven o'clock train to Wellington, changing at Hamilton. I've organized tea and sandwiches for them at a quarter past six—it's all part of the service. Not at all, Sergeant, you're most welcome. And please give my best to Mrs. Evans and all the little Evanses."

\*\*\*

"Detective Chief Superintendent Jennings? It's Tom Higgins in Rotorua again."

"Yes, Tom?"

"I have an update on Gretchen."

"Let me get Peter."

"I'm here, Warren. What's up, Tom?"

"The owner of the Lake Hotel here just phoned Sergeant Evans to tell him that Gretchen and the young man are back at his hotel. Apparently they're taking the 7 a.m. train for Wellington tomorrow, changing at Hamilton."

"Now why would the hotel owner do that?"

"Joe Kaplan was in British military intelligence in the First World War, quite high up I gather. He's one of the nicest men in this town, and definitely one of the brightest. I'm certain he suspects something. After all, he's been running his hotel for years and this is the first time I've ever sent anyone to inspect his register, let alone Sergeant Neil Evans in civvies. For someone as sharp as Kaplan, the mere appearance of Evans out of uniform would be enough to get him thinking harder than perhaps you would like."

"Can you go over the hotel and talk to Kaplan? A person with his background may be of some help to us."

"Certainly. It's just a five-minute stroll from here. I'll get back to you."

***

"Good afternoon, Tom. I think I know what brings you here. Come into my private office and shut the door. You're obviously here on business, so I'm not going to offer you a Speight's, but would you care to join me in a cup of tea?"

"That would be very nice, Joe. Thank you."

"Now, I'm guessing that this visit is apropos of a telephone call I made a few minutes ago to Sergeant Neil Evans, your new plainclothes detective-in-training. Am I right?

"Right as always, Joe. Now, this is much too important to wait for tea and small talk, so I'm going to cut straight to the chase. Joe, what can you tell us about Gretchen Konrad?"

"You said 'tell us,' not 'tell me.' That means you've been in touch with headquarters. That's interesting, because I was thinking of contacting one of my old friends at headquarters myself."

"And why is that?"

"I've heard Gretchen speaking a number of times. I even made it my business to chat to her at breakfast this morning, and you know how much I love getting up early. Well, Tom, her accent intrigues me. She says she's from Bathurst in New South Wales, and I'm sure that her passport and her other documents will support that. But she speaks with an American accent. There's nothing wrong with that—the Yanks are on our side once again and they've entered the war more than two years late once again. But underlying that American accent is a German accent. Joe, I'm almost sure that Gretchen was born in Germany or Austria."

"Well, she does have a German name. Are you sure that you're not being influenced by that?"

"Yes, I thought of that last night. And that's why I dragged myself out of bed at the crack of dawn to talk to her at breakfast. Tom, her first language is German, I'm sure of it."

"There's nothing wrong with that, Joe. There are many fine immigrants from Germany living here in New Zealand. Some of them are refugees from Hitler and some came here earlier to find a better life."

"Yes, I know what you're saying, Tom. But these 'fine immigrants' of yours aren't sexually involved with a policeman 10 years younger than they are."

"Dammit, Joe, how did you work out that he's a policeman? She's been with him day and night for three days now, and we don't think that she even suspects that he's supposed to be following her."

"I have to say that your young constable has a most unusual way of following a suspect."

Chief Inspector Higgins sighed. "Joe, I wish I could tell you everything. But I can't tell you more than I know. And I certainly don't have the security clearance to know everything. I'm just the middleman here. I really think it would be better if you spoke to headquarters. Can I please use your phone to call Detective Chief Superintendent Warren Jennings in Wellington and ask him to speak to you? Once the two of you start talking, I'll just go straight back to the police station, for obvious reasons. Oh, there'll probably be a third person in on your conversation, an Australian detective superintendent named Peter Mudge."

\*\*\*

"Mr. Kaplan? This is Warren Jennings."

"Please call me Joe—everyone else does."

"I'm Warren, and Peter is listening in on the extension."

"Fine. How can I be of service?"

"Joe, before Tom Higgins telephoned, I had a conversation with a certain friend of yours. He told me that in the last war you had the highest possible security clearance, and he gave me permission to speak to you freely and answer any questions you may have."

"That could only have been Franklin O'Malley. We're so lucky that he's still living in New Zealand—any day now I expect him to be summoned back to London. Please give him my warmest regards."

"I'll do that, Joe. Now, what can you tell us about Gretchen Konrad?"

"I've been an hotelier for more than 20 years. Yes, it's an odd profession for someone with my background, as Franklin must have told you, but that's how it is. As an hotelier I can tell you that nowadays it occasionally happens that an unmarried woman in her 30s or 40s will travel to a place where she's unknown in order to pick up a good-looking younger man there. She'll spend a week or two with him, paying all expenses, and then return home. Both parties are fully cognizant of the situation at all times—they're both in it just to have a good time, with no obligation of any kind on either side. So, when Gretchen Konrad walked in with a young man whom she addressed as Wes, I naturally assumed that that was the situation. She was clearly in charge and financially responsible for everything, and he's young and handsome.

"Then I realized that this was a most unusual situation. First, I was sure that Wes was a police constable in civvies. His haircut, the way he stood, the way he looked around the lobby of the hotel—everything shouted 'I'm a policeman' to me. He was out of uniform, so he was on leave. But we're so short of police here, with the young men away at war, that policemen aren't getting any leave, other than compassionate leave. And this seemed to be a case of passionate leave, rather than compassionate leave—Wes appeared to be to be utterly smitten with Gretchen.

"So, the first question I asked myself was: What's Wes doing here? And the only answer I could find was: He's supposed to be tailing her, but she's somehow seduced him. Do you remember the sirens in Homer's *Odyssey*? They sang so sweetly that they caused passing sailors to steer their ships onto the rocks and drown. But Odysseus plugged the ears of his sailors with beeswax, so his ship sailed safely past. It seems to me that, before you instructed Wes to follow Gretchen, you should've plugged his ears with beeswax.

"And then I began to wonder: What's Gretchen doing here? She's an Australian who was brought up in America, but it sounded to me that her first language was German. And we're at war with Germany. Furthermore, why is she travelling around New Zealand? These women come to a place, they find a man, stay there with him for a week or two, and then they go home. Yes, they may take day trips. But Gretchen told me that they'd arrived by bus from Tauranga. I'm in Rotorua, a major tourist town, because of all the geothermal activity around here, especially at Waiotapu. But Tauranga? Farmers, bankers and timber merchants go to Tauranga—there's a good reason why that area is called the Bay of Plenty. But tourists don't go there."

"And what did you conclude?" Peter asked.

"I thought that she was a Nazi agent, travelling around New Zealand to get information of some sort for her German masters, using Wes as a cover. And I was about to stroll over to Tom Higgins's office and tell him what I thought, when Sergeant Neil Evans walked in. He asked me if he could copy Gretchen's register entry. Clearly, the police were onto Gretchen. Tom didn't need my tuppence worth. It's hard enough for him to run the show these days with the few men he has left without my sticking my nose into things and making his life even more difficult. So I left it at that. This morning Gretchen paid her bill and left for the Waiotapu geothermal area with Wes in tow.

"But about 45 minutes ago they returned to the hotel, wanting a room for the night. I tried to subtly discover their plans by asking them if they needed an early breakfast, and Gretchen then informed me that they're taking the first train in the morning to Hamilton, changing there for Wellington, as I'm sure Tom Higgins told you.

"I immediately phoned Neil Evans, and the rest you know. The reason I was concerned is that Wes appears to be totally under Gretchen's control. To put it bluntly, I'm not convinced that he's still functioning as a policeman. She's with him 24 hours a day, every day, but if he were to get an opportunity to sneak away and report to you, he may not take it."

"Joe, you've hit multiple nails on the head. We've known for nearly three years with absolute and total certainty that Gretchen is an *Abwehr* agent. Ever since the war started, she's just sat in Bathurst and waited for instructions from Berlin. So we just sat in Bathurst and waited."

"Ah, yes," Joe said. "Coke's motto was *'Prudens qui patiens'*—The prudent man is patient."

Unfortunately, Joe Kaplan had pronounced the last name of the great English jurist Sir Edward Coke correctly, that is, to rhyme with "book." Not surprisingly, Peter and Warren thought that Joe was referring to the ubiquitous and greatly respected antipodean explorer, Captain James Cook, so they nodded sagely to one another.

"Joe, do you have any ideas as to how we should proceed?"

"Well, for a start you might want to think about pulling Wes out. In my opinion, he's no use at all to you in his current emotional state, and he may actually change sides."

"That might backfire. I need to explain to you that there's an operation underway to ensure that Gretchen travels to an island near Tudor Island."

"You mean Coopers Island?" Joe asked.

"Yes, Coopers Island. We need her to send a report to Germany about an installation there. I'm concerned that, if Wes walks out on her, she'll be so upset that she'll immediately return to Australia."

"I said nothing about Wes leaving her. Here's what I suggest that you do."

# CHAPTER TWENTY-ONE

*Hamilton, New Zealand*
*Tuesday, September 15th, 1942*

Much to the amazement of everyone concerned, the train from Rotorua pulled up at Hamilton railway station five minutes early, giving Wes and Gretchen ample time to change platforms to board the train to Wellington. Gretchen knew from her journey north that, unless the train from Rotorua arrived exceedingly late, the stationmaster at Hamilton would hold the Wellington train for connecting passengers—the friendliness and helpfulness of New Zealanders extended to their railway system. Nevertheless, the sense of urgency of her mission never left her, and the fear that she might lose a day because a train was a few minutes late was always present at the back of her mind.

Gretchen and Wes boarded the Auckland to Wellington express as soon as it stopped at Hamilton station for 10 minutes. Gretchen had not objected to walking hand-in-hand with Wes when they were in provincial towns, but she decided to observe the proprieties in public from now on. In particular, she indicated to Wes that he was to sit opposite her in the train, not next to her.

As the train started to move out of the station, an Army sergeant entered their carriage at the far door. Wes was amazed to see that the soldier was his Hamilton police colleague, Ambrose Milton. He had last seen Ambrose three days before, on the morning of the day he had travelled to Tauranga, and on that occasion Ambrose had been wearing a police uniform. Before Wes could say anything to Gretchen, Ambrose waved, came over and sat next to him.

"Wes, it's great to see you. I just hope that your leave is going better than mine. In fact, there's no way that anyone's leave could be worse than mine. I came here to spend my leave with Emma—you remember Emma, we've been going out since we were 14. Anyhow, I didn't tell her that I was coming, and when I got back to Hamilton this morning, I walked over to the dairy where she works. I walked in, and she looked at me like I was a ghost.

"'What are you doing here?' she asked. I told her that I was on a 10-day leave from the Army— it's usually seven days, like you have, but I'm stationed so far south that I got 10 days. 'Why didn't you write to me first?' was her next question. I told her that I'd wanted to surprise her. Then she surprised me. 'I'm going out with Denis Cummings now,' she said, 'and we're getting married in two months.' You could've knocked me down with a feather. I asked her why she hadn't told me, and she said she didn't want to upset me while I was away defending the country! I just walked straight out of the dairy in a daze, and came back to the railway station. My immediate reaction was to go directly back down south, to where I'm posted—there's no point in a 10-day leave when the girl you love has left you for someone else. But now I have other plans."

Long before Ambrose came out with the Police Commissioner's name, "Denis Cummings," Wes realized that this charade was part of some complex operation. Ambrose was simply not distraught enough for someone who had just been dumped by the woman he loved. Wes decided to take his lead from Ambrose. But first he needed to introduce Gretchen.

"Gretchen, I want you to meet Ambrose. We've known one another since high school. Ambrose, Gretchen and I have been hiking around Tauranga and Rotorua. Gretchen is on holiday here from Bathurst in Australia."

Ambrose got up from his seat and shook hands with Gretchen. She looked at him closely. Everything about his triangular face was pointy: his nose, his ears, his lips, his chin. Even his eyes seemed to be placed within narrow slits with sharp ends. What a contrast to her beautiful Wes.

"So you're on a 10-day pass," she said.

"Yes, and what a waste it's going to be."

"Where will you spend it?" Gretchen asked.

"As I told you, I first thought of going back to my base," Ambrose replied, "but I'm sure it'll be more fun to stay in Wellington. Where are you two off to?"

Now that Ambrose was with them, Wes didn't want to exhibit his subservience to Gretchen. So, before she could answer, Wes said, "Gretchen is interested in unusual mines."

"Really? That's fascinating," Ambrose said. "How did your hobby start?"

Wes once again decided that he should reply. Before Gretchen could say anything, he repeated the explanation she had given to Jock.

"Do you still have your grandfather's collection of rock samples?" Ambrose asked.

"Yes, I've kept it all these years to remind me of him."

"You must have loved him very much."

"I certainly did," Gretchen said. "He was a wonderful man."

There was a short pause in the conversation. Then Ambrose asked her, "Where are you going next?"

Wes wanted to answer again, but Gretchen had not told him her plans. This time he had to let her reply.

"I'm going to visit a mine at Akaroa, and then on to Coopers Island."

"Gretchen, I see two problems there," Ambrose said.

"Oh?"

"Well, the first is that Wes here is on a seven-day leave. He has to be back at his base by one minute to midnight this Friday. You're going to arrive in Wellington tonight, that's Tuesday. That gives him three days to go with you from here to Akaroa to Coopers Island and back to his base. That can't be done—it takes a full day to travel the length of the South Island. And the trip involves crossing the Cook Strait in both directions, but the ferries don't sail in extreme weather. And that's not the only problem.

"To get from Wellington to Coopers Island," Ambrose continued, "you take the ferry from the North Island across to the South Island, and then you travel by train the entire length of the South Island, from Picton in the north to Dunedin in the south, and from there via Gore to Invercargill, which is the southernmost town in New Zealand. The train actually goes about 20 miles farther, to Bluff on the coast. From there, you take the ferry to Tudor Island."

"And?"

"And civilians are forbidden to travel south of Gore. People who have a valid reason for travel are issued special passes, which are checked at Gore. If you don't have one, they order you off the train."

There was silence for a while. It was clear that Gretchen was digesting the information she had received.

Finally she asked Ambrose, "What exactly is forbidden? For example, what if we hire a car at Dunedin and drive to Bluff?"

"Gretchen, I'm sure you know there's strict petrol rationing in New Zealand, so there wouldn't be much point in hiring a car. The real issue, though, is that travel anywhere in the area south of the 46th parallel is forbidden to civilians unless you have a pass. So, even if you managed to somehow get petrol coupons, your car would be stopped at the roadblock north of Gore and impounded. They've issued passes to everyone living in the area who needs to travel in and out. Even soldiers stationed in that part of New Zealand must have those passes when they go on leave so that they can return to the area."

"Is that how you know about all this?" Wes asked.

"No comment." Ambrose delivered this response with a big wink directed toward Gretchen.

Again a lengthy silence ensued. Then Gretchen asked Ambrose, "Okay, how about travelling to Tudor Island by boat from a port located north of the 46th parallel? From Dunedin, say?"

"Gretchen, I have to say that you catch on very fast. But the government has thought of that, too. Boats on the east coast are strictly forbidden to cross the 46th parallel. But it wouldn't just mean confiscation of the boat. In addition, the captain will go to jail for a long, long time, assuming that his boat isn't sunk by the navy or the coast guard."

"And what about boats from ports on the west coast?" Gretchen asked.

"Ports such as what?" Ambrose replied. "If you're hiking around New Zealand, you must have a map with you. Look at the west coast of the South Island."

Gretchen took the touring map out of her rucksack. She examined it for a moment.

"I see what you mean. The southernmost port on the west coast appears to be Greymouth, and that must be about 500 miles by sea from Tudor Island."

"It's not just the distance. It's about a 400-mile journey on the Tasman Sea, the second roughest sea route in the world, and from there into Foveaux Strait—and that's the roughest there is. If you ask someone in Greymouth to take you to Tudor Island by boat, he'll ask you why you want to travel via that route. And unless you have a really, really good answer, he'll call the police. Do you have a really, really good answer, Gretchen?"

For the third time, there was a long silence. Then Gretchen asked Ambrose. "There's a way to get to Tudor Island, isn't there?"

Instead of "no comment" and a wink from Ambrose, this time there was no response at all.

Gretchen tried a different approach. "Wes, did you know that the southern tip of New Zealand is forbidden to tourists?"

"I had no idea."

"So it's not common knowledge, then?"

"I don't think so. But why would the military make a big announcement?" Wes asked. "The only effect of that would be to draw attention to the area, which is probably the last thing they want to do."

"Ambrose, you just said that I catch on fast. Well, it seems to me that the reason that you know about all this is because you're stationed in that area."

Ambrose was saved from having to respond because the train had started to slow down.

"We seem to be stopping at Okahukura," Wes said. "Isn't this train supposed to go nonstop from Hamilton to Wellington?"

"The only place that the Auckland to Wellington express train stops is Hamilton, where we got on," Ambrose said. "This is most unusual."

As the train came to a standstill, Wes stuck his head out of the window. "It's the blue puggarees. Two military policemen just got on. And we're moving again. Can you believe it, the express stopped at Okahukura for two MPs?"

"Don't military police wear red caps?" Gretchen asked.

"Yes, in just about every army in the world, but not in New Zealand. Everyone in our Army has a lemon squeezer hat, just like mine," Ambrose said. "The hat has a wide band, called a 'puggaree'—I have absolutely no idea why. As you can see, my puggaree is khaki and red, for infantry. The military police have blue puggarees."

"But if the rest of the world wears red, why do Kiwis wear blue?"

"The military police sometimes have to calm down a situation. Blue is a restful color, and you know what they say about 'a red rag to a bull,'" Ambrose explained.

As he finished his explanation, the two military policemen entered their carriage. They stopped in front of every man who looked as if he was between 18 and 46 years of age and asked to see his papers. Finally they reached Ambrose and Wes.

"May I see your pass?" one of the MPs asked Ambrose. And at that instant, Wes realized that he was in big trouble. He'd told Gretchen that he was on a seven-day pass, and he hadn't contradicted Ambrose when his colleague had stated that Wes was on leave, just as he (Ambrose) was. But Wes couldn't hand over his police identification, because that would give the game away to Gretchen. What was he to do?

The MP glanced briefly at Ambrose's pass and handed it back to him. Now it was Wes's turn.

"May I see your papers, please?" the MP asked. He had been trained to treat men dressed in civvies as exempt from military service, unless their papers indicated otherwise.

Wes just sat there.

"Show them your seven-day leave pass, Wes," Gretchen said.

Wes continued to sit there.

"Are you an active duty soldier on leave?" the policeman asked, a lot less politely than before.

Again there was no response from Wes.

"Then where's your pass? And why are you out of uniform?"

For the past four days, Wes had managed to come up with answers, excuses and explanations. Now his mind went completely blank.

"You're under arrest," barked the other military policeman. He handcuffed Wes. Then he reached under Wes's seat.

"Is this rucksack yours?"

Wes nodded dumbly.

"Come along now."

The two military policemen escorted Wes to the back of the train. Ambrose and Gretchen just sat dumbfounded in total silence. And then the train slowed again. This time Ambrose lowered the window and looked out.

"We've stopped at Taumarunui. They're getting off the train with Wes. This isn't good."

The train started up again. Wes stood on the platform with a military policeman on each side holding an arm. One of policemen held Wes's rucksack in his other hand. As the train disappeared around a bend into the distance, the first MP removed the handcuffs.

"Sorry about that, Mr. McFee, but orders are orders. We were instructed to make the arrest as realistic as possible. And you certainly cooperated by saying nothing at all. Well done, sir!"

"But why?"

"Why what, sir?"

"Why was I arrested?"

"But weren't you told, sir?"

"Told what?"

"That we were coming to arrest you, sir."

"No, I was told nothing."

The two military police looked at one another.

"Then we're doubly sorry, sir. Look, sir, here's a travel warrant to get you back to Hamilton. If you'll please cross to the other platform, the local should be here in about 10 minutes. Our orders are to catch the next train to Wellington. Good luck, sir."

\*\*\*

Ambrose and Gretchen looked at one another.

"What can we do to help Wes?" Gretchen asked.

"What can we do? You said that Wes told you that he was on a seven-day pass. But he had no pass. In other words, Wes was absent without leave, or AWL as we call it."

"What's going to happen to him?"

"He's going to spend a long time in a military prison. And it's going to be most unpleasant for him."

"Is there nothing we can do?" Gretchen pleaded.

"Nothing. Going AWL in wartime is a really grave offense. It's almost treasonous."

Again there was a long silence.

"Gretchen, was Wes serious?" Ambrose asked. "Are you really interested in unusual mines?"

She nodded.

"Because your grandfather was a geologist?"

She nodded again, her eyes filling with tears. Then she blew her nose. It was clear to Ambrose that Gretchen was deeply upset by Wes's arrest.

"And do you really want to go to Akaroa and then Coopers Island to see the mines?"

"Yes, I do." She sniffed and blew her nose again.

"Akaroa is easy. You take the train to Christchurch, and then a bus to Akaroa. Wouldn't that be enough for you?"

"Not really."

"You want to go to Coopers Island to see the mine there, as well?"

"Yes."

Ambrose looked round. The nearest passengers were four rows away. But he nevertheless lowered his voice.

"Do you know where I'm stationed?"

"Coopers Island?"

"Yes. And do you know what I do there?"

"You guard the mine?" she asked.

"Right again. There are 24 of us soldiers guarding it night and day, in three squads of eight men each."

"What kind of mine is it?"

"They haven't told us. They don't tell us anything."

"Is there a way for me to get to see the mine?"

"Legally?" Ambrose asked.

"Preferably."

"I can tell you how to get to Tudor Island legally. It's the least I can do to help my friend

Wes. However, if I do and you're caught, I'm going to find myself in the cell next to Wes."

"I thought you just said it was legal."

"It's legal because no one in the military has thought of it yet, so it hasn't yet been prohibited. However, once they find out about it, it'll be illegal from then on. But they'll undoubtedly find a way of finding me guilty of something serious, even though the route is currently perfectly legal. That's what the army is like."

"So you're prepared to tell me about this route because of your friendship with Wes, who wanted to take me but couldn't?"

"Yes."

"I've found New Zealanders to be the nicest people I've ever met, but what you're willing to do for your friend goes above and beyond anything I've experienced anywhere."

"I'm sure you'd do the same for your friends."

There was another long silence while Gretchen thought intensely. As always, the four "Various" mines came into her mind. The Akaroa mine was probably unimportant. But there was no question that the fourth mine, the one on Coopers Island, was the key to everything.

When she got back to Wellington, she decided, she'd send a radio message to Berlin. But could she state that a promethium mine existed on Coopers Island solely on the strength of what Ambrose had just told her? She was now certain that there was a mine on Coopers Island, and that the mine was of major military importance. But so far no one had mentioned promethium or element 61. And until that happened or she saw the mine for herself, there was no way she could inform Berlin that she had confirmed the location of the vital mine that was going to change the entire course of the war.

# CHAPTER TWENTY-TWO

*Between Palmerston North and Wellington, New Zealand*
*Tuesday, September 15th, 1942*

As the train sped on toward Wellington, Gretchen realized that the only way she could get to Coopers Island would be if Ambrose were willing to divulge the legal route to the island that he had worked out. But his attitude toward her was odd. He kept telling her that he knew how she could reach the island, but then he withdrew into silence. Was he teasing her? That was possible. But access to an otherwise forbidden area is rarely a subject for teasing.

Was he testing her? That seemed much more likely. He did not want to be locked up for telling her how to get to Coopers Island. But how could she convince him that she was honest and trustworthy and would never reveal the name of the person who supplied the information to her? She turned to Ambrose.

"You've certainly had a traumatic leave so far. First, the situation with your girlfriend, and now the event with Wes. Could I suggest how you might want to spend the rest of your leave?"

"Go ahead. I'm listening."

"I don't like travelling alone. So, I invited Wes to join me. But now he's in jail somewhere. My arrangement with Wes was straightforward: separate rooms and I pay for everything. I'll offer you the same deal. What do I expect in return? Absolutely nothing. No strings attached—anytime you're bored with my company, off you go, with no hard feelings."

"Are you serious?" Ambrose asked. "You want me to come along with you? You'll pay all costs and there are no obligations of any kind?"

"No obligations of any kind on either of us. That's the deal," she said. "Wes had no problems with it, and I think you'll feel the same way."

"What's the catch?" he asked.

"There's no catch. How can there be one? You're on your own for the rest of your leave, I'm on my own for the rest of my holiday, but this way we both have company. And as I told you, you can leave any time you want to."

"My dad always says that when something sounds too good to be true, it *is* too good to be true."

"Your father is quite right," Gretchen said. "But this is one exception. I'd suggest that you ask Wes to confirm that. Unfortunately, neither of us is going to have the opportunity to talk to him for a while. It's extremely sad."

"Let me think about it."

"No worries. When you've made up your mind one way or the other, let me know."

Ambrose leaned forward and rested his chin on the palm of his open right hand. There was no question that he was deep in thought. Gretchen wondered how often he thoroughly analyzed anything—not too often, she felt. She sat back and opened her magazine.

She was halfway through an interesting article when Ambrose finally spoke.

"Let me see if I've got this straight. You want to visit two mines: one in Akaroa, one on Coopers Island."

"Right."

"You don't like travelling alone—you want someone to come with you."

"Correct."

"In return, you're willing to pay all my expenses. Furthermore, I can leave at any time."

"Yes."

"But there actually is one catch, at least for me: You're a really attractive woman, but you insist on separate bedrooms. Is that non-negotiable?" Ambrose asked.

"It's totally non-negotiable. And if you're not prepared to accept that, then let's forget the whole thing now. I'm sure that I can find someone else who's willing to accept my condition."

"Whoa, Nellie! Hold your horses. I accept."

"Unconditionally?"

"Unconditionally. Your room is your room and my room is my room. At all times."

"You really mean that?" Gretchen asked.

"I do."

"Fine. That's settled then. Now, do you have somewhere to stay in Wellington tonight?"

"No, I don't. Why do you ask?"

"I have a friend, a former colleague really, who's going to be extremely angry if I don't stay at her flat tonight," Gretchen said. "But I obviously can't invite you along, can I? So, here's what I suggest: When we arrive in Wellington, we'll find a hotel for you. I'll pay in advance for your room tonight and for your breakfast tomorrow morning. We'll have dinner together. Then I'll stay with my friend, and we'll meet at the ferry station tomorrow morning. It's right by the railway station on Wellington Quay. Does 8:30 sound good to you?"

"That sounds fine," Ambrose said. "In a way, I'm glad that we're going to go our separate ways tonight, because I want an early night. I got up at the crack of dawn this morning, and I've had a bloody awful day so far, other than your offer, that is. It probably would be a terrible idea for me to go out and get blind drunk, which is what I was going to do. So, it's an early night for me, and I'll meet you at the ferry at half past eight."

Working at persuading Ambrose to come along with her had briefly diverted Gretchen from thinking about Wes. The three days she had spent with him had been blissful. But now she had to pull herself together, put all personal feelings aside and locate the promethium mine.

# CHAPTER TWENTY-THREE

*Hamilton, New Zealand*
*Tuesday, September 15th, 1942*

Detective Constable Wesley McFee walked into the office of Chief Superintendent Morgan, the station commander at Hamilton.

The mail train had crept at a snail's pace over the 100 miles from Taumarunui to Hamilton, stopping at every station en route, no matter how minor. During the six-hour journey, Wes experienced an extensive range of contrasting emotions, including puzzlement, fear, lust, vengefulness, disappointment, and, above all, incandescent rage. When the train finally crawled into Hamilton railway station, Wes was ready to explode.

But as he strode from the railway station to the police station he became considerably calmer—perhaps it was the effect of being back in his hometown. As he entered the charge office, the man behind the wide wooden counter said, "Well done, Wes! Morgan would like to see you right away to congratulate you personally."

As Wes walked in, Chief Superintendent Morgan rose to his feet. With a big smile on his face, he came round to the other side of his desk and shook Wes's hand.

"Congratulations, Wes, on a good job well done! You're a real credit to the force."

"Thank you, sir. But I don't understand what's going on."

"Nor do I, my boy. This is a Top Secret operation, and I'm not in the loop. I'm going to make a trunk call to someone who'll tell you everything, or, perhaps, everything that you're allowed to know. We're at war, and national security is paramount, of course."

"What does national security have to do with it?" Wes asked, his confusion increasing to a level that he was having the greatest difficulty in handling.

"You'll learn everything in a minute. Is that Jennings? This is Morgan in Hamilton. I've got Wes McFee here. I told him that you'd answer his questions. Here, Wes, this is Detective Chief Superintendent Jennings in Wellington."

"Good afternoon, sir," Wes said as respectfully as he could.

"Well done, Wes! We're all very proud of you."

"What's going on, sir? Why did they arrest me this morning? The MPs said that I should have been told about it, but no one said a word to me, and they couldn't tell me anything at all."

"Slow down, Wes. Let's start at the very beginning. By the way, Detective Superintendent Mudge from the Bathurst Police in Australia is also in on this call."

"Bathurst, sir? But that's where Gretchen comes from."

"Exactly, Wes. That's why he's here in New Zealand. Now, on Saturday morning I spoke to you and told you to put on hiking clothes, pack a rucksack, and go to the station. I gave you the description of a woman and told you to follow her to Tauranga as discreetly as possible. Under no circumstances was she to suspect that you were following her. Is that right?"

"Quite right, sir."

"What did I tell you about the woman, other than her physical appearance and the clothes I believed she was wearing?"

"Nothing, sir. That was all you said to me."

"And why do you think that was?"

"Information is given on a need-to-know basis, sir."

"Absolutely correct, Wes. But you were with her for three days. What have you learned about her during that time?"

"Her name is Gretchen Konrad. She's about 35 years old, about 5 feet 7 inches tall. Blonde hair and blue eyes. Slender build. She lives in Bathurst, New South Wales, but before that she lived in Chicago, in the United States. She's a vet, a large-animal vet. She's on holiday in New Zealand. She has a hobby—she's interested in unusual types of mines. But she's not a geologist or anything like that."

"Did you examine the contents of her handbag? Look at her passport or anything like that?"

"Without a search warrant, sir?"

"I was just asking, Wes."

"No, sir, I didn't go through her things."

"Now, returning to your instructions, I told you to follow her without her discovering you. But you ended up spending three days in her company. You were with her literally day and night. What happened in the train from Hamilton to Tauranga?"

Wes started to explain.

Warren Jennings gently led him through the events of the past three days, ending with the two military policemen arresting him on the train.

The only thing Wes omitted were the three nights of passion.

When Wes was finished, Warren asked him, "When were you going to report to us?"

"Report to you, sir?"

"Yes. You were told to report to Inspector Urquhart at Tauranga. You went to the police station with Gretchen. You left a clever message—that bit about Commissioner Cummings was really brilliant. As a result of your quick wittedness, Urquhart was able to follow you to the waterfall. But after that you made no attempt to communicate with the police. Why not?"

"I was with Gretchen, sir. If I'd walked into a police station, she'd have realized that she was being followed, and you'd explicitly instructed me to not let that happen."

"You didn't think of leaving a note for the police with the hotel receptionist?"

"No, sir. That never occurred to me."

"I see. Now, I know that I didn't tell you the reason that you were to follow Gretchen. Did you ever wonder what she'd done, or what I suspected that she'd done?"

"No, sir."

"Never?"

"Never, sir."

"But you're a trained policeman, a detective with a number of years of experience. Surely you know that we don't just choose a person at random and instruct one of our overworked policemen to drop everything and follow her?"

"Well, sir, more than once I've been ordered to tail an innocent person in the hope that she would lead me to the guilty party. And meeting Gretchen was all so sudden, sir. I waited on the platform here in Hamilton and I saw her get off the Auckland train. I followed her to the Tauranga train. As I told you, she disappeared and then she suddenly sat down opposite me. We got to talking. She seemed such a nice person that it never occurred to me that perhaps she'd done something wrong. We sort of became friends, and friends don't suspect one another."

Warren Jennings thought that now was the right time to open Wes's eyes.

"Wes," Warren said, "you said that Gretchen has an interest in mines. Unusual mines."

"Yes, sir."

"What do we get from mines?"

"What do you mean, sir?"

"You've studied geography at school, and you know that there are different kinds of mines. What sort of mines do you know?"

"Well, sir, there are coal mines, and iron mines, and mines for copper, and so on. There are even sulfur mines."

"And what are coal and iron and copper and sulfur used for?"

"All sorts of things, sir."

"Yes, of course. But if you were fighting a war, you'd need weapons and ammunition. What are guns and bullets and shells and tanks and ships made from?"

There was a long pause. Warren did not want to interrupt Wesley McFee's thought processes, because it was important that he discover the truth for himself.

"Sir, are you saying that Gretchen is some sort of spy?"

"Well, Wes, can you come up with a better explanation?"

"Maybe she's just interested in mines, sir."

"Do you really believe that, Wes?"

Again, a long pause.

"No, sir. I don't."

Wes swallowed. "But if she's a spy, why didn't you arrest her?"

"Well, Wes, as you well know, when we find one member of a gang of, say, pickpockets, we don't arrest him. We watch him and then we arrest the whole gang. It's the same with a spy ring. But it's much more important with German spies—we dare not let even one of them escape."

A short silence ensued as Wes digested what Warren had said. Then Wes said slowly, almost on the point of tears, "She was making use of me, sir."

"Actually, Wes, she wasn't."

"How can you say that, sir?"

"Wes, she had no idea that you're a policeman, let alone that I ordered you to follow her. That's why we had you arrested. It was the only way to get you out of the difficult situation you were in without her finding out about you. So, as far as Gretchen is concerned, you're just an ordinary New Zealander, a soldier who went absent without leave. You say that she made use of you. But what did she gain by befriending you?"

Wes thought for a moment. "Nothing, sir. Nothing at all. But why did she behave the way she did with me?"

"It had nothing to do with her being a spy. She arrived in Bathurst in 1938, and she lay low until about two weeks ago. Then she received a radio message from Germany telling her to go to New Zealand. She was to find a particular mine of great military importance. On the train she bumped into a handsome young man. She started talking to him. She became infatuated with him, just as you became infatuated with her. So you did the natural thing—you had an affair with her."

"But I love her, sir, and I know that she loves me."

"Now think hard about that, Wes. Are you really in love with her? I know that you've had three wonderful nights with her, but is that really love? Or is it just passion?"

Again, there was a long silence. Then Wes sighed heavily.

"I see what you mean, sir."

"Good. One other thing, Wes: I know that you're a loyal Kiwi, and that you put your country before all else. It's absolutely essential that nothing should stop Gretchen from getting to the mine on Coopers Island."

"But Ambrose told us that the whole area is out of bounds to civilians."

"It's out of bounds to civilians, but we allow spies to travel there and report to Germany."

"Report what to Germany, sir?"

"Wes, what I'm about to tell you is classified Top Secret. You are not to breathe a word to a soul. Is that understood?"

"Yes, sir."

"This morning we had to arrest you to extricate you from the situation you were in, through no fault of your own. However, if you let slip anything that I'm about to tell you now, we'll arrest you for real. And you'll be lucky to escape with just a life sentence. You know what the penalty for treason during war time is, don't you?"

"Yes, sir, I do."

"Wes, in the strictest possible confidence, the mine at Coopers Island produces a metal that's going to win the war for us. And we want Germany to know about it."

"But why, sir? Why would we want to tell them something like that?"

"If they know they can't win, they'll surrender and bring this war to a quick close. Once Hitler finds out about the mine, it'll be all over."

"But why don't you just tell him about it, sir?"

"Do you think he'd believe us?"

"Why not? You can show the evidence to him."

"He'd think it was a forgery. No, he's got to be told about it by one of his own agents. So, we've set up an elaborate plan that will result in Gretchen inspecting the mine on Coopers Island and telling the Germans everything about it. That's what this is all about, and that's why we had to pull you out this morning without Gretchen realizing that you're a policeman, and a brave and resourceful one at that.

"Wes, on behalf of the Government of New Zealand, I salute you, and I thank you for your services to the people of New Zealand. Goodbye, Wes, and God bless you."

Warren replaced the phone on its cradle. His Australian colleague turned to him.

"Do you think he believed that load of guff?"

"Well, Peter, Wes isn't the brightest candle on the Christmas tree. I was careful to embed all the fiction in solid facts that he knows to be true. Also,

I never reprimanded him and I never made him feel bad about what he's done, so there's no reason to think that he's going to mull over what I've just told him. On the contrary, I think he's going to bask in glory."

"You don't think you overdid it a little at the end? Wasn't that bit about 'on behalf of the Government of New Zealand' just a shade over the top?" Peter asked.

"No, I don't think so. The important thing is that we don't want him to go running after Gretchen or try to contact her in any way. That really would upset the applecart."

"Joe Kaplan advised us to keep Wes in jail until the whole thing is over. Do you think Joe was right?"

"Well, it's too late now," Warren said.

"It probably isn't. But if we arrest him after what I just told him, he's going to make an almighty stink when he finally gets out. I'm afraid that *alea iacta est*, which is how our good friend and erstwhile classics professor Joe Kaplan would put it, before helpfully supplying the English translation."

"Which is?"

"The die has been cast."

# CHAPTER TWENTY-FOUR

*Wellington, New Zealand*
*Tuesday, September 15th, 1942*

The train slowed as it neared Wellington. Gretchen suddenly realized that exactly a week earlier she had taken a taxi from the railway station to 29 Captain Cook Terrace. At that time, she had no idea at all why the *Abwehr* had summoned her to New Zealand, and 'Walter Bennett' was just a name in a radio message to her from Berlin. Now she had a specific mission, one that might totally change the course of the war.

During the previous tumultuous week, her emotions had swung from utter misery to paradise and back to utter misery. Both extremes had taken a toll. In addition, the forcible removal of Wes from her life had brought back memories of those terrible three minutes with Walter. But somehow the knowledge that she could singlehandedly win the war for Nazi Germany kept her going.

The train came to a halt with a slight jolt. Ambrose alighted first and politely assisted

Gretchen to climb down the stairs from the carriage to the platform. They strolled toward the exit of the huge neo-Georgian building, turned right and started walking in the direction of the Parliament Buildings.

"First things first," Gretchen said. "We need to find a hotel for you. Do you have any preferences?"

"No. The nearest one will do just fine. Look, there's one across the street."

"I don't think so. The Masonic Hotel has a terrible reputation. Let's walk another block and see. There's one over there. How does the London Hotel look to you?"

"As long as the room has a comfortable bed, it'll be perfect. I just want to sleep."

Gretchen led the way to the London Hotel. The receptionist said that a single room was available and Gretchen paid her for it in advance. Ambrose wrote his personal details in the hotel register on the next open line.

"Leave your rucksack in your room, Ambrose. I'll be waiting down here for you."

Ambrose went upstairs as fast as he could. He wanted to phone Warren Jennings quickly, without arousing any suspicion on the part of Gretchen. Ambrose looked around the room—no telephone. He dumped his rucksack on the bed, locked the door and rejoined Gretchen downstairs.

"What'll it be: fish and chips, or steak, eggs and chips?" Gretchen asked.

"I love beef and so I never say no to steak. On the other hand mutton and lamb aren't exactly my favorite foods. I'm from a sheep farm, and that's all we ate, day after day. Before I joined the army, I helped my dad run the farm. And I'll be going back when the war is over. Sheep farming is in my blood. It's all I've ever done and all I want to do."

"I'm a large-animal vet," Gretchen said, "so I've visited lots of sheep farms."

"So, we've got something in common: sheep!"

They saw a restaurant on the other side of the road.

"How does this place look to you?" Gretchen asked.

"Do they have steak on the menu? That's all that matters to me."

After a good meal, Gretchen turned to Ambrose. "I've enjoyed our dinner, but I've got to go to my friend's flat now. I'll see you at the ferry station tomorrow morning. Sleep well!"

*** 

"Detective Chief Superintendent Jeffries? It's Detective Sergeant Milton here. I phoned your office, but they told me to phone you at home and they gave me this number. I hope that's all right."

"Yes, it's fine, sergeant. What's happened?"

"Sir, I'm talking to you from the manager's office at the Arthur Hotel. The manager, Mr. Peterson, has been extremely helpful to us. He's standing right next to me."

"I see. Please go on."

"On the train to Wellington, the subject of our enquiries told me that she was going to spend tonight at the flat of a friend, actually a former colleague of hers. The subject paid for a room for me at the London Hotel and then we went to have dinner together. After the meal, she got up and said she had to go to her friend's flat. Of course, I followed her at a distance. She turned left as she exited from the café and started walking rapidly in the direction of the station. But then she turned left at the first corner she came to, then left again, and headed back in the direction of the Arthur Hotel."

"Did she take any evasive action at all?"

"Not as such. She could've turned right when we exited from the café and that would have taken her straight to the Arthur Hotel. I think that she wanted to be sure that I didn't see her entering the Arthur Hotel after she'd told me that she was going to stay with a friend. It wasn't really evasive action—she just didn't want me to know where she was actually going."

"She doesn't suspect that you're a policeman?"

"I'm sure she doesn't, sir. Once she was out of my sight around that first corner, she headed straight for the Arthur Hotel. That's not the way that someone who knows that they're being tailed behaves, at least not in my experience as a detective."

"I understand. Go on."

"Through the glass front door of the hotel I saw her standing at the reception desk, then she signed the register. I saw afterwards that she wrote her own name and her Bathurst address, and that she's in Room 203. Anyhow, she didn't go upstairs immediately. She waited for the receptionist to call the porter, she had a few words with him, and then she went up. When she was out of sight, I entered the hotel lobby.

"A few minutes later the porter went upstairs carrying two suitcases. One had 'Veterinary Instruments' painted on it. That suitcase was fastened with a chain and a lock. When the porter was upstairs, I asked to see the manager in his office. I identified myself to Mr. Peterson and asked him if I could please speak to the receptionist. He willingly agreed, and he was kind enough to man the reception desk so that Miss Templeton could talk to me in private. She told me that the subject had asked for a single room for one night. While she was signing the register, she stated that she'd stayed at the Arthur Hotel a few days earlier and had left two suitcases with the porter. Miss Templeton had called the porter over and asked the subject to describe her two suitcases to him.

"I thanked Miss Templeton, then asked her if I could speak to the porter. He came to the office almost immediately. He told me that, after the subject had described her two suitcases to him, he went to the storeroom, located the suitcases and took them up to Room 203. One thing, sir, that I think you should know. One suitcase had a lock and a chain; it was marked 'Veterinary Instruments.' But the porter said that the suitcase didn't clink the way a box containing lots of metal objects would. Instead, it seemed to contain a solid object."

"Thank you, sergeant. I'm quite sure that I know exactly what's in that suitcase. Go on."

"The subject and I have arranged to meet tomorrow morning at half past eight at the ferry station. I'm sure she'll be there—she wants certain information from me."

"I understand. Don't say any more about that on the telephone. Is there anything else I should know?"

"No, sir. That's it."

"You've done very well indeed, Detective Sergeant Milton. I'm going to arrange to get you out of the Arthur Hotel without her seeing you. I'm sending two detectives to relieve you. As soon as they tell you that the coast is clear, leave the Arthur Hotel immediately, go straight to your room at the London Hotel and stay there until breakfast time. The subject may decide to join you at your hotel for breakfast; it wouldn't be a problem if she chooses to do that. After breakfast, whether or not she joins you, go directly to the ferry station. If your route takes you past the Arthur Hotel, don't even glance in its direction. Is that understood?"

"Yes, sir."

"Fine. Now let me have a word with Mr. Peterson."

Ambrose handed the handset to the manager.

"Peterson here."

"Mr. Peterson, this is Detective Chief Superintendent Jennings. First and foremost, I'd like to thank you for your cooperation. We greatly appreciate it when members of the public are so helpful."

"Not at all, Detective Chief Superintendent. It's always a pleasure to assist the police."

"In that case, may I ask you to do us another favor, please?"

"Of course. How can I help you?"

"As I'm sure you realize, we believe that the woman in Room 203 can assist us with our enquiries. I'm going to be sending two men to your hotel. One will wait at the other end of the second-floor corridor, watching her room and the fire escape. The second will sit somewhere in the lobby where he can watch the stairs. Would it be possible for them to use your office as a command post? I expect that they'll be out of your hair by nine tomorrow at the latest."

"Of course, Detective Chief Superintendent. And I'll arrange for the night porter to bring them tea."

"Thank you. That would be most kind of you. You've been extremely helpful. Now may I speak to Detective Sergeant Milton again, please?

\*\*\*

As soon as the porter had left Room 203, Gretchen locked the door behind her, leaving the key in the lock, and started composing her message to the *Abwehr*. She informed Canaris that both Tauranga and Rotorua had proved to be false leads. She was now all but certain that the mine was on Coopers Island and enumerated her three reasons for arriving at that conclusion: The mine was one of the four on the "Various" list; civilians were barred from travelling to the area south of the 46th parallel; and the military were protecting the mine. She added that she had met a soldier on leave who said he and 23 other men were guarding Coopers Island. She was going with him to Akaroa, just in case the mine was located there, and then on to the island—the soldier had told her there was a way to circumvent the ban on civilians.

She unlocked the suitcase containing the transceiver and took out the codebook. She encrypted the message, and then carefully checked her work. She was about to take the transceiver out of its suitcase and place it on the table in her room when she heard a key being inserted in the door lock. She quickly shut the suitcase again and pushed it under the bed. The scraping noise from the lock continued.

She went to the door. "Who's there?"

"What are you doing in my room? Why can't I unlock the door?" an inebriated voice said.

"This is my room. What's the number on your key?"

"Er, it's 302."

"Well, this is 203."

"Oh. Sorry to have disturbed you." The words were slurred.

"Goodnight," Gretchen said. She heard footsteps walk away from her room and go up the staircase.

\*\*\*

Detective Sergeant George Papadopoulos was standing in the shadows at the other end of the second-floor corridor. He heard slow footsteps on the staircase, and a few seconds later he saw a tall man with black hair reach the second floor. The man was smartly dressed in a navy blue suit, white shirt, dark tie, and black Homburg hat, but the lighting was too dim for the detective to be able to discern the pattern on the tie at that distance—as part of the war effort, many light bulbs had been removed to reduce electricity consumption. The man turned left, walked slowly to Room 203 and inserted a key in the lock. The door did not open. The tall man then spoke to Gretchen, but Papadopoulos was too far away to hear the words of the conversation through the locked door. Then he saw the man return to the staircase and walk slowly up the next flight of stairs.

The detective was torn. The tall man who had been outside Gretchen's room was presumably a confederate, so Jennings would want to know the fullest details about him. On the other hand, if

Papadopoulos followed the man upstairs, he would be deserting his post. While he was investigating upstairs, Gretchen might well leave her room via the fire escape. He decided to take a chance and followed the man upstairs. Papadopoulos saw the tall man unlock Room 302, open the door, enter and slam the door shut behind him. The detective quickly returned to his observation post in the second-floor corridor.

\*\*\*

For the first time since arriving in New Zealand, Gretchen Konrad started to worry that the authorities might be onto her. Yes, the man on the other side of the door had certainly sounded drunk, but he could have put that on. But was it really likely that a fellow guest suffered from alcohol-induced dyslexia? Wasn't it more likely that a policeman was trying to find out if Gretchen was in her room? If she started transmitting in 10 minutes' time, at half past ten, as instructed, would the secret police burst into her room, arrest her, and take the transceiver and the all-important codebook?

Once more she had no choice. Gretchen reopened her suitcase, took out the transceiver and Morse key, put them on the table, draped the aerial around the room, plugged the set in and switched it on, and put on the headphones. Then she sent her message out into the ionosphere.

When she had finished, her hands were shaking. She quickly repacked the suitcase and chained it closed. The episode with the drunken guest had so unnerved her that she forgot to listen at eleven for a possible message from Germany.

\*\*\*

"We've got the message. And the direction-finding people tell me that it was sent from the Arthur Hotel. Everything ties up nicely," Warren Jennings said.

"How soon can we get it to the three professors?" Peter Mudge asked. "I arranged for them to be standing by in the mathematics seminar room at Victoria University, waiting for the five-letter groups."

"There's a military dispatch rider downstairs with his motorcycle. He says he knows exactly where the Department of Mathematics is. He claims that at this hour of the night it'll take him under five minutes to get there."

"Excellent. And this time we'll have two bites of the cherry. First we'll let the three profs have a go at it tonight. With their previous experience, they should have most of the message for us within an hour. And tomorrow morning, as soon as Gretchen has left her suitcases with the porter, we'll lay our hands on the codebook and decrypt every word," Peter said.

"In any case, this is all just a precaution," Warren said. "We both know exactly what that message says: She's on her way to Coopers Island with Army Sergeant Milton."

"And after you've decrypted the message tomorrow morning, don't forget to put the codebook back in the suitcase. Once she's seen the mine and discovered that it produces promethium, she's going to race back to Wellington to tell her Nazi friends. And after she's sent them the information, with the aid of that codebook, we'll arrest her."

# CHAPTER TWENTY-FIVE

*Berlin, Germany*
*Tuesday, September 15th, 1942*

Admiral Wilhelm Canaris addressed the members of his executive team.

"Gentlemen, you have in front of you the message Gretchen Konrad transmitted an hour ago from New Zealand, together with all the other messages sent to and from her since this operation commenced. Comments?"

A hand went up near the end of the table.

"Yes, Horstmann?"

"Admiral, this is Allied deception. Gretchen 'just happened' to get a list of mines in New Zealand that includes this mine on Coopers Island. And the Coopers Island mine 'just happened' to be one of only four mines on that list with a special marking. And Gretchen 'just happened' to meet one of the 24 soldiers guarding this mine on Coopers Island. And this soldier 'just happened' to know a way to get her onto Coopers Island to see the mine for herself, even though no civilians are allowed to travel south of the 46th parallel. I'm sorry, but I don't believe in coincidences. And I certainly don't believe in four coincidences."

"But are they really coincidences?" a voice asked.

"What do you have to say about this, Donndorf?"

The colonel adjusted the monocle in his right eye and then addressed Horstmann. "With all due respect, Detective Chief Superintendent Horstmann, I view all four of the points you raised from a totally different perspective. We sent a message to Gretchen Konrad that she received in Bathurst on the night of Wednesday, September 2nd, Australian time. For the sake of argument, let's suppose that the Allies intercepted the message. And that's not an unreasonable assumption—after all, we sent it in plaintext. But our message didn't mention mines. Here it is in the file. It just tells Gretchen that her brother is ill. The first mention of mines is in our coded message that arrived in New Zealand on Thursday morning, September 10th, at 1 a.m. From now on, all times I mention will be New Zealand times.

"First, let me address the issue of the list of mines that Walter Bennett gave Gretchen in Wellington. We don't know precisely when he handed it to her, but she told us about it in her radio message sent to us on Friday night, September 11th at 10:30. If this is Allied deception, that would mean that the enemy had, at most, a day and a half to somehow decrypt our message, prepare a doctored list of mines, and give the list to a person in the Department of Lands and Survey whom they knew Bennett would contact. To me, Detective Chief Superintendent, that would indeed be a coincidence. Let me say the same thing in a different way. It would appear that on Thursday morning, September 10th, right after they decrypted the message, Gretchen asked Walter to get her a list of all the mines in New Zealand. Gretchen told us that Walter acquired the list from 'a colleague in the Department of Lands and Survey.' If this is indeed Allied deception, how did they know to give a doctored list of mines to Walter's friend? That is, how did they know that Walter would ask him?

"Second," Colonel Donndorf continued, "I want to address the issue of the special markings for the four mines on the list. If I understood you correctly, Detective Chief Superintendent Horstmann, you considered that the mine on Coopers Island 'just happened' to be one of four mines with special markings. But if the Coopers Island mine is indeed the promethium mine, then it would undoubtedly have a special marking. That is, the authorities would only permit the word 'promethium' to appear in a Most Secret military document, and never on a list in the Department of Lands and Survey. As far as I'm concerned, the fact that the mine on Coopers Island has a special marking on the list only strengthens my belief that the promethium mine is there.

"Third," the colonel went on, "I turn to the 'coincidence' that Gretchen met one of the 24 soldiers guarding Coopers Island. When she arrives on the island, she'll see if there are indeed 24 soldiers there guarding the mine. If there are, there would have to be barracks, a mess, showers, latrines, armaments, barbed wire around the mine, communications systems, and so on and so forth. And all this must've been built, from scratch, between the earliest time that the Allies could have decrypted our message, that is, on Thursday morning, September 10th, and the earliest that Gretchen could possibly have arrived at the mine, which would be on Saturday night, September 12th. So, Detective Chief Superintendent, the Allies would need to set everything up and have the 24 soldiers guarding the mine there within less than 72 hours. That would not be a coincidence, Detective Chief Superintendent. That would be a miracle.

"And fourth," Donndorf continued without a pause, "the same argument applies to the issue of the 46th parallel. When Gretchen arrives there with that soldier, she'll see for herself whether there are control points on the roads, the railway lines and the ports to prevent civilians from travelling south of the 46th parallel without a pass, and if the locals have the necessary passes to enable them to carry out their daily business on both sides of the parallel. And if this has been set up, again all this must have been done within less than 72 hours.

Again, this would be another miracle, not a coincidence.

"There's one final point that I wish to make," he added, pausing dramatically until everyone around the table was looking expectantly at him. A miniscule adjustment to his monocle followed. Finally Colonel Donndorf spoke.

"Let's assume that you're right, Detective Chief Superintendent, and that this is indeed an Allied deceptive move. That is, there's no promethium mine on Coopers Island, but the New Zealand authorities want Gretchen Konrad to travel there and discover that for herself. Why would they do such a thing? If there's no promethium mine there, why go to all the trouble and expense to trick an *Abwehr* agent into going to the southernmost tip of New Zealand so that she can send a message to us here to tell us that there's no mine?"

"And what do you say to that, Horstmann?" Admiral Canaris asked.

There was no reply from the end of the table.

Admiral Canaris broke the silence. "In the light of the information we've received and the discussion we've just had, is there any point in taking this any further? Surely I should just inform the High Command of the Armed Forces that there's definitely a promethium mine on Coopers Island, and send a message to Gretchen instructing her to stay in Wellington and await further orders?"

This time Major von Grauschild put up his hand.

"Yes, Major? What do you have to say?"

"Admiral, I think that there's one other possibility that perhaps could also explain all the known facts. Suppose that there's a mine on Coopers Island that contains a mineral of vital importance to the Allied war effort, but it's not promethium—it's something else that's absolutely essential. That would explain why, when Bennett obtained a routine list of mines from his friend, the mine on Coopers Island was one of four that bore a special marking. That would also explain the soldiers on the island, and why civilians aren't allowed to travel south of the 46th parallel."

Every pair of eyes around the table focused on Major von Grauschild.

"So, what's going on? It seems to me that the Allies want to discourage our tanks from attacking their forces. One way to do that is to make the High Command of the Armed Forces believe that the Allies have a highly effective anti-tank shell that can destroy our Panzers from a considerable distance. To achieve this deception, they decide to plant some doctored photographs and deceptive information on one of our agents in Egypt.

"Now, months ago the Allies put everything in place on Coopers Island in order to protect this vital mine with its critically important mineral. They also instituted the prohibition on travel at that time, for the same reason. Then they learn that Gretchen is coming to New Zealand, and that she's looking for the mythical promethium mine. Everything is ready and has been for good while. They simply wait for her to come and visit

Coopers Island. They don't have to do anything—
the fly will eventually come to the spider's web.
After all, there are only four special mines on the
list. And when she gets close to the web, she just
happens to meet a soldier who knows a way to get
her across the 46th parallel and onto the island.
When she arrives there, they show her the mine
and tell her that it contains promethium. None of
us have seen this rare-earth metal and Gretchen
certainly hasn't. When they tell her it's a
promethium mine and show her a large lump of
what they claim is promethium, she's in no way
equipped to contradict them. Completely satisfied,
she sends us a radio message that she's found the
mine on Coopers Island and it's full of
promethium, enough to change the course of the
war. We believe their disinformation and hold our
tanks back instead of attacking remorselessly."

"Grauschild," said Canaris, "do you really
believe what you're saying? Or have you
constructed some sort of straw man for us to try to
knock down?"

"Admiral, I think that my scenario and Colonel
Donndorf's are both possible. The only way that
you can determine which of us is correct will be
after Gretchen Konrad visits Coopers Island and
reports back to Berlin."

"So our only hope now is Konrad," Admiral
Canaris said. "She has to travel from Wellington to
Coopers Island and then back to Wellington to get
Bennett's codebook and her transceiver so that she

can tell us what's really happening on Coopers Island. Fortunately, I think she's going to succeed."

# CHAPTER TWENTY-SIX

*Wellington, New Zealand*
*Wednesday, September 16th, 1942*

Warren Jennings greeted Peter Mudge as he walked into his office at police headquarters the next morning by saying, "We've got problems."

"What happened last night?" Peter asked.

"It's not just last night, it's this morning, too. But I'll start with last night. At about 10:20 p.m., a tall, well-dressed man knocked on Gretchen's door. Detective Sergeant Papadopoulos was standing at the other end of the second-floor corridor, right by the fire escape. He saw the tall man knock on her door and speak briefly to Gretchen. Sergeant Papadopoulos was too far away to be able to hear what the man said, let alone listen to her reply, if any. Also, the lighting in the corridor was dim, so he's not completely positive as to what he saw. The man then went upstairs. Papadopoulos followed him and saw him unlocking Room 302.

"Sergeant Papadopoulos couldn't leave his post to tell us, so we only found out about the incident when Gretchen went downstairs to breakfast this morning. All we know so far is the register entry of the man in Room 302, namely, Heinrich Apfelbaum of Auckland."

"German first name, German last name," Peter commented.

"Yes."

"You'd think that an *Abwehr* agent would have the sense to change his name to Henry Apple or Henry Tree."

"Just like Gretchen Konrad changed hers to Margaret Conrad?" Warren asked.

"I take your point. What you're saying is that if you have a German background but you've anglicized your name, people will get suspicious. But if you keep your Teutonic name, you're publicly proclaiming that you have nothing to hide."

"Exactly."

"Is it too soon to have found out anything about Heinrich Apfelbaum?"

"Much too soon. We've told Auckland to put all available men on the job, but that's probably only one or two people, the way things are going these days," Warren said.

"There's something else," Peter added. "We thought last night that Gretchen made Ambrose sleep in a different hotel so that she could transmit to Berlin—she didn't want him to see her suitcases, and so on. We were right about that, but it now seems that she had an additional motive, namely, communicating with the tall man, whose real name may or may not be Heinrich Apfelbaum. But I have to say that he certainly chose a bad time to visit her, arriving just before she was due to transmit."

"Maybe he simply didn't know that she has a radio. And maybe that's why she didn't open the door to him—she didn't want him to see the transceiver. Through the door he told her whatever it was that he'd come from Auckland to Wellington to tell her, and that was that. I told you that it was a brief conversation, but it was certainly long enough for him to warn her, for example, that Ambrose Milton is a detective sergeant in the New Zealand Police Force."

"Please keep me informed regarding Apfelbaum," the Australian detective superintendent requested. "If there's an *Abwehr* cell in New Zealand with two members, namely Bennett and the tall man, then the *Abwehr* has probably put at least two spies in Australia, and up to now, we know about only Gretchen. My government will be most concerned if it turns out that Apfelbaum is also an agent. Worse, notwithstanding the address in Auckland that the tall man wrote in the register, he may in reality be a second Australian agent also sent to New Zealand to locate the promethium mine."

"I understand, Peter. I'll certainly keep you in the loop."

"Fine. Changing the subject, you said that there were further problems this morning."

"Yes. As I'm sure you remember," Warren said, "last night the three professors weren't able to decrypt every word of Gretchen's message. They managed to work out about 90 percent, but that was it. We told them to go to bed, because the remaining 10 percent didn't look too important. Of course, we'd called them in only because we had to know as soon as possible if Gretchen had transmitted anything that we hadn't anticipated. We knew—but we didn't tell them, of course—that we'd get our hands on the codebook in the morning, and that would enable us to find out the rest of her message. So, soon after midnight, I dismissed the three-man decryption squad."

"And what does the rest of the message say?" Peter asked.

"That's the whole point. When she left the Arthur Hotel this morning, Gretchen asked the porter to store her suitcase of clothes, but she's traveling with her rucksack and her other suitcase, presumably containing her transceiver, as well as the codebook."

"Damn. That's a double problem. No codebook and no way of knowing where the next transmission is coming from."

"I'm 99 percent certain that the next place that she'll use her transceiver will be in Cookville on Tudor Island, after her visit to Coopers Island," Warren said.

"Agreed. But getting our hands on that codebook could be extremely useful to the Allies. Who knows how many other *Abwehr* spies are using that code? At the very least, I'd love to send a copy to MI5, and they would certainly know who else needs to have it."

"I suppose I could instruct Ambrose to search for it among her things," Warren suggested.

"That's probably a bad idea. He'd have to find some way to open the lock, take out the codebook, relock the suitcase, get the book to us so that we can copy it, and then put it back exactly where it was after we've returned it to him, all without Gretchen finding out. Remember, we've drummed into him that he's not to share a room with her, no matter what excuse she comes up with. It would've been hard enough for Wes to temporarily abstract the codebook while cohabiting with Gretchen, but it'll be almost impossible for Ambrose to achieve anything at all, let alone without her finding out. No, Warren, that isn't going to work."

\*\*\*

"Tell me again why you're carrying that suitcase of veterinary instruments with you," Ambrose said. "You said that your former colleague is no longer working as a vet, and she wants you to take all her instruments back with you to Australia. Can't you find someone in this country to give the instruments to? There must be lots of vets in New Zealand."

"My friend isn't working as a vet because the New Zealand Veterinary Association won't recognize her qualifications. She claims it's because she's a woman. So, she's given me her instruments to take back to Australia with me. She was adamant that, in view of the treatment she's received from the authorities in Wellington, her instruments were not to remain here."

"But couldn't you leave that big, heavy suitcase in Wellington, and pick it up on the way back?"

"Ambrose," Gretchen said, "we've been through this once already. There's no guarantee that I'll go home via Wellington. I may sail back to Australia from Dunedin or even from Invercargill."

"Invercargill isn't a port city."

"You know very well that I meant Bluff—it's the port of Invercargill. Look, you volunteered to carry the suitcase. If you're unhappy about it in any way, I have no problem with carrying it myself."

"Don't worry, I'll carry it."

"Well, either please stop complaining or let me carry my own suitcase. Look, the ferry has almost arrived in Picton. Wasn't that a wonderful trip through the beautiful Marlborough Sounds?"

"Yes, certainly," Ambrose said, "but the first part of the trip, across the equally beautiful Cook Strait, wasn't so wonderful. Did you see how many passengers were sea-sick?"

"I think it was worth it. The last part of the trip along Queen Charlotte Sound was unforgettable."

# CHAPTER TWENTY-SEVEN

*Akaroa, New Zealand*
*Wednesday, September 16th, 1942*

They took a train from Picton to Christchurch, and from there a 50-mile bus ride landed them in Akaroa. Across the road from the bus stop was a French restaurant.

"Would you like to eat here?" Gretchen asked.

"I'd love to. I've never eaten French food."

After their superb meal, Gretchen asked the owner if she could suggest somewhere for them to stay.

"I have a room that I rent out. Would you like to see it?"

"Yes, please, but where can my friend stay? Do you have a second room?"

The proprietor seemed a little taken aback by Gretchen's request, but quickly recovered. "My neighbor two doors down also has a room. I'll go and ask her if it's available for tonight."

Both rooms were vacant. Gretchen asked Ambrose to put her suitcase and rucksack in her room so that they could see something of the village in the late afternoon light.

"Utterly charming is the only way to describe Akaroa," Gretchen said as they walked around. "The water in the harbor is such an intense blue. And the colonial houses have such beautiful flowers."

After they had seen much of the village, Gretchen turned to Ambrose. "There's something odd going on. I've been looking closely at my NZMS 1 map, and the mine in Akaroa appears to be located right in the middle of this beautiful place. Something's wrong here. Let's go to the police station and ask them where the mine is."

Ambrose did not want to go anywhere near the police station in case a colleague recognized him. But he had no choice—he could not think of a good excuse to remain outside while Gretchen obtained information.

They walked into the charge office. The constable behind the counter greeted them both politely and then asked, "How can I help you?"

"We're looking for the mine in Akaroa," Gretchen said.

The policeman smiled. "Miss, you'll be pleased to know that I'm not allowed to give you that information."

"I don't understand," Gretchen said, somewhat more harshly than she had intended. "I've come here all the way from Australia to see the mine, and you're telling me that I should be pleased that you *can't* tell me where it is?"

"Miss, do you know what sort of mine it is?"

"No. What do you mine here?"

"Thallium."

"Thallium? What's that?"

"Well, I can't rightly say, miss, but there's one thing that I do know, because my superiors have drummed it into me. Thallium is a deadly poison. They used to use it to kill rats, but too many people have died accidentally just from handling the stuff. I'm sorry you've come all this way for nothing, miss, but there's no way you'd be allowed anywhere near the mine. And I assure you that it's for your own good. We want people to come to Akaroa to have a good time, to enjoy the beaches and the walks and the harbor and see our pretty village. But we don't want dead tourists. Is there anything else I can help you with, miss?"

Gretchen shook her head.

"No? Well, in that case, enjoy your stay in Akaroa."

Gretchen and Ambrose left the police station. Her first reaction was anger at having come all that way for nothing, but then she thought it through more carefully: The "Various" entries for the first three mines had all been correctly assigned. This encouraged her to believe that the Coopers Island mine was indeed the one she sought.

Gretchen invited Ambrose to sit next to her on a bench overlooking a park that fronted the harbor. "Ambrose," she said, "I've crossed the Akaroa mine off my list. Now tell me: How do we get to Coopers Island?"

"Easy as pie. Take out your map. We cross the South Island from east to west, from Dunedin to Milford Sound, all the time staying north of the 46th parallel."

"But Milford Sound is in the middle of nowhere."

"Yes, but that's part of the trick. Tomorrow morning we take a bus back to Christchurch, and then a train all the way down south to Dunedin. From there we take a train inland to Middlemarch, and a bus from Middlemarch to Queenstown. Then we take two buses to get from Queenstown to Milford Sound. That puts us on the west coast."

"Why two buses?"

"Because of the Homer Tunnel."

"What's that?"

"I'll tell you when we get there."

Gretchen asked her next question with a touch of anger in her voice. Ambrose quickly realized that she did not like to be told to wait to get an answer.

"And how do we get from Milford Sound to Coopers Island?"

"By boat. In fact, two boats: one from Milford Sound to Tudor Island, and a second one from there across Raphael Channel to Coopers Island."

"But I thought boats were forbidden to cross the 46th parallel."

"Only on the east coast of the South Island."

"By why should a captain take us along the west coast from Milford Sound to Tudor Island?"

"Because you're a penguin expert."

"I'm what?"

"An expert on penguins. I'll tell you more when we get to Queenstown. Now let's get some sleep."

"Just a minute. There's a problem, a very big problem that you've overlooked."

"What's that?"

"You told me that I'd need a pass to travel south of the 46th parallel."

"That's right."

"So what's going to happen when I arrive at Tudor Island without a pass?"

"As I told you, you need a pass to cross the 46th parallel. It's a travel pass, not a pass that gives you permission to be south of the 46th parallel. Travel passes are checked at Gore, and that's it. When you get to Tudor Island, everyone will assume that you're there legally, like everyone else on the island. Now can we please go back to our rooms and hit the hay, as they say in the movies?"

\*\*\*

"Peter, something unexpected has happened in the course of our investigation of the tall man, Heinrich Apfelbaum. A three-man team in Auckland spent most of the day finding out everything they could about him. He and his late wife immigrated to New Zealand from Austria in 1930. He has one child, a boy, Oswald, age 24. His wife died five years ago in a road accident—a motorist ignored a pedestrian crossing and hit her. She died instantly. Apfelbaum's an accountant in a solo practice. His clients love him. They say he's absolutely honest and won't tolerate the slightest attempt by a client to cheat on taxes. He's doing extremely well financially because of his excellent reputation."

"So what's the problem?"

"They went to see him at his home this evening, to ask him what he was doing in Wellington. They expected an answer like 'I have a client there' or 'I needed to see a medical specialist' or some other good reason."

"And?" Peter asked.

"He exploded with rage and threw them out of his house. The team leader says that, on the basis of what they'd found out about him during the day, his behavior this evening was totally unexpected and completely out of character."

"Did they say something that set him off?"

"On the contrary. Far from being an antagonistic interview, their sole purpose was to find a good reason to tell us that Apfelbaum is unquestionably innocent in this matter. They just wanted to find out from him why he knocked on Gretchen's door. They expected an explanation that would totally exonerate Apfelbaum. Instead, he was on the point of physically assaulting them."

"That's not the behavior of an enemy agent," Peter pointed out.

"No, it isn't. In any event, he must be fully aware that we can't let the matter rest there," Warren said. "I think that you and I will have to travel to Auckland tomorrow. Do you agree?"

"I've had an idea. Did the squad in Auckland look at Apfelbaum's bank records?"

"Not that I know of. Why?"

"Oh, it's just a long shot. But could you arrange to have the records waiting for us when we arrive there tomorrow afternoon? Would that be a problem?"

"The bank manager will probably want some sort of search warrant, but I'm sure that the local magistrate will be cooperative. After all, this is certainly a matter of national security."

# CHAPTER TWENTY-EIGHT

*Dunedin, New Zealand*
*Thursday, September 17th, 1942*

They arrived in Dunedin after a two-hour bus ride from Akaroa to Christchurch followed by a seven-hour train journey from Christchurch. As the train drew into the station, Gretchen looked out the window and gasped.

"Yes," Ambrose said, "it's the most beautiful railway station in the whole world. Let's explore it before we find somewhere to stay the night."

They inspected the building, constructed in the Flemish renaissance revival style. Outside they admired the clock tower, the pink granite pillars in front, and the red terracotta shingles and copper-domed cupolas on the roof. "The overall effect is truly gorgeous, inside and out," Gretchen said. "I can't tear myself away."

"Don't worry, we're coming back here. For many reasons we're not taking a bus directly from Dunedin to Queenstown. The bus route goes far too close to Gore for my liking—I don't want any unnecessary problems that might be caused by your getting anywhere near the 46th parallel. Also, the train we're taking from here to Middlemarch goes through the Taieri River Gorge. It's one of the great train journeys of the world. The views from the train down to the river below are breathtaking, and just wait until you see the old wrought-iron viaducts that the train traverses. And finally, if we go by train, we'll have to come back to this beautiful station tomorrow."

***

"Mr. Apfelbaum?"

"Yes. Who are you?"

"Who in Wellington is blackmailing you?"

"What did you say?"

"Mr. Apfelbaum, on the fourteenth day of the last four months you've withdrawn 100 pounds in cash from your bank account. Someone is blackmailing you. Who is it?"

"Who are you? What do you want? How did you get that information?"

"We're from the police. I'm Detective Chief Superintendent Jennings and this is Detective Superintendent Mudge from Australia. May we come in, please?"

"I'd rather you didn't."

"Wouldn't you prefer to talk in private? Let's go inside."

Jennings and Mudge escorted Heinrich Apfelbaum into his front room. The two policemen sat down, and indicated to the terrified accountant that he should do the same.

"I have nothing to say to you," he said.

"Mr. Apfelbaum," Jennings said, "I think I know why you're being blackmailed but that's *not* why we're asking you these questions. We're here on a totally unrelated matter of national security. What we need to know from you is this: Two nights ago you were staying at the Arthur Hotel in Wellington. Why did you knock on the door of Room 203 at about 10:20 p.m.?"

"If I tell you, will you go?"

"That depends on what you tell us."

"I had too much to drink. I was intoxicated. I misread my key. I was staying in Room 302 that night, but I read it as 203."

"And the reason you were drunk, Mr. Apfelbaum, was because you were so frightened by the situation you're in. Is that correct?"

"Yes."

"The bars close at six, but you were so terrified that you were willing to take the risk of possibly being arrested for going to a speakeasy and drinking bad liquor made by a bootlegger. Is that correct?"

"Yes."

"Mr. Apfelbaum, you don't have to answer this question. I think that you're being blackmailed because your son Oswald is a deserter, and the blackmailer knows where he is. Am I correct?"

Heinrich Apfelbaum covered his face with his hands but said nothing.

"Mr. Apfelbaum, let me give you two pieces of advice. The first is this: As you know very well, the blackmailer won't stop demanding money until you don't have a penny left. And when you've been bled dry, he'll inform the authorities about your son in order to get a reward. So giving money to the blackmailer is no use at all. And my second piece of advice is that there are two different military crimes: desertion, and absence without leave. Desertion is extremely serious. You know this, and that's why you're paying the blackmailer. A lengthy absence without leave is serious, too, but considerably less serious than desertion. Yes, your son will go to jail, but probably for just a month or two.

"So, tell your son to report back to his camp immediately. Once he's been arrested for being absent without leave, give the police all the information you can about the blackmailer."

Jennings and Mudge rose and left the house. Apfelbaum did not move. He remained seated with his face in his hands.

***

The next morning Gretchen and Ambrose returned to the Dunedin railway station to travel to Middlemarch. Soon after leaving the platform, the train took them past a bustling industrial zone. This area was of great interest to Gretchen. The anti-tank shells made from a promethium alloy were presumably manufactured in a place situated relatively close to Coopers Island that had access to the other necessary components. Judging from the piles of raw materials stacked outside the factories that she saw within the city limits, Dunedin was well supplied with iron, steel, copper, and coal, so supplies of those essential materials could also easily be sent by train to, say, Invercargill. It occurred to her that the presence of a secret munitions factory there might be another reason why civilians were forbidden to travel to the area south of the 46th parallel.

Their train soon left the main line leading to Gore and Invercargill, and instead turned west in the direction of Middlemarch. First, they saw large farms on both sides. Then, the track started to climb up to the Otago Plateau. Below them the wide Taieri River flowed through forests of intense green. The scenery was utterly breathtaking. Much to their disappointment, the train finally reached the end of the line at Middlemarch. The passengers who were travelling to Queenstown all piled into the waiting bus, which set off immediately on its four-hour run.

Ambrose and Gretchen arrived in Queenstown, situated on the side of 50-mile long Lake Wakatipu. They found rooms in a hotel near the bus stop and went to eat. They were ravenous—the only food they had eaten since breakfast was a shared sandwich they had managed to buy at the teashop at one of the train stops. Not only was there just the one sandwich left, but also the owner had politely but firmly insisted on a deposit of one pound for the teaspoon to stir their cups of tea. She explained apologetically that teaspoons were in short supply, and she had to hang onto her few remaining spoons.

After their meal, Gretchen walked with Ambrose to the edge of the lake.

"Ambrose, we're in Queenstown. I need to know how we get to Coopers Island from here. And don't give me that drivel about penguins again."

"Gretchen, please be careful. As of tomorrow afternoon, you'd better be a penguin expert, or you won't get to the island."

"Are you serious?" she asked.

"I am. But first, I have to tell you about Milford Sound and Fiordland. Take out that map of yours. Here we are in Queenstown. Fiordland is this huge region to our southwest. It consists of part of the Southern Alps and all these fiords."

"Including Milford Sound?"

"Yes. During the ice age, stones at the bottom of slowly moving glaciers ground down rocks and cut their way to the sea, creating U-shaped valleys. Then, when the earth warmed again, the glaciers melted, the level of the sea rose, and the valleys became fiords like beautiful Milford Sound."

"Where's that tunnel you told me about?" Gretchen asked. "I can't see it anywhere on the map."

"Homer Tunnel? It's right here, between Milford Sound and Queenstown. The last time we looked at this map together you saw that there aren't any ports on the west coast of New Zealand until you get as far north as Greymouth. That's because this mountainous region is so inaccessible. Until around 1890, the only way to get to Milford Sound was by sea. Then a man named William Homer had the idea of drilling a tunnel through the mountain so that tourists could get to Milford Sound from Queenstown."

"He wanted to bore through a mountain just to enable tourists to see Milford Sound?"

"Just wait until we get to Milford Sound," Ambrose said, "and you'll understand. Anyhow, it took Homer nearly 50 years to persuade the government to fund the project. Work finally started in 1935. But the politicians provided far too little money. Only a handful of men worked on the tunnel and they had to use picks and shovels. Finally, they broke through—and then the war started, putting an end to the whole endeavor.

"Tomorrow we'll take a four- or five-hour bus ride from Queenstown to the eastern opening. Then we'll get off the bus and clamber through the unfinished tunnel—people can get through it with some difficulty, but it's impassible to vehicles. Hopefully there'll be another bus waiting on the other side to take us to Milford Sound."

"And when we get there?" Gretchen asked.

"There's a boatman named Horace Grosvenor who's obsessed with penguins. There are nearly 20 different species of penguin. Six of them live and breed in New Zealand: the rockhopper, the little blue, the Fiordland crested penguin, the Snare, the erect-crested penguin and one other. Oh yes, the yellow-eyed penguin. Remember that name—those yellow-eyed penguins are going to be very important to you.

"Now," Ambrose continued, "Fiordland crested penguins are found in Fiordland—there's no surprise there. But they're also found on Tudor Island. And yellow-eyed penguins live and breed on the east coast of New Zealand south of Dunedin, but also on Tudor Island. So, if you're a penguin expert, where's the best place to look for both Fiordland crested penguins and yellow-eyed penguins?"

"On Tudor Island, of course."

"Good, you've been listening. Anyhow, Horace Grosvenor is just crazy about penguins. He earns a living by taking tourists to see the wonders of Milford Sound in his boat, but he'd far rather take people to visit the penguins. So, we're going to ask him to take you to Tudor Island so that you can provide veterinary services to the penguins. Your unbelievably heavy suitcase with your equipment that I've lugged halfway around the world—or so it seems—is going to prove to be extremely useful, for once. And when we arrive at Tudor Island, we'll find a way to get you across Raphael Channel to Coopers Island. The distance is only 200 yards, so I don't anticipate a problem—"

"Other than the fact that the area is totally off limits to civilians, and there are 24 soldiers stationed there with strict orders to shoot first and ask questions afterwards," Gretchen said.

"Well, yes, other than that."

"As in: 'Other than that, Mrs. Lincoln, did you enjoy the play?' Look, Ambrose, I'm most grateful to you for all your help, and I'm extremely impressed with your scheme to get me to Tudor Island. I'm sure you'll find a way to get me to Coopers Island, such as finding me a spare Army uniform to wear for a night visit, when the other soldiers won't be able to see that I'm not what I seem."

"Now that's a first-class idea. Why didn't I think of it?" Ambrose asked. "Actually, there's a much easier way. Unless things have changed since I went on leave, Major MacKenzie is the only officer on the island. His office is in a house that they built years ago for the forest ranger. It's right next to the jetty, which is on the south side of the island. There's a beach on the north side—the locals call it Mystic Beach. We'll row to the beach, walk through the rainforest, turn left and arrive at the mine, which is on the east side of Coopers Island. Of course, I'll have warned everyone in advance that you're coming through, so no one will shoot at you. In fact, no one will see you."

"Because I'll be invisible? C'mon—you've got to be kidding me!"

"No, you really will be invisible. No one will want to get into trouble for letting you inspect the mine, so everyone will be extremely careful to pretend that they can't see you.

"And now it's dark and it's getting cold and we have an early start tomorrow. So let's get some sleep."

# CHAPTER TWENTY-NINE

*Fiordland, New Zealand*
*Saturday, September 19th, 1942*

The lengthy bus ride from Queenstown to the Homer Tunnel was exhilarating. The elderly bus driver drove for miles along on the shores of Lake Wakatipu. Leaving the lake, the road meandered south to Lumsden, then west to Te Anau, situated on Lake Te Anau, even larger and just as beautiful as Lake Wakatipu. Next, the bus headed north along the side of Lake Te Anau, and entered an alpine region. The mountain peaks glistened in the sunlight. Dense rainforests covered the lower slopes. And the waterfalls and rivers were bursting from the copious rain that fell almost every day.

"Why didn't we just drive northwest from Queenstown to here, instead of this 200-mile detour we've just taken?" Gretchen asked. "I'm not complaining about the gorgeous scenery, but surely a straight line is the shortest distance between two points, even in New Zealand?"

"You know all about geometry, but your knowledge of geography is just a little weak. The direct route would have to go through two major mountain ranges. It would start with a 15-mile tunnel, then a 3-mile bridge over Lake Wakatipu and then another 15-mile tunnel. So, it would cost millions and millions, and you wouldn't be able see these breathtaking mountains."

Gretchen smiled. "Give me geography over geometry any day."

The bus drew up at the parking area at the entrance to the Homer Tunnel. The passengers took their backpacks and suitcases and started down the dimly lit tunnel, almost a mile long. The granite walls and ceiling seemed to press in on them, and the rocky ground was unkind to their feet.

Nearly half an hour later they reached the end of the tunnel. An alpine vista greeted them: sheer peaks surrounded by glacial valleys. They were relieved to see a bus waiting for them and they all climbed aboard. The glorious beauty that they had previously seen paled in comparison as the bus driver slowly and carefully crept along the remaining 10 miles to the sound over a badly maintained gravel road that twisted its way down to the head of the fiord. Here the mountains were higher, the waterfalls bigger, and the temperate rainforest an even more intense green.

When the bus finally came to a stop at Freshwater Basin at the start of Milford Sound, Gretchen felt sad—she had hoped that the magical trip from the Homer Tunnel would go on forever. But then she saw the sound stretching out in front of her, with even more spectacular scenery, and she realized that the best still lay ahead.

Ambrose led Gretchen to the jetty. "Is Horace around?" he asked a man leaning against a post.

"He's in there, having a cup of tea."

"You need to carry your suitcase now, with the lettering showing," Ambrose instructed Gretchen as they walked into the café. Seated at the first table by the door was a bear of a man with gentle features. He was about 40 years old with light brown hair. His beard had not been trimmed for months, and his clothes had been patched in more than one place.

"Hello, Horace, I'm Ambrose. You took me on your boat two years ago."

"I'm sorry, but I don't remember you. I take so many tourists around the sound."

"No worries. Horace, this is Dr. Gretchen Konrad. She's a vet, as you can see from the lettering on her instrument suitcase. She specializes in birds. She wants to go to Tudor Island to treat any penguins that need medical attention."

"Of course. I'd love to take you there. It's going to be an extremely rough trip, miss, but it's only 24 hours, so I'm sure you can handle that."

Gretchen managed a smile. "No worries."

"Now, Horace, how much will you charge us for the trip?"

"Well, seeing it's for the penguins, it'll be five pounds."

"That's ridiculous. Do you still charge four pounds for the two-hour trip on the sound?"

"Yes. That's what all of us charge for a boatload of tourists. Standard charge around here."

"So you if you charge two pounds an hour, and it takes you 24 hours to get there and 24 hours to get back, that makes 48 hours, plus the time to rest on Tudor Island before you head back. Gretchen, give Horace 100 pounds."

"That's ridiculous. I couldn't take 100 pounds. That's robbery."

"No, it's not. Either you take the money, or we're not going, and the penguins are going to miss out on the medical treatment that many of them so badly need."

"Miss," said Horace, "I'll take your money because your friend has forced my hand, but I want you to know that I'm accepting it under duress."

"That's fine, Horace," Gretchen said. "Now, when do we leave?"

"How about right away? Those penguins can't wait. I'll get Charlie, my crew—he must be somewhere about—and we'll head for Tudor."

He led them to where *Callisto* was moored on the jetty. It had a cabin located in the middle of the deck, with four rows of forward-facing benches each seating four passengers. Forward of the cabin was the wheelhouse. Horace's boat looked too small to safely navigate the sheltered waters of Milford, let alone the Tasman Sea that loomed threateningly at the mouth of the sound.

Gretchen stood at the bow with Ambrose for the first hour as they sailed down what Rudyard Kipling called the eighth wonder of the world. Sheer cliffs lined both sides of Milford. To their left and right, waterfalls tumbled all the way down the mountains; Horace stopped his boat right in front of each of two tall waterfalls that were exceptionally beautiful. As *Callisto* left the second one, three dolphins suddenly appeared and leapt above the surface, before plunging in again and circling the boat. An unexpected squall of rain struck, but neither Ambrose nor Gretchen moved from the open deck to the shelter of the cabin— the view was mesmerizing.

As they neared the exit to the sea, Gretchen saw two seals poke their heads out of the water and peer at the *Callisto*. Gretchen was about to point them out to Ambrose when a rising swell hit the hull.

"Come inside quickly, right now!" Horace yelled.

The rest of the trip to Tudor Island was a nightmare for the two passengers, but especially for Gretchen. She had many times heard the old joke that, 'when severe seasickness first strikes, you are afraid that you are going to die. And as it gets worse, you are afraid that you are not going to die.' Gretchen lay face down on one of the benches, and rapidly progressed from stage one to stage two. As bad as the four days on the *Star of Adelaide* had been, this was much, much worse. And the fact that the endless tossing of the boat did not affect Horace or Charlie in the slightest only added insult to injury.

The boat proceeded steadily down the west coast of the South Island and then turned east. When *Callisto* passed Solander Island and entered Foveaux Strait there was a sudden pause in the wind and the tide. The pitching, rolling and yawing of the boat all but ceased. In reaction to the unexpected hiatus in the violent motion, Gretchen slightly weakened her grip on the bench. And then everything resumed with a vengeance. Gretchen was thrown off the bench onto the deck where she lay, holding tightly onto the leg of another bench, until Charlie had tied *Callisto* up at Cookville jetty.

Gretchen gingerly got up and looked around for Ambrose. He came over to her and put his arm around her. She walked unsteadily up to Horace and thanked him for bringing her to Tudor Island.

Then she asked Charlie where he had stowed their luggage. While she waited for him to bring the baggage, Gretchen swore a solemn oath to herself that she would never ever set foot on a boat again. And then she quickly unswore it—she had to get to Coopers Island.

# CHAPTER THIRTY

*Tudor Island, New Zealand*
*Sunday, September 20th, 1942*

Horace helped Gretchen clamber out of *Callisto* onto the Cookville jetty and handed her suitcase and rucksack up to her. Ambrose followed.

On the other side of the wooden jetty, the Bluff–Tudor Island ferry awaited. A man wearing the uniform of an army colonel stood on the jetty between the two vessels. Ambrose saluted him. He returned the gesture. Then the colonel asked, "Name?"

"Milton, sir."

The colonel opened the manila folder he held. A metal clip fastened the pages, but they still flapped wildly in the wind. Eventually, the colonel found what he was looking for.

"Milton, you're back a day or two early."

"Yes, sir."

"Actually, that's excellent. You've been transferred to Wellington, effective immediately. Here are your orders. Good thing the ferry's here."

"But what about my stuff on Tudor Island? I've been billeted with Mrs. Tompkins."

"We'll have your kit sent on to you in Wellington. Hurry up, man, the ferry's about to depart."

Ambrose saluted, smiled warmly at Gretchen and boarded the ferry. The deckhands immediately untied the lines, and within a minute the ship was on its way to the mainland.

Gretchen just stood there, utterly dumbfounded. The colonel came up to her. "You look lost. I'm Colonel Wetherby. Can I help you?"

Gretchen said nothing.

"That looks like Horace Grosvenor's boat. Did old Horace bring you here from Milford Sound?"

"Yes."

"Good God, you must be starved. Come with me."

He took her suitcase in his left hand, and with his right hand he took Gretchen's left arm and deftly steered her to the Tavern of the Seas Café near the base of the jetty.

"Good afternoon, Miranda. Lovely day, isn't it? The wind's dropped a bit, it's only gale force now. I say, this lady has just arrived from Milford. She needs some of your delicious food to recover from the rigors of the journey. Will steak, eggs and chips suit you, m'dear? And Miranda, a whisky and soda for me and a glass of lemonade for the lady. Thank you."

He turned to Gretchen again. "The name's Wetherby, Colonel Eustace Wetherby. I'm the officer commanding the Home Guard in this part of New Zealand. My wife and I came out to New Zealand right after the war—the First World War, that is. Some of the men seem to think I came here after the Boer War. I'm old, yes, but I'm not that old!" Colonel Wetherby chortled to himself.

"Anyhow, we lived in Auckland for nearly 20 years until she passed away in '37. Pneumonia got her, poor thing. I got lonely and bored—we had no children. So I got involved in the Home Guard. I could see that this war was coming and I wanted to play my part. And how did they reward me for all my hard work?"

He stroked his bushy white moustache as he paused briefly.

"A week ago they sent me out here, m'dear, to Ultima Thule—beyond the borders of the known world. Actually, it's a wonderful place for a lonely old man like me. There are only 300 islanders, so everyone knows everyone else. And, more importantly, everyone looks after everyone else. The villagers deliver food to the older folk a few times a week, and they in turn help to look after the younger children. You repair your neighbor's roof, and he fixes your plumbing problem. It's like that on all small islands, you know. It's particularly important now, with almost all the men folk gone to war. In fact, this island is almost all women and children. On the other hand, Coopers Island—you can see it over there, across Raphael Channel—is all men. The members of the garrison there are in the Home Guard, too. They're all First World War veterans, like me. We're all billeted here on Tudor Island.

"Ah, your food. Eat up, m'dear, we've got to keep your strength up." He raised his whisky glass. "Your very good health!"

Even Colonel Wetherby could not continue to talk while swallowing whisky and soda. This gave Gretchen the chance to introduce herself.

"Colonel Wetherby, I'm Gretchen Konrad."

"How d'you do, m'dear? And what brings you to this part of the world? Not penguins, I hope? Grosvenor keeps bringing people here to see his dratted penguins. The island will soon be overrun with penguin people."

Gretchen had realized immediately that, with Ambrose gone, her only hope of seeing the mine lay with Colonel Wetherby. "I'm a vet, so Horace brought me here to Tudor Island in the hope that I'd heal sick penguins, assuming there are any that need medical attention. But that's not why I'm here. I have a rather strange hobby—I'm interested in unusual mines. I met Sergeant Milton on a train from Hamilton to Wellington. He mentioned that he was guarding a mine. So I persuaded him to let me come here with him to see the mine."

"So Milton told you he was guarding the mine, did he? I say, that was rather indiscreet of him, you know. Tell me, Miss Konrad, did he happen to mention to you what kind of mine it is?"

"No, he didn't. But someone I met subsequently in Wellington told me that it's a promethium mine."

Eustace Wetherby started laughing. He laughed so hard that he started to cough uncontrollably. Gretchen was about to call Miranda over to assist when the colonel finally managed to stop his coughing.

"M'dear, you're the victim of a joke that seems to have spread from the southernmost tip of New Zealand all the way north to Wellington. By now, it's probably reached Auckland. Next week, the Japs on the Solomon Islands are going to be laughing their heads off, by Jove.

"First and foremost, let me inform you that the mine in question is a gold mine, the richest gold mine in New Zealand, and one of the richest in the entire British Empire. In wartime, gold is, well, it's worth its weight in gold. So the New Zealand government assigned Home Guard soldiers to Coopers Island as a first line of defense. If they think there's a problem, their orders are to immediately summon help from the mainland.

"Once the war started, mining had to stop—every able-bodied man was needed for the war effort. So the mine became dormant. One of the men guarding the place looked down the shaft, saw nothing, and announced, 'We're guarding an empty mine.' On hearing that, another of the Home Guard, a retired professor of chemistry, said, 'No, it's a promethium mine.' M'dear, how much do you know about promethium?"

"Nothing. Why?"

"Well, to understand the joke, you need to know that promethium is radioactive—it decays quickly. It's like a saucer of water. If you leave it in the hot sun, the water soon evaporates until the saucer is dry. Where's the water? It's in the atmosphere in the form of water vapor. Well, promethium decays rapidly into other elements. So, if there were a deposit of promethium in a mine somewhere, every last promethium atom would soon have transmuted itself into other elements, leaving a mine without any promethium in it. And that was the chemistry professor's witticism—he joked that the empty mine was a promethium mine. And his little quip has apparently spread all over New Zealand. I must tell him about it when I see him again, when he goes off duty on Coopers Island and comes back here to Tudor Island to eat and sleep. He'll be tickled pink.

"And while we're on the subject of being on Coopers Island, would you like to visit the mine, m'dear? I should be able to arrange something for tomorrow, or the next day at the latest. How can I contact you? Where are you staying?"

"I've no idea. Is there a hotel or a guest house on Tudor Island?" Gretchen asked.

"No, I'm afraid that there's nothing like that here. But many of the islanders take in paying guests, including Miranda here. I say, Miranda, is your guest room available for Miss Konrad?"

"Yes, Colonel, it is."

"Well, that's settled then. I suggest you get some sleep, after what you've been through—the waters around New Zealand are no place for a memsahib. I'll come over here in the morning and discuss the arrangements with you."

*** 

"Major MacKenzie? It's Eustace Wetherby here, across Raphael Channel."

"Oh, hello, Wetherby. Through my binoculars I saw Gretchen Konrad arriving on Horace Grosvenor's boat. I also saw that you disposed of Ambrose Milton quite smartly—that was neatly done. How did your pitch go down with Gretchen?"

"I'm sure she fell for it. Of course, what she's been through over the past 24 hours must surely have dulled her wits just a little. However, though if I may say so myself, I put on a jolly good performance."

"I'm glad to hear it. Will you be bringing her over for a tour of the mine tomorrow morning?"

"That was what I suggested to her. Have your men had a chance to salt the mine yet?"

"Two of them started on it this morning. I think they've done an excellent job. They painted a few rocks in the Day Room—I'm no expert, of course, but to me they look like real gold nuggets. This afternoon, when the paint was almost dry, they carried them from the ranger's house over to the mine and displayed them artistically at the bottom of the shaft. By the way, how are you going to explain to her why the mine suddenly peters out after about 50 feet?"

"Well, it's one of the richest gold mines in the entire British Empire, you know," Wetherby said.

There was a guffaw over the line from the Coopers Island end. "Yes, Wetherby, I know."

"So, what they took out so far was almost pure gold, like the nuggets now at the bottom of the mine—there was no need to dig any further to meet New Zealand's current needs."

"Tell me, Wetherby, have you ever thought of working as a used car salesman?"

This time a chuckle came from the Tudor Island end. "No, I haven't, but now that you come to mention it—"

"Changing the subject as quickly as I can, do you think she's going to come over tonight?"

"She seems absolutely exhausted, and I don't think that she's putting it on. After all, she spent 24 hours travelling from Milford Sound to here in Horace Grosvenor's boat. That tub is hardly capable of smooth sailing on a duck pond, let alone the two wildest waterways in the world. Anyhow, we'll keep a watch at this end. If the guard here on Tudor sees her leaving Cookville in the tinny that just happens by sheer chance to be lying on the beach opposite your jetty with its oars in place for some unknown reason, he'll let you know. In the meantime, I assume that your men have been told not to let her see them?"

"Of course."

"What reason did you give them? After all, when they arrived you told them that they're there to guard against intruders and that they have to radio Invercargill in case of invasion."

"I told them it was a training exercise."

"Did they believe you?" Wetherby asked.

"They are New Zealand's most experienced soldiers, so they never ever believe anything at all that they hear from an officer. The other day I tried to tell them that two plus two equals four, but they all knew better than to accept it when it came from me."

Wetherby chuckled again. "Well, I don't care what they choose to believe or not, just as long as they stay out of her way. In the best case, you'll be able to give them some advance warning that she's en route to Coopers Island."

"And in the worst case, they'll see her but they'll make very sure that she doesn't see them," Major MacKenzie said. "As you observed, she's probably too exhausted to try anything tonight. But leave the oars in the tinny for her, just in case— what she'll see here will be much more convincing if she rows over to Coopers Island on her own. Otherwise, we'll see the two of you tomorrow morning. How does eleven o'clock sound to you? We'll give her a nice cup of tea and some Griffin's biscuits, and then you and I will escort her to the mine, which will be gleaming with gold, as we've been instructed."

"That sounds excellent, Major MacKenzie. Until tomorrow then, unless the guard on the jetty here spots her rowing across Raphael Channel to your island, in which case he'll phone you at once."

# CHAPTER THIRTY-ONE

*Tudor Island, New Zealand*
*Sunday, September 20th, 1942*

Fighting against her physical and mental exhaustion, Gretchen forced herself to compose a message to send to the *Abwehr* during her transmission window. It read: "The mine on Coopers Island is a rich gold mine. There is no such thing as a promethium mine. Promethium is radioactive and decays quickly into other elements. A promethium mine cannot possibly exist. In order for Germany to get the gold, I will visit the mine tomorrow and report fullest details to you."

She realized that the second and the fourth sentences essentially said the same thing and that she could have worded the last sentence more clearly, but she was too exhausted to care. She encrypted the message using Walter's codebook. Gretchen then took the encrypted message and decrypted it, finding that, in her exhausted state, she had made two serious encryption mistakes. She corrected her errors and rechecked her work. It was absolutely essential that there should be no mistakes whatsoever in this message, undoubtedly the most important one she would ever send.

Finally she was satisfied. Now she had to stay awake for another three hours. The bed looked so inviting, but she knew that, once she lay down, there was no way she could wake up at 10:30 to send her message.

She decided to go for a walk. The guest room had an exterior door, which meant that she could leave at any time and later return without disturbing Miranda. As she had hoped, the icy wind and the cold night air kept her alert. The village was relatively small, and within an hour she had walked along every street she could find. So she retraced her steps, passing each house a second time, taking care to walk more slowly than before. Finally, she returned to Miranda's house at ten o'clock, set up her transceiver and waited. At the appointed time she switched on the set, put on her headphones, and sent her message. Then she sent it again, just in case in her exhausted state she had made a Morse error. When she had finished, she wondered if Miranda had heard the tapping of the Morse key, but she was too tired to worry about it. The important thing was that she had sent her message to Germany—what happened to her after that was irrelevant.

She switched off the set, coiled the aerial and replaced the radio in her suitcase. Without taking off her clothes, she collapsed onto the bed.

\*\*\*

As soon as he received her message, Admiral Canaris ordered his executive team to assemble in an hour's time.

When everyone was present, he opened the meeting. "You all have copies of Gretchen's latest message in your folders. It was sent twice—both messages are identical in every respect. First, I would like Colonel Donndorf to report on the scientific accuracy of the contents."

"Thank you, Admiral Canaris. I tried to contact all the scientific experts to whom I spoke earlier regarding promethium and alloys. Some of the professors were unavailable on such short notice, but those whom I was able to consult told me that it is likely that all isotopes of promethium are indeed radioactive, just like technetium, element 43. That would explain why no one has been able to find element 61 in nature. In brief, there's no reason to believe that Gretchen's statements are incorrect."

"Thank you, Donndorf. Gentlemen, it seems irrefutable that the information agent JULIUS sent us is wrong. He appears to have fallen for an Allied deceptive trick. We now need to analyze the deception in detail to determine the motives behind the Allies' attempt to foist disinformation on us. Then we can decide how to capitalize on our skill in having seen through their deceit.

"Let's start with the photograph of the ammunition boxes. One box is marked 'Pm' for promethium and 'NZ' for New Zealand. In retrospect, both those markings were cleverly chosen. The Allies chose Promethium for their deception because no scientist had managed to find it yet, so no one knew its properties—there was no way for us to challenge any claim made for the rare-earth metal. That was an exceedingly ingenious move. Also, they cunningly chose New Zealand for the location of the promethium mine because they believed that we couldn't possibly send an agent to that far corner of the British Empire to check anything. I'm delighted to say that they were completely wrong in that regard.

"Now look at the photograph showing the damage to the tank supposedly hit by the promethium alloy shell from a distance of 3,000 yards. How can we tell what actually caused the destruction? Yes, a British superweapon, the promethium alloy anti-tank shell, could certainly have caused it. But there are many ways to destroy a tank. For example, they could have used high explosives and blown it up. Alternatively, suppose that they fired a conventional anti-tank shell at the tank from a distance of, say, 100 yards. Then the British removed the second anti-tank gun and took the photograph that we see in front of us. If that's what they did, I, for one, was totally fooled."

A hand went up.

"Yes, Wilczek?"

"What about the photograph of the generals?" Major von Wilczek asked. "How was that forged? Do all Allied generals have doubles to pose for pictures?"

"No, I don't think so," Canaris said. "That photograph could have been taken on a completely different occasion. Alternatively, the generals were gathered there for another weapons trial, and the trick with the two tanks was simply an additional part of the proceedings. Any other questions?"

There was silence.

"Fine. Now we come to the hard part. Are we unanimously agreed that there's no promethium mine and therefore that there's no anti-tank shell made from a promethium alloy that has these remarkable properties?"

He looked around the table as everyone nodded.

"Does anyone disagree?"

No one moved.

"Good. We are in unanimous agreement. Now, why did the Allies want us to believe that they have a miraculous anti-tank shell?"

There was total silence around the large table.

"Doesn't anyone have an idea?"

A tentative hand went up.

"Yes, Horstmann?"

"In view of the surprising reluctance of the military experts to stick their necks out, this ignorant policeman will at least get the ball rolling."

There were smiles all around the table.

"I'm certainly not an expert on armor, but the answer seems rather obvious to me, perhaps because Major von Grauschild suggested it nearly a week ago at one of our meetings. Field Marshal Rommel has achieved his many victories by going on the attack rather than adopting a defensive stance. The enemy want Rommel to think that if he advances with his tanks, this time the Allies will destroy them with their anti-tank shells before our tanks can get close enough to fire at the anti-tank guns."

"So what should we advise Rommel to do?" Canaris asked.

"The Allies view their anti-tank guns as inadequate," Horstmann replied, "and Rommel needs to capitalize on this. He should attack even more strongly than he has done up to now, if that's possible."

"Are there any dissenting views?" the admiral asked his team members. "None? In that case, I have an announcement to make. *Herr* Hitler has been closely following *Fraulein* Konrad's activities. And in the light of her discovery regarding the non-existence of the promethium mine, the *Führer* has awarded her the *Kriegsverdienstkreuz* (War Merit Cross). He will present the medal to her personally when she comes here after the final victory, but in the meantime, I have been instructed to warmly congratulate her on her award when we next send a message to her. In the meantime, I expect to hear from her tomorrow regarding the gold mine.

# CHAPTER THIRTY-TWO

*Tudor Island, New Zealand*
*Monday, September 21st, 1942*

Gretchen awoke with a start at three. It was pitch dark outside. She knew that she had overlooked something of critical importance, and for her peace of mind she had to resolve the issue right away, even though her body was desperately in need of a long sleep. She thought for a minute, and then it came to her: Ambrose had told her he was 28 years old, but Colonel Wetherby had said that all the men on the island were First World War veterans like him. How could this be? And Ambrose was a sergeant in the regular Army, but the men guarding Coopers Island were supposedly in the New Zealand Home Guard. Also, Ambrose had been whisked away from her the moment he arrived on Tudor Island. In addition, it seemed to her as if the departure of the ferry had been delayed to wait for him. Gretchen's eyes opened wide as she realized the truth: It *had* been held for Ambrose until he arrived so that they could get him off the island immediately.

The more she thought about it, the more inconsistencies and contradictions she saw. Ambrose had introduced her to Horace Grosvenor as Dr. Gretchen Konrad—but she did not recall telling Ambrose her last name. At the time she wondered if he had inspected a hotel register after she had entered her personal details, but now she realized that he had not had the opportunity to learn her name that way.

So, Ambrose was a plant, probably a policeman of some kind. Ambrose had joined Wes and her in the train. And that meant that Wes was a policeman, too—no wonder he did not want her to come into the police station at Tauranga. And what about Colonel Wetherby? He had sounded like an actor playing the role of an elderly British colonel with all his "m'dears." And that "memsahib" near the end was a bad slip—if Wetherby had really been in India, he surely would have mentioned it, the same way that every other Englishman she had met who had served in India always did.

Who else was actually a policeman? What about that man in Tauranga who gave her a ride from the mine to the bus stop? What was his name again? Oh, yes, Jock. He just happened to be at the mine (or rather, the power station) when she and Wes reached the metal door—was that just another coincidence? Surely not. And the reason that Wes came running after her to accompany her to

Rotorua was presumably because Jock instructed him to be with her.

On the other hand, no policeman could possibly get involved with a suspect the way Wes had. Wes loved her; he had told her so many, many times. But she had climbed naked into his bed and seduced him. He had tried everything he could think of to resist her, but beyond a certain point he could not help himself. And from that point on, he had had to play the role of a besotted lover. And then he had been arrested. That was probably staged, too, so that a new policeman, Ambrose, could escort her to Coopers Island. And how indescribably stupid she'd been not to realize that it was more than yet another coincidence that Wes's friend Ambrose just somehow happened to be a soldier who was posted to Coopers Island. He had been extremely cunning, imparting that information to her at the precise time when she was so terribly upset by Wes's arrest and in no fit state to judge whether what he was saying was credible.

And what about that nice hotel owner in Rotorua? What was his name again? Joe something or other? Oh, yes, Joe Kaplan. He had been just a mite too friendly and asked her a few more questions than hotel owners usually did. Maybe he was a retired policeman. But no one had known that she and Wes were heading for Rotorua, let alone that they would choose the Lake Hotel, so what had they done that had made Joe Kaplan so suspicious? No, that was the wrong way of looking at it. The authorities in Rotorua definitely knew that she and Wes were going there—Jock must have telephoned his opposite number in Rotorua. And without a doubt the Rotorua police station commander must have ordered a detective to follow them from the bus stop. And then, when they were safely in their room at the Lake Hotel, the detective tipped Joe off that she was a German spy.

But why that circuitous travel route from Dunedin to Milford Sound via Queenstown, culminating in that nightmare sea voyage? Surely with his police contacts, Ambrose could have taken her past the checkpoint near Gore? And then she realized with a sudden shock that there was no prohibition of any kind at all against travel south of the 46th parallel. She had been led along that road from Dunedin to Milford Sound precisely to prevent her finding out that she could have travelled freely by train from Dunedin via Gore and Invercargill to Bluff, and from there by ferry to Cookville, where she now was. From the time she arrived in Auckland on the *Star of Adelaide*, Gretchen had been a puppet, with the New Zealand police pulling the strings.

How could they have arranged everything so quickly here in New Zealand? The answer to that question was obvious—the Australian authorities must have known all the time that she was a spy. But how was that possible? There was no doubt whatsoever in her mind regarding the answer to that question—the stolen radio. They must have picked up the 1939 message that she sent to Berlin in plaintext. And what about the plaintext message that the *Abwehr* had sent her more than two weeks previously? They must have read that, too. Was her New Zealand contact, Walter Bennett, also a policeman? That was unlikely—what Wes did with her was one thing, what Walter had inflicted on her was quite another. She needed to warn Walter that the police were on his trail. And then she thought: No, that animal deserves everything that is going to happen to him.

Then she remembered the list of mines. The people in the Department of Lands and Survey must have instructed their typist to deliberately slightly misalign the stencils before typing "Various"—that would focus her attention on those four mines and, in particular, the mine on Coopers Island. They clearly did not care about the order in which she visited the four mines, just as long as at some point she arrived at Tudor Island to meet "Colonel Wetherby." And the list obviously helped them to keep track of her. They were fully aware that the four mines were in or near Tauranga, Rotorua, Akaroa and Coopers Island, so those were the four places where they watched for her. What a total idiot she had been!

And what about the man who had knocked on the door of Room 203 of the Arthur Hotel just before she was due to transmit? Was he really a drunk, or was he a policeman, too? She could not work it out. If he was a policeman, why did he have to knock? They must have known that she was in there. Was it to put her off her stroke before her radio transmission? Possibly yes, but how could they know that she was scheduled to transmit to Germany at 10:30 p.m.? And then it struck her: Walter must have told them. So they must have arrested Walter already, and that coward would unquestionably have told them everything he knew in order to save his neck. Had he told them about the way that he had blackmailed her into satisfying his lust? Probably not. Everything else, yes, but surely not that—surely he would be too embarrassed to tell anyone what he did to her that night?

The epiphanies continued steadily, one after the other, like newly assembled cars coming off a fast-moving production line. If the authorities knew that she was a Nazi spy travelling from Sydney to Auckland to meet her "brother," then they must have known about Walter from the time she had received that plaintext message sent by the *Abwehr* more than two weeks before. That meant that they must have staked out Walter's house in Wellington and they certainly had been waiting there when she drew up in the taxi. And they must have been listening to her radio messages. At least those messages were in code—no wonder the *Abwehr* had made such a fuss when she had transmitted that lengthy plaintext message to them just before the war started.

So the New Zealand authorities had watched and waited while she stayed in Walter's house. In fact, they probably planted a listening device in his house, so they understood precisely why she walked out on him on Friday morning. Gretchen shuddered uncontrollably—they knew what Walter had done to her. Mentally she had arrived at a point where she could somehow manage to live with this dirty secret—what she could not handle was others knowing what he had inflicted on her.

Gretchen finally understood what was really happening to her: The New Zealand authorities had manipulated her into travelling to Tudor Island so that she would send that message to Germany informing the *Abwehr* that the promethium mine did not exist. Which meant that the promethium mine did exist, and, therefore, she had to see it with her own eyes to be able to provide first-hand evidence to the Third Reich. She could not wait until Colonel Wetherby—or whatever his real name was—organized a tour of the mine for her. He had probably arranged to have a few specimens of iron pyrite or fool's gold displayed to trick her into believing that Coopers Island housed "one of the richest gold mines in the British Empire." No, she had to examine the excavation herself right away, before they had a chance to disguise the fact that this was a promethium mine, not a gold mine. And then she would send another radio message to Berlin, this one based on eyewitness information. She would reveal the true facts to Admiral Canaris and the *Abwehr*. And Nazi Germany would triumphantly win the war.

She took out the area map that she had bought after the saleslady informed her that the NZMS 1 maps for Tudor Island and the surrounding islands had not yet been issued. She studied the replacement map as carefully as she could. The scale was barely adequate, but she could see the key features. Coopers Island was roughly square, approximately one mile long by one mile wide, with a trail that ran north–south down the middle. But the only jetty was on the south side, so there had to be a path that led to the mine, which she recalled was on the east side of the island. The path to the mine presumably branched off the main trail at some point.

When she landed at Tudor Island the previous afternoon, Gretchen had noticed the house on Coopers Island overlooking the jetty that Ambrose had mentioned to her, so she quickly realized that it would be futile for her to row straight across Raphael Channel—she would be spotted immediately. Then she remembered that Ambrose had told her that there was a beach on the north side where she could land a boat. No, she was wrong there, her memory was playing tricks. Ambrose had not said that—the assistant at the stationery shop in Wellington where she had bought her maps had told her about the beach. No, she was still wrong—Ambrose and the assistant had both told her. So, once she was ashore at Mystic Beach she would walk through the rainforest along the main trail, turn left when she reached the path to the east, and finally reach the promethium mine.

Gretchen unlocked the suitcase in which she stored the transceiver and removed the Colt M1911A1 pistol she used for shooting cattle, horses and sheep that she needed to put out of their misery. Then she took out two ammunition clips, each containing seven .45 ACP cartridges. She loaded the pistol with one clip, stuck the weapon in her waistband and put the other clip in the pocket of her trousers. She locked the suitcase. Then she grabbed her flashlight and quietly left the house. During her circuits of the village, she had seen three tinnies lying on the beach, and one of them had oars in it. She crept over the rocks and walked through the sand to the boat. She pushed the tinny into the sea, waded into the icy water, jumped in and started rowing as quietly as she could.

# CHAPTER THIRTY-THREE

*Raphael Channel, New Zealand*
*Monday, September 21st, 1942*

As the rowing boat slid forward into the moonlit channel, Gretchen was intensely aware of the forest ranger's whitewashed house that overlooked the jetty on Coopers Island and, equally importantly, offered a view of Tudor Island and its jetty. She realized that, from the time she had clambered over the rocks onto the beach, a watcher at the front window could have spotted her making for Coopers Island. But there was nothing she could do about that. She looked over her left shoulder as she turned the tinny and headed west along the southern side of Raphael Channel. She noticed that the building was in darkness, so there was no way of knowing if someone in that house had observed her in the boat.

After some 600 yards, the L-shaped channel turned sharply to the right and ran due north. Gretchen rowed slowly along the west coast of

Coopers Island. Then she saw sharp rocks perilously close to the tinny, so she moved toward the center of the channel, keeping a safe distance from the shore. Eventually she reached the northern exit of Raphael Channel and turned into Foveaux Strait. Again looking over her left shoulder, she could see the white sands of Mystic Beach gleaming in the light of the waxing gibbous moon.

She rowed hard toward the shore, aided by the wind and the powerful current. The tinny landed smoothly on the white sand. She jumped out and pulled the boat onto the beach. She saw a pole in front of her with a sign on the top that warned that every part of the island was out of bounds to civilians. Gretchen smiled grimly to herself as she read that, and then tied the tinny to the pole, in case the tide came in while she was on the island.

She looked around. The beach seemed to be deserted. It was about 75 yards wide. The distance from the shore to the forest was roughly 50 yards. Gretchen swiftly headed across the sand to the shelter of the trees. As she neared the deciduous rainforest, she drew her pistol from her waistband.

Through the trees she saw the trail about 10 yards to her left. It led in a southerly direction from a gap in the bushes in the center of the edge of the beach to the ranger's house and the jetty. Her initial thought was to step back onto the edge of the beach and walk along the sand to the gap where the trail began. After that, she would walk along the trail until she reached the path that branched off and led eastward to the mine.

Then Gretchen thought about the Home Guard soldiers that the military had posted on the island. Ambrose had told her that eight men at a time patrolled Coopers Island, day and night. Presumably they used the trail to get from one side of the island to the other, so the risk of her encountering a soldier was greater if she used the trail. On the other hand, if she blundered through the dark forest, slipping on moss, slithering through clumps of giant ferns, and disturbing wildlife, the noise would alert the guards. Furthermore, the soldiers presumably knew the forest well from their unending patrols through the thick vegetation, whereas she had no idea of the topography. After weighing up the alternatives for a few seconds, Gretchen decided that she would walk as quietly as possible along the trail, listening for approaching footsteps. If she heard something, she would just duck into the rainforest and hide behind a tree. If the worst came to the worst, of course, she had her pistol. But a veterinarian carrying an M1911A1 pistol was a losing proposition against a First World War veteran armed with a rifle. And with that gloomy thought, Gretchen started down the trail.

*** 

Lance Corporal Lewin looked down from his perch in the huge southern beech tree in which he had concealed himself. Major MacKenzie's instructions to his three squads had been clear: The purpose of the training exercise was to observe the intruder, without her seeing anyone and without obstructing her in any way. The eight members of the squad that included Lewin had met to decide how to carry out the exercise. In their opinion, there were only four ways that the intruder could get onto Coopers Island. She could land by parachute on the wild grasses that covered the flat open space next to the mine. She could also land on Mystic Beach, provided she took the greatest care not to come down in the fringing forest or on the dangerously sharp rocks that surrounded the sand. The other two alternatives were to arrive by boat at the jetty or on Mystic Beach.

Lewin had told the other members of his squad that he would sit and watch from a tree that offered an excellent view of Mystic Beech. The tree was situated at the north end of the trail that led from the beach to the jetty and just to one side of it. He was wondering what would happen if the woman tried to drop onto Mystic Beach by parachute—would he have to rescue her if she missed the target landing area? His orders were clear: He was to see but not be seen. But if the intruder were hanging suspended in the air from her harness with her parachute caught in a tree or if she lay on the rocks badly injured, surely his duty to save her life would take precedence over the rules of the training exercise?

Lewin's musings were interrupted by the sound of rowing. He looked out to sea and saw a tinny, with a woman at the oars, rounding the rocky head on the west side of Mystic Beach. He approvingly noted the professional way in which she beached the boat and tied it to the pole.

And then he noticed the pistol in her hand. From where he sat in the tree, she seemed to be holding an M1911 handgun, the standard semi-automatic service pistol used by the American Army in the First World War. In an instant, Lewin's whole attitude to the training exercise changed. It was one thing to play hide-and-seek with a woman in a moonlit forest. But being hunted by a woman with an M1911 was quite another.

Next, he remembered that this was a training exercise, so it was certainly within the bounds of possibility that the pistol was unloaded. After all, the object of the exercise was simply to observe the intruder without her seeing him. At the end of the training exercise, the members of the squad would certainly be questioned regarding the route that the intruder had followed, and Major MacKenzie would inform the members of the squad if the woman had spotted any of them in the course of her foray onto the island. Handguns simply did not enter into it.

Questions suddenly popped up in Lewin's head: Why did the training exercise involve a woman? That made no sense at all. And why an armed woman? That made even less sense. Perhaps, he thought, there were two women involved here. The first woman, the participant in the training exercise, was still to arrive on the island, whereas the woman now on the beach in front of him was a genuine intruder who had to be stopped. Was that the situation? And, if so, what was he supposed to do about it?

The woman darted from the beach into the forest. He could no longer see her—there was a giant eucalyptus tree between them. Then he observed her returning to the edge of the beach and walking along the sand before re-entering the forest at the gap in the trees at the start of the trail. As she walked along the trail, she passed almost directly under where Lance Corporal Lewin was sitting some 15 feet above her head.

His two years of experience as a sniper on the Western Front took over. As Gretchen moved forward, he noiselessly took his rifle and aimed it at the far end of the barrel of her pistol. He squeezed the trigger.

The last time that Lewin had fired at a target was more than 20 years before, and the lack of practice took its toll on Lewin's sharpshooting skills—the bullet thudded harmlessly into the ground nearly a foot to the right of its intended destination.

Nevertheless, he achieved his aim of disarming Gretchen, because the sudden loud muzzle blast directly above her head shattered the silence of the nocturnal forest and shocked her into dropping her pistol onto the ground. She did not hesitate for an instant. She ran as fast as she could in the direction of the jetty.

Lewin waited until he could no longer hear her hiking boots thudding on the trail. Then he climbed down. In the moonlight, the massive trunk of the southern beech tree cast a shadow that darkened the area where the handgun had fallen, so he scrabbled around in the dirt until he found it. He walked out of the forest to the edge of the beach so that he could examine the weapon closely. It was a Colt M1911A1, a newer model than the one he knew from the Great War. He noticed a tiny dent on the right side of the pistol almost directly below the rear sight—Lewin wondered if the weapon had fallen onto a stone. Other than that, the handgun seemed to be intact. He was tempted to fire it at the nearest tree to test it out, but wisely restrained himself. After all, concealment was a key component of this rather unconventional training exercise, and the less noise the members of his squad made, the better for all concerned.

Next he realized that the only way the woman could leave the island was to return to her tinny. So he removed the clip from her pistol and placed the empty gun in the boat—it never occurred to him that she might have a second clip in her pocket, let alone that there might be a bullet in the chamber. Then he returned to his post in the southern beech tree.

***

Sergeant Clayton hid behind a large silver fern. He had taken up his station as close as he could get to the place where the path to the mine branched off the main north–south trail. Suddenly he heard a rifle shot from the direction of the beach. It was difficult to judge in the forest, particularly at night, but he thought that the sound came from a distance of about half a mile away, perhaps a little farther. Almost immediately afterwards, he heard running footsteps. The steps slowed noticeably after 30 or 40 seconds. Then the sound grew louder. There was no doubt in his mind—someone wearing boots was running toward him. He trained his rifle on the trail, aiming through the fronds.

He saw a woman in hiking clothes, blonde hair disheveled, with a wild expression on her face, coming down the trail in his direction. This, it seemed, was the woman of the training exercise.

Clayton saw the woman slow as she reached the T-junction and then walk swiftly down the path to her left, almost running in the direction of the mine. The sergeant lowered his rifle. He had no idea what was happening, but at least he had observed the woman without her noticing him.

\*\*\*

Bert Troy hid in the wooden guard hut next to the mine. When the members of the squad met to plan for the training exercise, Bert had immediately shouted that he wanted to be in the guard hut. He was certain that the woman would land by parachute in the grassy area, and he wanted to be the first one to spot her. He was surprised when everyone readily agreed, some enthusiastically. It was only later that he realized that the intruder would undoubtedly head for the mine. On her way there, she would certainly peer into the otherwise empty hut. And there she would observe Bert Troy, trying in vain not to be observed. But by the time he had worked this out, it was too late to change. His seven comrades had already snapped up the other spots.

Troy heard footsteps coming towards him. He peered gingerly through one of the openings in the guard hut. A woman moved swiftly across the flat open space in the direction of the mine. Her gaze was fixed on the shaft in front of her. Bert ducked down swiftly. As he did so, he realized that the woman had a strange expression on her face. Just before the war started, he had seen a production of *Hamlet* at the St. James Theatre in Auckland. In her last scene before drowning herself, the actress playing Ophelia had an almost identical look about her as she wandered through Elsinore Castle, behaving exceedingly strangely. Like his two comrades before him, Bert was puzzled, but for a different reason—he certainly had not expected that a crazy woman would participate in the training exercise.

\*\*\*

After everything that Gretchen had been through for the past week, being shot at and dropping her pistol had pushed her over the edge. Even though she was now totally defenseless, she abandoned any attempt at concealment and ran at full tilt away from the Home Guard soldier above her in the tree who had fired at her. She slowed as she tired, but was still moving at faster than a walking pace when, through the gloom of the forest, she saw the path to the mine branching off to her left. She continued at the maximum speed she could manage in her exhausted state, and a few minutes later she left the rainforest and found herself in a flat open space, covered in wild grasses. She wondered if that was where the promethium ore was dumped before they transported it to the jetty, or if that was where they had stored the equipment while they were digging down to where the promethium deposit lay.

Gretchen rushed towards the mine. In front of her was the mineshaft. She reached the edge of the hole in the ground, switched on her flashlight and pointed it downward. All she could see was darkness. Then she observed the ladder on the side nearest her.

She began climbing down. Gretchen noticed that the top and the bottom of the ladder had horizontal posts that were cemented into the rock. After about 25 feet, the ladder came to an end, and her flashlight illuminated a second ladder, fastened to the shaft below the first ladder and, for some reason, a short distance to the side of it. With some difficulty, she transferred her weight from the bottom rung of the first ladder to the top rung of the second, and then continued to descend.

Gretchen Konrad soon reached the last rung of the second ladder. The bottom of the shaft was about two feet below her feet. She shone her flashlight around in total bewilderment. Of all the four mines she had visited, this was the most grotesque. It was just a cavity in the ground, about 50 feet deep, cut vertically down through bare rock. And then she saw the gold nuggets, and she immediately realized that she had been wrong again—this was indeed one of the richest gold mines in the British Empire. And she understood why the mine was guarded day and night.

Gretchen suddenly thought of her beloved Wes. As a motor mechanic, he would never be able to afford to buy expensive jewelry for her. So, while she was down here, why not steal some of the enemy's pure gold, to be fashioned after the war into a necklace or a bracelet? She took her Swiss Army knife out of her pocket, held the nugget in place on the ground with her left hand and tried to slice off a piece of gold. Gretchen knew that gold is a soft metal, so she was surprised when her knife could not cut into the lump to even the slightest extent. She shone her flashlight on the nugget and noticed what seemed to be gold on the fingers of her left hand, even though her knife had been totally unable to penetrate the hunk of solid metal. She rubbed the nugget with her right hand

and more gold paint came off, this time onto her hand.

She rushed to the next nugget. This time she rubbed it with her sleeve, and the gold color rubbed off onto the material, exposing bare rock. Then she remembered that gold is heavy, about seven times heavier than a quartz rock of the same size. So she picked up the smallest nugget, and quickly discovered that it was as light as a rock, rather than heavy as a lump of gold. "They've salted the mine with gold-painted rocks," Gretchen said to herself.

This was not a promethium mine or even one of the richest gold mines in the British Empire—it was just a hole in the ground.

Gretchen climbed back up to the surface. What did this mean? Why had she been directed to this place? Was there a promethium mine somewhere else in New Zealand, or had Colonel Wetherby been telling the truth regarding the radioactivity of promethium? After all, he'd lied to her regarding the existence of a rich gold mine, so why should she believe anything he'd said?

And what was she to tell the *Abwehr*? That she'd managed to penetrate the defenses of Coopers Island and found a barren pit containing rocks freshly coated with gold-colored paint? That she could no longer tell the enemy's truth from lies, or facts from fiction? That the promethium mine was now as realistic as the pot of gold at the end of the rainbow? Or that she had finally come to the end of the road? She slowly retreated to Mystic Beach.

***

On her way to the mine, Gretchen had passed by Bert Troy. He'd peeped at her from his hiding place in the guard hut and seen by the look on her face that she was tottering on the brink between sanity and madness. Troy watched her walk back toward the forest. She moved like an automaton.

It seemed to Sergeant Clayton, hiding behind the large silver fern, that Gretchen looked right through him, unseeing. Finally, she walked underneath Lance Corporal Lewin, who was stunned to see the change in her. His reaction again was that there were two different women involved, and that this time he had encountered the participant in the training exercise. Then he took a second look and saw that the person coming toward him along the trail was the same woman as before, but now utterly defeated.

***

Gretchen walked across the sand, untied the tinny, pushed it into the water and climbed in. She placed the oars in the rowlocks and started to row back to Tudor Island the way she had come.

The relentless current and the gale-force wind now pushing mercilessly from the southwest in tandem grabbed the tinny and whisked it away from the island. She fought with all her strength to bring the tiny craft closer to Coopers Island, preferring to be dashed onto the razor-sharp rocks than swept out to sea. But her efforts were futile. No matter how hard she struggled against the combined elements, the thundering tempest and merciless surge drove the tinny inexorably toward the middle of Foveaux Strait. Time went by and still she rowed futilely, unable to give up.

As she weakened, images started to flash through her mind: her bedroom in her childhood home in Bremen; the dachshund belonging to her communist lover; her office in Bathurst; Walter Bennett; a huge German American Bund rally in Chicago; and her beloved Wes.

The images blurred and finally faded to a dull gray nothingness. Gretchen passed out from exhaustion.

# CHAPTER THIRTY-FOUR

*Coopers Island, New Zealand*
*Monday, September 21st, 1942*

"Lance Corporal Lewin," Major MacKenzie said, "tell me again what you saw."

"Well, sir, it was dark—only the moon illuminated the beach. But from my tree I could see her as she pushed the tinny into the water and got in. She started rowing back in the direction from which she'd come."

"So you mean westward, toward the northern entrance of Raphael Channel?"

"Yes, sir. Westward. But I saw the boat being forced in a northeasterly direction by the wind, which had shifted direction and was blowing gale force again. No matter how hard she tried to row, she kept moving northeastward."

"Could it have been the current that forced the tinny to go in the wrong direction?"

"Yes, sir, the current or the wind. Or both, sir."

"Go on."

"When I saw her being pushed away from Raphael Channel, I climbed down from the tree and ran to the beach to see if there was anything I could do to save her, perhaps by swimming out to the tinny and helping her. But the boat was travelling too fast—there just was nothing I could do. I'm sorry, sir."

"No, Lewin, you did the right thing. If you'd tried to save her by swimming the Foveaux Strait you'd have drowned long before you reached her, let alone when you tried to get back with her, against the current and the wind."

"Yes, sir, I know that, but I still feel bad about it. Realizing that there was nothing I could do, I just stood on the beach and watched. And soon the boat was carried beyond the rocks on the east side of Mystic Beach, and I couldn't see her any more—those huge boulders blocked my view."

"Did you know that the Air Force sent up a Supermarine Walrus to look for her?"

"I heard a plane soon after sunrise. That must have been the Walrus."

"Yes, it took off from Bluff Harbour. They found nothing. But it's a huge ocean and she's in a tiny boat."

"How's she eventually going to end up, sir?"

"The Antarctic Circumpolar Current runs strongly from here. So if they don't find her soon, either the wind and the waves will overturn the boat, plunging her into the icy water, or her tinny will be pushed round and round Antarctica for years. Eventually, it'll hit an iceberg and sink."

\*\*\*

"Detective Chief Superintendent Jennings? This is Major MacKenzie on Tudor Island."

"Any sign of that tinny yet, major?"

"Nothing so far. The pilot of the Walrus had to return to base—his fuel was running low. He has considerable experience with air–sea rescue and he knows these waters well, so maybe he can locate her. Anyhow, he's taking off again as soon as they've refueled his plane. I'll let you know as soon as we hear anything.

"But that's not why I phoned you," MacKenzie continued. "We've found the radio and the codebook that you asked me to look for. They were in a suitcase in the room she was renting here. The suitcase was marked 'Veterinary Instruments.' It was chained and locked. I didn't know what to do, not being in the police and not having a search warrant, so I phoned Dunedin and spoke to the Chief Magistrate there and gave him your name. Anyhow, he phoned me back not long after, and he gave me permission to open the suitcase, which I did by cutting the chain. And inside was a Marconi transceiver as well as a German codebook."

"That's excellent news. We really need to get our hands on that codebook right away—we need to decode the message she sent out last night from Cookville that we picked up in Dunedin. If you could arrange to get the codebook to Invercargill, we'll have it flown here. Now that I come to think of it, we're probably going to need all her things. Please put the radio and codebook back in the suitcase and tie it firmly shut with a rope or something. Then I'd appreciate it if you could pack everything else of hers that you find there into her backpack."

"That's no problem. I'll arrange to have the suitcase and backpack transported to Invercargill as quickly as possible."

***

"Gentlemen," Admiral Wilhelm Canaris said, "it's been three days since we last heard from Gretchen Konrad or Walter Bennett. This is a worrying development—she promised to report on the gold mine. One possibility is that the New Zealand authorities have arrested them both. We'll get to that later. First, I want to discuss what we know—then we can try to discover what's going on.

"In Gretchen's last message, sent from Tudor Island, she made two statements of critical importance. First, there's definitely a mine on Coopers Island, but it's a gold mine, a particularly rich one. Incidentally, that's exactly what Major von Grauschild put forward at a previous meeting. He suggested that there's a mine on Coopers Island and it contains a metal of utmost importance to the Allied war effort, but it's not promethium.

"The second vital statement in Gretchen's message was that promethium doesn't exist in the natural state because it's radioactive and decays quickly into other elements. Accordingly, there cannot be such a thing as a promethium mine or, for that matter, a promethium alloy anti-tank shell.

"Donndorf, will you please update us regarding the scientific and metallurgical information you've obtained?"

"Thank you, Admiral. We last met on extremely short notice, so I couldn't contact all my experts regarding the radioactivity of promethium. I have subsequently done so, and the decision is unanimous. They all said that it's likely that promethium is radioactive. In more detail, they told me that they expect that there are a number of different isotopes of promethium, but that it's plausible that all of them are radioactive with half-lives so short as to make it impossible for promethium to exist for long in the natural state. The bottom line is that it's the unanimous opinion of Germany's leading chemists and metallurgists that Konrad's statement that a promethium mine cannot exist may well be scientifically accurate. Accordingly, there's no reason to disbelieve what she has told us."

"And that means," Canaris interrupted, "that the Allies cannot have made anti-tank shells out of an alloy of promethium. And that, in turn, means that the photographs and information that the Allies sold to agent JULIUS are disinformation.

"If Konrad and Bennett have been arrested," he went on, "they may well talk to save their necks. They'll tell the authorities everything. The Allies will learn that we know that the whole promethium operation is a deceptive trick. Accordingly, they'll expect us to deduce that their anti-tank weapons aren't up to the task. They know that we'll adopt appropriate tactics in the light of this knowledge. But there's obviously nothing they can do about it. They gambled and they lost. And, as a result of their inadequate deceptive plan, they'll lose the forthcoming battle at El Alamein. The lesson is clear: Disinformation that can be proved to be disinformation is a good source of information.

"I will now advise the High Command of the Armed Forces that we recommend that Field Marshal Rommel continue to attack strongly with his tanks in all forthcoming battles on the Western Front."

# CHAPTER THIRTY-FIVE

*Garden City, Cairo, Egypt*
*Tuesday, October 20th, 1942*

"Grey Pillars" was the name on the ornately decorated apartment building at 10 Tolombat Street, Garden City, a suburb of Cairo. The building originally housed Allied General Headquarters, which almost immediately outgrew it and now filled a whole neighborhood. Despite the many pressures from other military units competing for space, Colonel Marlowe and his Security Intelligence Middle East group somehow managed to stay on in Grey Pillars. But finally the intelligence unit grew too large for the available space, and they had to move to 6 Sharia Kasr-el-Nil. This apartment building had a questionable reputation—it housed a fashionable brothel. Colonel Marlowe moved the bordello to the third floor, where it provided useful cover for the activities conducted in the rest of the building.

Captain Wright knocked. On hearing the word "Enter!" in Colonel Marlowe's gruff voice, he opened the door.

"Come in, Wright, and sit down. I need to make use of your superlative acting skills once again. But to prepare you for your new role, I have to tell you what's really happening with the promethium—I'm afraid that, for the sake of security, I've had to slightly mislead you regarding some of the facts."

Wright said nothing.

"As you know," Marlowe continued, "General Montgomery is about to attack Field Marshal Rommel and his Afrika Corps across the El Alamein line. Monty has a secret weapon. Our American allies provided it in the form of 300 Sherman tanks—the best in the world. In particular, the gun on a Sherman has a longer range than any German tank. So, Monty wants Rommel to order his tank commanders to advance into the face of our tanks, so that we can destroy their tanks while our tanks are still outside their effective range.

"However, a secret weapon has to stay secret. General Montgomery decided that the best way to deflect German intelligence from learning about our new tanks was to inform them that we have a new anti-tank shell with superior capabilities. Then they'd expend all their energies on finding out every single detail of the new shell. And once they'd fallen for our deception, we made sure that they knew that this was all a bluff."

"But sir, why did General Montgomery want the Germans first to think we have the anti-tank shell and then discover that we don't have it after all?"

"Good question! Once the Germans knew for sure that the promethium alloy doesn't exist, we wanted them to ask themselves: Why would the British spend all that time, money and effort to try to deceive us into believing that they have a new anti-tank shell when they don't? And the only possible answer is: Because the British know that their anti-tank weapons are inadequate. And if they're inadequate, the correct tactic for Rommel to employ is to order his tank commanders to charge headlong into Allied positions—"

"From where our Sherman tanks will destroy them before our tanks come into effective range of their tanks."

"Precisely, Wright. Precisely."

"But what if the photographs I gave Kezerian worked too well? What if they fell for our deception?"

"Well, we knew that the antiquities dealer had forwarded the information you'd given him to his German contacts, and we hoped that the *Abwehr* would send an agent to New Zealand to locate the promethium. Our counterparts in that country told us about a suitable abandoned mine on Coopers Island. The shaft is about 50 feet deep, and contains a ladder leading to the bottom of the shaft—and nothing more. Now we needed some window dressing. The Kiwis put signs up around the island stating that it was out of bounds to civilians. They also arranged for 24 Home Guard soldiers to guard the mine and enforce the prohibition on civilians coming to the island. To ensure that news of the tremendous military importance of the mine would get around quickly, they billeted the troops on nearby Tudor Island and made them travel back and forth all the time. We hoped that reports about the mine would soon reach the ears of German military intelligence. In the event, the *Abwehr* sent a woman agent to New Zealand to investigate. She was based in Australia. Because the Australians knew all about her and were listening to her radio messages, it was no problem at all to feed her the clues that would lead her to the mine. And when she got there, she learned that promethium is radioactive and decays into other elements, so there can be no such thing as a promethium mine, let alone a promethium anti-tank shell."

"But what if she ignored your clues and didn't find the mine?" Wright asked. "Or what if the Germans didn't send an agent to New Zealand in the first place?"

"Ah! That was Plan B. We'd arranged to have a technical article published in a British research journal that would make it clear to a scientist that we couldn't possibly be mining promethium. We know that the Germans study our scientific literature line-by-line in case one of our boffins gives away a secret by mistake. In fact, when the rather gifted actor who pretended to be a colonel on Tudor Island met the German agent and told her about the mine, he gave her a simplified version of the contents of the article, which she duly radioed to Berlin. Once we knew that the *Abwehr* had the information, there was no need to publish the research article."

"So you had all bases covered?"

"Yes, I think so, Wright."

"Sir?"

"Yes?"

"What happened to the German agent after she arrived at the mine?"

"What exactly are you asking, Wright?"

"Well, sir, you said that she found the mine and sent a radio message about promethium to Berlin. What happened after that?"

"Wright, you should know better than to ask a question like that. Operational information is given out on a need-to-know basis."

"I'm sorry, sir."

"And so you should be. However, I don't think it will do much harm if I tell you the part that isn't classified Top Secret, provided you keep the information to yourself. She fled Coopers Island in a row boat and was swept out to sea. Like us, the Kiwis use the amphibious Supermarine Walrus as a rescue plane for downed aircrew, so they sent up a Walrus to look for her. The pilot has lived in that area all his life and he had a good idea where to look for her. He and his crew spotted her boat on their second search. He was able to land his plane in the middle of the Foveaux Strait, which is no mean feat of airmanship, I can tell you. When they got to her she was unconscious, so he flew her straight to Dunedin Hospital."

"Did she survive her ordeal at sea?"

"Why are you asking me all these questions, Wright?"

"Well, sir, if she's alive we can turn her and persuade her to send disinformation to the *Abwehr*."

"Wright, I know you are going to find this extremely hard to believe, but your duties do not include instructing the British intelligence services how to do their jobs."

"Sorry, sir."

"Wright, this conversation has gone on long enough. That's all I'm going to tell you regarding the *Abwehr* agent."

Colonel Marlowe paused again. Then, as he continued, a look of determination appeared on his craggy face. "In 637 AD there was an almighty battle at Al-Qadisiyya, in what is now the Kingdom of Iraq, between the Arab Muslims and the Sassanid Persians. Even today, the Arabs refer to it as 'the mother of all battles.' Well, we're about to start the mother of all battles here on the El Alamein line. And I have no doubt that General Montgomery and the Eighth Army will be victorious in the Battle of El Alamein."

# CHAPTER THIRTY-SIX

*Vicinity of El Daaba, Egypt*
*Friday, October 23rd, 1942*

"Gentlemen," Lieutenant General Stumme said to his staff officers, "as you all know, I'm in command of the Afrika Corps while Field Marshal Rommel is on sick leave in Germany. He's been gone for almost a month now. But before he left, he drew up detailed plans for our next offensive.

"However, we're currently unable to execute his plans—I don't have to tell you that we're desperately short of fuel for our tanks. The Allies are somehow discovering when our convoys are about to cross the Mediterranean Sea to resupply us, and Royal Air Force planes based in Egypt are sinking our ships—two more fuel tankers were sunk last night about 30 miles off the coast as they approached Tobruk.

"The thorn in our flesh is Security Intelligence Middle East, headed by Colonel Marlowe. They've set up a spy network in southern Italy to inform them when our ships are sailing for Tobruk.

Marlowe's people then pass the details on to Royal Air Force Headquarters at Grey Pillars, and their planes easily find our conveys. They're currently sinking about half our ships but almost all our fuel tankers. Unfortunately, the *Luftwaffe* has been unable to stop them—they don't have enough fuel, either.

"And another thing. The Security Intelligence people in Cairo have been trying to deceive the *Abwehr* into believing that the Allies have this powerful new anti-tank shell that will change the course of the coming battle. Admiral Canaris himself has informed me that the shell doesn't exist, and that the purpose of their disinformation campaign is to try to dissuade us from our usual offensive tactics. We don't have enough fuel to start the next battle by attacking the enemy, but once we counterattack we'll do so with the full knowledge that the Allies' anti-tank weapons are inadequate.

"Cairo is well defended against air raids. But when the Allies start the battle, their attention will be diverted to the El Alamein line. That will give the *Luftwaffe* the opportunity to wipe out the Security Intelligence Middle East group. A few bombers will specifically target their headquarters building at Number 6, Sharia Kasr-el-Nil.

"Field Marshal Rommel expects that, when we counterattack, we'll break through the Allied line and reach Cairo. But by the time we get there, the Security Intelligence group will have fled, probably to Jerusalem. If our bombers use high explosives to reduce their building to a pile of rubble before they have a chance to escape, the Security Intelligence Middle East group will never have another opportunity to plot against the Third Reich."

"But General Stumme," asked a staff officer, "isn't Number 6, Sharia Kasr-el-Nil the location of the finest bordello in Cairo? I was so hoping to celebrate our victory there."

The general grinned broadly, showing two gold teeth. "Major Kappler, I'm bitterly disappointed in you. It pains me deeply that you, of all people, should be fooled by that *Schweinehund* Marlowe who's running the Security Intelligence organization. The brothel of which you so longingly speak is on the third floor, but the rest of the apartment building is filled to overflowing with Security Intelligence staff. So I'll ask the *Luftwaffe* to use their special bombs, the kind that just bypass the third floor and leave the rest of the building a heap of smoking ruins. That way, you and I will both get the greatest satisfaction.

"Any other questions?"

Major Kappler raised his hand. "I heard that one of our spies in Alexandria has provided us with a map showing the defenses of part of the El Alamein line. Is that correct?"

"Our spies in Egypt have provided us with two Allied maps. Superficially they're identical. But there are a number of critical differences. For example, one vitally important area is marked 'firm and fast' on the one map and 'generally impassable' on the other. Our intelligence people say that the British are trying to trick us into sending our tanks into sandy areas, doubling or even trebling the consumption of our precious fuel. The problem is that we don't know which map to believe. In fact, both may be deceptive."

General Stumme concluded his remarks. "Gentlemen, the battle could start any minute now. Or it might take months before Montgomery feels ready. We must be prepared at all times of the day or night."

\*\*\*

That night was calm and clear, with a full moon. At 9:40 p.m., a carefully planned Allied artillery barrage started, arranged so that the first rounds from nearly 900 guns would all land at precisely the same time across the entire length of the 40-mile front, from the Qattara Depression in the desert to El Alamein on the Mediterranean coast. The bombardment continued for more than five hours.

In response, the *Luftwaffe* sent up Stuka dive-bombers to try to destroy the field artillery, but with little effect. While the air attack was in progress and with the Allied anti-aircraft crews concentrating their efforts on the dive-bombers, four Heinkel medium bombers headed straight for Cairo. An RAF Spitfire scored a dead hit on one, and anti-aircraft fire downed another two. But one plane managed to reach Garden City, Cairo, and dropped a bomb on Number 6, Sharia Kasr-el-Nil.

# CHAPTER THIRTY-SEVEN

*Alexandria, Egypt*
*Thursday, February 11th, 1943*

The convoy of cars bringing senior Allied officers arrived at the British Military Hospital in Alexandria. General Bernard Montgomery climbed out of the first car and strode vigorously to the front door, where the matron was waiting to greet him. The expression on her face was a mixture of limitless compassion and unbending sternness in equal quantities. As always, the general's uniform was impeccable in every respect, but the matron's outfit, especially her stiffly starched white linen headdress, made Monty look like a raw recruit who had not yet learned how to prepare his uniform for inspection.

"Good morning, matron. How nice to see you again. Is Wright in a private room, as I ordered?"

"Of course, General Montgomery."

"And does he know why he's there?"

"No, sir. Your aide left strict instructions about that."

"Excellent. I see that my colleagues have all assembled here now. Would you please be so kind as to take us to Wright's room?"

The matron led the way, followed by a troop of generals and their aides-de-camp. She opened the door of a room and announced, "Captain Wright, sir."

Captain Wright had been napping briefly. He suddenly awoke to see that the small room was filled with generals, colonels and other senior officers, wearing a variety of different uniforms. Red tabs and red cap bands of senior staff officers were everywhere. Wright thought he was dreaming until General Montgomery approached the bed.

"At ease, Major Wright!"

As an officer trained at Royal Military College Sandhurst, Wright knew better than to correct a general regarding his rank. So he said nothing. Then he saw that the general was holding out his hand. In his open palm lay two brass crowns, the insignia of a British Army major. Monty smiled and then placed the crowns on the bedside locker.

"You've been promoted, Wright. When you're fully recovered your batman will sew these crowns on your epaulets in place of your captain's three pips. And because you were largely responsible for winning the Battle of El Alamein, I and the others have come here this morning to decorate you."

He paused, nodded, and an aide-de-camp, distinguished by the braided gold aiguillette looped over his left shoulder, came forward bearing a small purple velvet cushion on which lay the medal of the Distinguished Service Order.

"Atten-shun!" General Montgomery intoned. "Major Wright, the Distinguished Service Order is awarded to officers 'for distinguished services during active operations against the enemy.' To mark your invaluable services leading to the victory at El Alamein, I hereby award you the Distinguished Service Order."

He reached down to the cushion, lifted the white enameled silver-gilt cross bearing the gold Imperial Crown, and pinned the red ribbon with narrow blue edges on the pillow next to Major Wright's head. He saluted the injured man.

Then he returned to his place and announced, "General Bondieu will now award you the *Croix de Guerre*, the War Cross. *Mon général, s'il vous plaît.*"

A short man wearing the uniform of a brigade general in the Free French Forces came forward, shorter even than General Montgomery. His exceedingly tall aide-de-camp accompanied the general; the aide carried his own small cushion bearing a bronze cross with swords, hanging from a green and red striped ribbon. The gross disparity in their heights added to Wright's sense of unreality.

The French general announced loudly, "*La France vous remercie de votre galanterie.*"

He fastened the ribbon on the pillow next to the DSO and saluted Wright. The aide-de-camp leaned forward and whispered in Wright's ear, "Ze general 'e say, '*La France*, she sank you for your *galanterie*.'"

The two French officers returned to their places.

"Next," General Montgomery ordered, "Lieutenant General Lobachevsky of the Red Army General Staff will award you the Order of the Red Star."

A Soviet general stepped forward, accompanied by a colonel. General Lobachevsky was tall, totally bald, and built like a professional wrestler. His aide was as tall as the general and as muscular. Her hair looked as if it had been in an all-out, no-holds-barred fight with a combine harvester on a collective farm on the vast steppes of Soviet Central Asia and lost the brawl. She wore no make-up and it was obvious that she cared little for her personal appearance. Good manners demanded that Major Wright observe the two Soviet officers directly for only the shortest possible time. But that momentary glance was enough; he instantly detected from their body language that the General and his aide were considerably more than just professional colleagues.

General Lobachevsky made a lengthy speech in Russian, which his aide did not translate. Then she took a box out of a pocket of her baggy uniform, opened it and extracted a red-enameled medal in the shape of a five-pointed star. The silver shield in the center of the medal depicted a soldier carrying a rifle. The edge of the shield displayed the State political slogan, "Workers of the world, unite!" A silver hammer and sickle symbol was mounted below the shield. The medal had no ribbon, so General Lobachevsky placed it carefully on the pillow next to the French medal and saluted Wright.

His aide then announced in heavy accented but perfect English, "Comrade Lieutenant General Lobachevsky has awarded Major Wright the Order of the Red Star in recognition of his role in winning the battle of Stalingrad." Then she, too, saluted Wright, and both Soviet officers resumed their places.

"And now," Montgomery proclaimed, "Major General van der Merwe will award you the Union of South Africa King's Medal for Bravery. This medal is awarded for noncombatant acts of gallantry."

By this time, Wright's head was swimming. First Monty had thanked him for his part in winning the Battle of El Alamein, even though he had not participated in the fighting in any way. After all, he had been badly wounded just after the battle began when the German plane dropped a bomb onto the building in Cairo in which he was stationed. That was why he had been in the British Military Hospital in Cairo for a month, followed by nearly three months in this military hospital in Alexandria. But General Montgomery had awarded him the DSO 'for distinguished services during active operations against the enemy.' There was no possible way that he could have won the DSO for his role in El Alamein—he had not taken part in the battle.

Then came the French medal. Wright had no idea whatsoever why that medal had been awarded. In Cairo he had met a few Free French officers socially, but he had not had any professional dealings with the French, let alone fought alongside them (or anyone else, for that matter) in the Battle of El Alamein.

Regarding the two Soviet officers, while in hospital he had heard about the victory at Stalingrad. But Stalingrad was in the Soviet Union, and he had never in his whole life been there, let alone fought at Stalingrad.

And now he was getting a *non*combatant's medal from a South African general. This contradicted the award of the DSO.

Major General van der Merwe was tall and thin. His nose was long and straight, and beneath it he sported a triangular moustache. His eyes were oval shaped. Judging from the expression on his face, the general had no sense of humor whatsoever. He carried a wooden box, which he now opened. He took out a silver medal depicting dairy farmer Wolraad Woltemade on his horse, bravely plucking survivors of the wreck of the ship *De Jonge Thomas* from the turbulent seas of Table Bay in 1773 and dragging them to the shore, until he and his exhausted horse disappeared beneath the stormy waves. The edge of the medal bore the words "For bravery—*Vir dapperheid*" in relief letters. Attached to the medal was a long blue neck ribbon with narrow orange edges.

General van der Merwe slowly placed the medal on the pillow next to where the Order of the Red Star lay. He turned and looked directly at Major Wright; the other generals could see only the back of the South African general's head. Then his face dissolved into a huge grin, he winked broadly at Wright and announced loudly, "*Jou luie vabond, klim onmiddelik uit die bed uit!*" Then he saluted and returned to where he had been standing. Wright's mouth dropped open. He alone in that hospital room had understood that the dour-looking General van de Merwe had said in Afrikaans, "You lazy scoundrel, get out of bed immediately!"

"Right," General Montgomery said. "Everybody out—I want to talk to Major Wright alone. Matron, please get me a comfortable chair—this may take a while."

# CHAPTER THIRTY-EIGHT

*Alexandria, Egypt*
*Thursday, February 11th, 1943*

"Major Wright, would it be correct to say that you're wondering what's going on?"

"Am I dreaming, sir?"

"No, you're not—you're wide awake. I've come here to tell you about our victory at the Battle of El Alamein and our victory at Stalingrad, and the role that you played in both battles, even though you weren't present either at Stalingrad or at El Alamein. It's a long story, but your doctor assures me that you're now strong enough to hear the whole thing, which is why I've waited until now to tell you what really happened.

"Your role in our overall strategy was to convince the Germans that we possessed the promethium anti-tank shell. And you succeeded so well that you've been promoted and awarded four medals."

"Sir, I was going to ask you about those medals," Major Wright said.

"Well, we award the DSO to officers 'for distinguished services during active operations against the enemy.' As far as we're concerned, your meeting with Aram Kezerian was precisely that. He's the leading Axis spy in Egypt—or he was. After our overwhelming victory in the Battle of El Alamein we arrested him. And as soon as we've driven the Germans completely out of North Africa, which shouldn't take more than another few weeks, we'll hang him—we won't need him any more. So, yes, he was the enemy. And your meeting with him was an 'active operation' from our point of view. What I'm saying is that you won the DSO for the one-on-one operation in the office at the back of his antiquities shop here in Alexandria, rather than the full-scale El Alamein battle in which you definitely did *not* take part.

"By the way, it really was rather bad luck that you caught that bomb so far behind the lines. The battle opened with an artillery barrage. Rommel sent up some bombers to try to destroy our field guns, but one pilot somehow ended up in totally the wrong place and dropped one of his bombs on you. Well, not on you personally, you understand, but you know what I mean. Did you know that an ack-ack crew in Garden City, Cairo shot him down before he could release any more bombs? I know it's not much in return for the nearly four months you've spent in hospital, but it's some small comfort to know that our men took revenge on your behalf. And your doctors tell me that there's a good chance that you're going to make a full recovery—it's just going to take a few more weeks. Anyhow, that's why we awarded you the DSO."

"But sir, what was all that about the Battle of Stalingrad? I've never been there."

"Well, Colonel Kovalevskaya, General Lobachevsky's aide-de-camp, explained the situation to me. It seems that once we'd convinced the German High Command how deficient the British anti-tank weapons really are, it became a doctrine of their High Command that all Allied anti-tank weapons are inadequate. Actually, that makes a lot of sense, because if one of the Allied countries could've produced a better anti-tank weapon, the others would've acquired it relatively quickly. So, what started as the German belief in the shortcomings of the British anti-tank weapons here in North Africa became the undoubted weakness of the Soviet anti-tank weapons in Russia, and in particular at Stalingrad. When the Soviets staged a massive counterattack there on 19th November, they used their T-34 tanks. In Stalingrad, it wasn't a question of tank gun range but rather winter maneuverability—the T-34 is more effective than a Panzer when it comes to moving over deep mud or snow."

"Sir," Major Wright asked, "are you saying that, when the Red Army counterattacked in the Russian winter conditions, the Germans used the same tactics that they'd used at El Alamein because they believed that the Soviet anti-tank weapons were inferior?"

"Precisely, Wright. And the result was the same as at El Alamein—overwhelming defeat of the German forces. And that's why you're one of only a handful of British citizens who holds the Order of the Red Star."

"Thank you for explaining that to me, sir," Wright said. "But what about the *Croix de Guerre*? As far as I can recall, I've had no dealings at all with the Free French, other than meeting a few of them socially."

"Well," Monty replied carefully, "that's just to keep General de Gaulle happy."

"What do you mean, sir?"

"This must stay between ourselves. Do you give me your word on that?"

"Of course, sir."

"Well, de Gaulle is driving Mr. Churchill crazy with his demands that France has to rank equally with Britain and America and the Russkies in every respect. So, when someone in Free French headquarters in London found out by accident that Britain was going to award you a DSO and that our Soviet allies were going to give you their Order of the Red Star, General de Gaulle put pressure on us to ensure that you got a gong from them, too. Rather pitiful, isn't it? Mr. Churchill is fighting two wars, one against the Axis Powers, the other against General de Gaulle."

"Fine, sir, that explains the *Croix de Guerre*. I suppose I'll have to wear it along with my other medals, even though it's really a travesty."

Monty smiled his rare smile and then nodded. "I'm sorry, Wright, but you have no choice."

Major Wright paused, swallowed and then somehow managed to pluck up enough courage to ask General Bernard Montgomery one last question.

"And finally, sir," he asked, "why did General van der Merwe give me the Union of South Africa King's Medal for Bravery? You announced that it's awarded for noncombatant acts of gallantry."

"Surely you know the answer to that, Major Wright? Don't you remember Corporal Dan, Klaas van Deventer's brother-in-law, who sold a bill of goods to an antiquities dealer and brilliant spy, the soon to be late and unlamented Aram Kezerian? Well, Corporal Dan's a South African. And what an excellent job he did, too."

# CHAPTER THIRTY-NINE

*Coopers Island, New Zealand*
*Wednesday, January 26th, 1944*

Joe Kaplan, his hair now snowy white, stood next to Detective Sergeant Wesley McFee. The stormy summer sky that arched over the Coopers Island cemetery was as dark as Wes's mood. The words of the uniformed military chaplain drifted in and out of his consciousness.

"…We have entrusted our sister Gretchen Konrad to God's mercy, and we now commit her body to the ground: earth to earth, ashes to ashes, dust to dust: in sure and certain hope of the resurrection to eternal life through our Lord Jesus Christ…"

Wes tried to concentrate on the funeral service, but it was hopeless. Two days earlier, Chief Superintendent Morgan, his station commander in Hamilton, had instructed Wes to travel to Tudor Island without explaining why he was needed there. Joe Kaplan was standing on the Cookville jetty when the Bluff ferry docked. He took Wes to the Tavern of the Seas Café so that he would be seated when he heard about Gretchen.

"Since September 1942," Joe told him, "Gretchen lived in Wellington. Sadly, last week she died of a brain tumor and we're here on Coopers Island for her funeral."

Wes was totally stunned. Memories started flooding back and emotions clogged his brain. He was unable to think clearly, let alone ask Joe questions about what had happened to her during the past 16 months. A few days after the two military policemen had separated him from Gretchen, he had asked Chief Superintendent Morgan about her. Morgan put a finger to his lips and invoked the Official Secrets Act. Wes assumed that the police had arrested Gretchen and she was now in prison, or perhaps they had executed her as a spy. He did not ask Morgan again.

Joe escorted Wes from the café and led him to the graveyard, a 15-minute walk. Neither man said a word. They arrived at the wind-blown cemetery overlooking Raphael Channel. Wes thought that the grassy slope, sprinkled with clusters of mature indigenous trees, was completely deserted, but then he noticed two men in uniform in the far corner near a huge kauri. As they neared the freshly dug grave, Wes recognized Assistant Commissioner of Police Warren Jennings, standing next to a military chaplain. Jennings introduced Wes to the Reverend Mark Connolly, and indicated to Major Connolly that he should now begin the funeral service.

During the ceremony, Wes kept going back in his mind to those 72 hours he had spent with Gretchen—there was no way he could ever forget them. Through his tears he saw Connolly close his prayer book and approach Jennings. The two men, now deep in conversation, started to walk slowly back toward the Cookville jetty. Joe put a fatherly arm around Wes's shoulder and gave him a gentle nudge to indicate that they should follow.

Just before the four men reached the jetty, Warren pointed in the direction of the Tavern of the Seas Café. They entered and sat at a table overlooking Raphael Channel. Miranda appeared, smiling.

"I'm so sorry that I have nothing stronger than tea," she apologized.

"No worries, Miranda. Tea is just what we need," the Assistant Commissioner of Police assured her.

They drank their tea in silence. Then Joe spoke.

"Wes, what I'm about to tell you falls under the Official Secrets Act. That's why Major Connolly was asked to perform the funeral. We've got Hitler against the ropes, but the war's not over yet, and we couldn't risk having a civilian clergyman, let alone gravediggers in the cemetery during the service."

"Risk? What risk?" Wes asked, clearly bewildered.

"It's absolutely essential that Canaris and the *Abwehr* learn nothing about Gretchen's life here in

New Zealand. In particular, they must never know that I was at her funeral," Kaplan insisted.

"Why not?"

"Because from the time she left the hospital, Gretchen worked for me as an Allied agent."

"An Allied agent? But she's a Nazi spy. I mean, she was a Nazi spy." And turning to Jennings, he added, "Isn't that what you told me, sir?"

The Assistant Commissioner nodded as Kaplan continued. "Wes, there's no doubt whatsoever that Gretchen was a Nazi agent. But before she joined the German American Bund (that's the American Nazi Party), she was an enthusiastic member of the Communist Party of America. Like many top agents, she was somewhat unstable. So much so that, when she came out of Dunedin Hospital and we moved her to an isolation cell in Wellington Women's Prison, it was easy for me to turn her."

"How?"

"Well, we often use threats. We tell captured spies that to save their lives they need to work for us. Or we bribe them—spies are usually extremely mercenary. But in Gretchen's case, I used love."

"Love?"

"Love, infatuation, passion, romance—call it what you like. You see, in the hospital she told us that, as she was losing consciousness in the tinny, she started to hallucinate. And the last image she saw was you, Wes. She referred to you as 'the love of her life.' I didn't try to analyze her feelings. I simply asked her, 'Gretchen, are you willing to work with me to help Wes win the war?' And that was that. From time to time I prepared encrypted disinformation for her to transmit to Germany by radio, and she cooperated fully. Based on the messages that they sent to her here in New Zealand, I have no doubt that she fooled the *Abwehr*."

Once more Wes was unable to speak.

"After the tumor was diagnosed," Joe Kaplan continued, "the doctors did everything they could to try to save her. She was strong again, having fully recovered from her ordeal. She desperately wanted to live and fought hard until the end, which came surprisingly suddenly. I'd wanted you to be at her bedside."

The four men sat in silence for a long while. Then Wes left the table and walked slowly back to the grave.

# AFTERWORD

*Coopers Island* is a work of fiction. All the characters are fictional; where we have given characters the names of historical figures, such as General Bernard Montgomery and Admiral Wilhelm Canaris, we have made up the statements attributed to them. All the commercial establishments in this story, including hotels, rooms to let, banks, cafés, restaurants and shops, are figments of our imagination, as is the *Star of Adelaide* and the other ships and boats. The descriptions and locations of the various police stations are also fictional.

We have predated some discoveries. Scientists at Oak Ridge National Laboratory in Tennessee found element 61 only in 1945 and announced the discovery two years later. At that time, they proposed the name "prometheum"; in Greek mythology, Prometheus stole fire from the gods for human use. The spelling was later changed to "promethium." Also, proof that Mata Hari was indeed a German spy surfaced only in the 1970s, so Gretchen Konrad could not have known about Major Röpell and Captain Hoffmann.

We have based "Tudor Island" on Stewart Island; yes, the pun is intended. Coopers Island is the old name for Ulva Island. There is a disused tin mine on Stewart Island. Ulva Island, situated in an inlet just off the east coast of Stewart Island, is pristine temperate rainforest, unquestionably the most beautiful forest that we have ever seen anywhere in the world.

No one can be expected to know everything about his or her country, so it is hardly surprising that some of the individuals in this story occasionally gave wrong information. For example, when Gretchen arrived in Auckland on the *Star of Adelaide*, the customs official at the exit from the cargo docks told her that "even though Abel Tasman was the first European to discover New Zealand after a nightmare journey sailing across what is now called the Tasman Sea, he never actually set foot in our country because he was too seasick!" It is certainly possible that Tasman was extremely seasick. We know from his diary that his crossing of the Tasman Sea in 1642 to New Zealand from the island that he named "Anthoonij van Diemenslandt" (but which is now called Tasmania in his honor) was considerably rougher than anything that Gretchen had to endure. However, the real reason why Tasman did not venture on land was that, when he sent a party ashore to get fresh water, Maori in canoes attacked one of his boats and killed four of his men. So he immediately sailed north to Fiji.

The shop assistant in Wellington who sold the maps to Gretchen informed her that, "The New Zealand government strongly encourages hiking in our beautiful countryside, so the Department of Lands and Survey has produced ... NZMS 1 maps." In fact, the NZMS 1 map project was started in 1935 in response to fears of war and invasion, not to promote hiking (or "tramping" as it is called in New Zealand). In passing, there was a good reason why she could not supply Gretchen with the NZMS 1 maps for the islands on the south coast of the South Island; none of the seven NZMS 1 maps planned for that area were ever produced.

When discussing the hats worn by military police in New Zealand, Ambrose told Gretchen that, "Everyone in our Army has a lemon squeezer hat ... [that] has a wide band, called a 'puggaree'— I have absolutely no idea why." The word "puggaree" comes from the Hindi word *pagri* meaning a turban.

On the other hand, some unlikely statements are actually correct. For example, during the steak dinner that Wes and Gretchen enjoyed on September 13th, 1942 in Rotorua, Wes assured Gretchen that one shilling and sixpence was the usual price for steak, eggs and chips in New Zealand. He explained that because the country was at war, "the government controls the prices of essential items, such as food. Fortunately there's almost no rationing." In fact, Wes was right; extensive rationing was introduced in New Zealand only from October 1942. This was despite earlier calls by some leaders to ration food, so that as much as possible of New Zealand's abundant agricultural products, like butter, bacon, eggs, milk, cheese, and meat, could be sent overseas to feed the British who were severely undernourished— German U-boats were sinking large numbers of the ships trying to bring food into Britain.

In the first paragraph of Chapter 35 we inform the reader that "Colonel Marlowe moved the bordello to the third floor, where it provided useful cover for the activities conducted in the rest of the building." From the viewpoint of security, it would have made more sense to move the brothel to the ground floor and restrict access to the other floors. But on page 27 of *The Deceivers: Allied Military Deception in the Second World War* (Scribner, 2004), Thaddeus Holt states that "[Lieutenant Colonel] Clarke gallantly permitted the ladies to continue their business on an upper floor, and they and the [Security Intelligence Middle East] staff would exchange cordial greetings when they met."

In some instances, speakers really should have provided explanations. For example, Ambrose Milton told Gretchen that his former girlfriend, Emma, worked in a dairy. Knowing that Gretchen came from Australia, he should have informed her that, in New Zealand, a "dairy" is a convenience store that sells a variety of items, not just milk products. Also, when speaking to Walter Bennett and Detective Chief Superintendent Jennings of the New Zealand Police Force, Detective Superintendent Mudge of the New South Wales Police Force used the term "sandgroper" to refer to someone from Western Australia. He should have warned his colleague that the term is somewhat pejorative. In that conversation, he also used the phrase "beyond the black stump." He probably thought that Jennings was familiar with that Australian expression denoting "in the middle of nowhere," but it would have been better if he had explained the phrase to the New Zealand policeman. (There was no need for Mudge to explain anything to Walter Bennett—that traitor and sexual predator is utterly beneath contempt.)

Our descriptions of actual places in New Zealand are as accurate as we could make them, with the exception of the locations of two of the mines. There is no sulfur mine at Waiotapu; sulfur deposits lie on the other side of Rotorua and have been mined at several sites there, including Tikitere. Also, the only thallium mine in New Zealand is at Rotokawa and not Akaroa. We took the liberty of shifting the mines so that we could share the beauties of Waiotapu and Akaroa with our readers.

Finally, as we have stated, this book is a work of fiction. But the friendliness, helpfulness and kindness of the people of New Zealand as described in this book are real.

# ACKNOWLEDGEMENTS

We would like to thank Rosalind Fischl OAM, Renée Glass and Bob Winner for their meticulous reading of the manuscript and their many helpful suggestions. We are most grateful for their assistance.

Malcolm Anderson and Mark Steadman, guides on the *Oceanic Discoverer,* were invaluable sources of information on numerous aspects of New Zealand: the people of New Zealand and their history, geology, flora and fauna (especially penguins). We particularly appreciated their passion for their country, and we hope that we have been able to share some of that enthusiasm with our readers.

We are most grateful to our publisher, Jennifer Chesak of Wandering in the Words Press, for her encouragement and enthusiasm. As before, it was a delight to work with an editor of Jennifer's caliber. In addition, she has once again designed a striking cover.

# STEVE SCHACH

After 26 years as a professor at Vanderbilt University in Nashville, Tennessee, Steve Schach, a Cape Town, South Africa native, recently moved to Sydney, Australia. Before he began writing thrillers, Steve wrote 13 best-selling software engineering textbooks, which are used in universities all over the world. Down Under, Steve intended to become a full-time grandfather, and limit his intellectual activities to solving cryptic crossword puzzles and avidly watching Sesame Street with his grandchildren. However, the urge to write proved to be far too strong to overcome. Wandering in the Words Press published his first thriller, *Old Bach Is Come*, in March 2013.

# SHARON STEIN

Sharon Stein is a pediatric radiologist. Born in Cape Town, South Africa, Sharon was a professor of radiology and radiological sciences at Vanderbilt Children's Hospital in Nashville, Tennessee, and an examiner for the American Board of Radiology. She is a former president of the Southern Pediatric Radiology Society. In 2009 Sharon moved to Sydney, Australia with her husband, Steve Schach, to be with their grandchildren. She is an accomplished cook and baker who loves to share her many recipes and techniques. *Coopers Island* is her first thriller.

www.ingramcontent.com/pod-product-compliance
Lightning Source LLC
Chambersburg PA
CBHW062006170626
46813CB00001B/52